Sue Miller is the author of several bestselling novels including *The World Below*. She lives in Boston, Massachusetts.

LOST IN THE FOREST

One minute John is the cornerstone of Eva's world, rock to his two teenage stepdaughters and his own son, Theo, the next he is tossed through the air in a traffic accident. His sudden death changes everything. Eva struggles with the desolation of loneliness, finding herself drawn back to her untrustworthy ex-husband. Emily, the eldest daughter, grapples with her new-found independence and responsibility. Little Theo can only begin to fathom the permanence of his father's death. But for the middle child, Daisy, John's absence opens up a whole world of confusion. Just at the onset of adolescence and blossoming sexuality, Daisy is exposed to the terrifying duplicity of life . . .

Books by Sue Miller
Published by The House of Ulverscroft:

THE WORLD BELOW

SUE MILLER

LOST IN THE FOREST

Complete and Unabridged

CHARNWOOD
Leicester

First published in Great Britain in 2005 by
Bloomsbury Publishing Plc
London

First Charnwood Edition
published 2005
by arrangement with
Bloomsbury Publishing Plc
London

British Library CIP Data

Miller, Sue, 1943 –
   Lost in the forest.—Large print ed.—
   Charnwood library series
   1. Traffic accidents—Fiction 2. Fatherless families
   —Fiction 3. Loss (Psychology)—Fiction
   4. Large type books
   I. Title
   813.5'4 [F]

   ISBN 1–84617–045–1

Published by
F. A. Thorpe (Publishing)
Anstey, Leicestershire

Set by Words & Graphics Ltd.
Anstey, Leicestershire
Printed and bound in Great Britain by
T. J. International Ltd., Padstow, Cornwall

This book is printed on acid-free paper

Grateful acknowledgment is made to Harvard
University Press for permission to reprint '1452: Your
thoughts don't have words every day' and '1726: If all
the griefs I am to have' from *The Poems of Emily
Dickinson*, edited by Thomas H. Johnson
(Cambridge, Mass.: The Belknap Press of Harvard
University Press.) Copyright © 1951, 1955, 1979,
1983 by the President and Fellows of Harvard College. Reprinted by permission of the publishers and
the Trustees of Amherst College.

Acknowledgments

I want to thank Dori and Doug Towne of Calistoga for their warmth and our long friendship. I'm grateful to Kathleen Cornelia and Phillipa Jones of the Diageo Company for their kindness. Sterling Vineyards and Beaulieu Vineyards were extraordinarily welcoming and gracious on one of my exploratory trips. I thank them. John and Sloan Upton of Three Palms Vineyards told me fascinating and funny tales of their start, and entrusted me with their album of photographs, which fed my imagination about the physical labor and pleasure involved in making a vineyard from scratch.

Nigel Newton, my British publisher at Bloomsbury, encouraged me and introduced me to Jon Kongsgaard, who shared with me a bottle of his own extraordinary wine and talked, over a long Napa lunch, about his life growing grapes and making wine. Tony Mitchell generously answered my nearly endless list of questions about vineyard management. Andy and Lilla Weinberger were kind and patient with me over the days I 'helped out' at Readers Books in Sonoma, pestering them with questions about their wonderful store and how it works.

Joan Wheelis rescued me and helped me think in new ways about this book.

Maxine Groffsky, my literary agent, and Jordan Pavlin, my editor at Knopf, are both essential to me for their keen intelligence about my work and their warm support. Doug Bauer is my sine qua non.

1

Emily telephoned, his older daughter. 'Can you come get us?' she said. 'It's an emergency.'

As usual, she didn't greet him, she didn't say *hello* at the start of the call. And also as usual, this bothered him, he felt a familiar pull of irritation at her voice, her tone. But even as he was listening to her, he was focused on steering the truck around the sharp curves in the narrow road, around several small heaps of rock that had slid down the steep hillside: he was feeling the pleasure he always took in the way the slanted afternoon light played on the yellowed grass and reddened leaves left in the vineyards, in the way the air smelled. He kept his voice neutral as he responded. 'When? Now?'

In the background, behind her, Mark could hear someone give a sudden *whoop*. Festivities, he thought. As ever. Eva's face rose in his mind — his ex-wife. At the least excuse, there was a gathering at her house: to celebrate a birthday — reasonable enough; but also for a project completed, a team victory, a skill accomplished. You learned to ride a bike, you got a party thrown for you.

'*Duh*. Yes, Dad, now,' Emily said. 'That's what I mean.'

He was headed north on 128 to a small vineyard he thought his crew should harvest tomorrow. He needed to check the grapes. But

1

he could probably get Angel to do it if he had to. His windows were open. The noise of the rushing air made his daughter's voice on the car phone sound distant.

'So?' she said. 'Can you?'

If his younger daughter, Daisy, had ever called him because of an emergency, it would have been a child's crisis — not making the basketball team, needing a ride somewhere that her mother or stepfather couldn't provide. But with Emily, this emergency was likely to be at least slightly serious, an emergency in near-adult terms. Terms he might even be sympathetic with.

But she would be *taking charge* again, and this was something he and his ex-wife had agreed that she should be discouraged — no, *freed* — from doing so often. He cleared his throat. 'Maybe I should talk to your mom,' he said. Yes. The approach to take.

'Dad!' she objected. He didn't answer for a long moment, and as if in response to this, her voice had changed when she spoke again. She sounded younger: 'Mom can't talk right now. That's why we need you.'

And with those words, *we need you*, it was settled. To be needed. Well. Mark thought of Emily's delicate oval face, her regular, pretty features, her curly dark hair, so like Eva's — all the things that were lovely about her. All the things that didn't piss him off. 'Okay,' he said. 'Okay, as it happens, I can come. As it happens, I will.'

She wouldn't be charmed. 'Now?' she said impatiently.

'Now. Or, gimme ten or so.' He was slowing, and as he pulled into a turnaround by the roadside, the truck bounced and his tires crunched on the dusty gravel.

'Okay.' She sighed, in relief it seemed. 'Just honk, though,' she said. 'We'll come out. Oh, and Dad?'

'Yeah?'

'It's for overnight.'

It could not be for overnight. He had plans. He had a date. He was going to get laid. 'Okay, sunshine,' he said. 'We'll work it all out.'

She sighed again and hung up.

Twenty minutes or so later, when he pulled up at the curb in front of his ex-wife's large Victorian house, the door opened before he hit the horn and his younger daughter staggered out onto the wide porch, carrying her sleeping bag, her pack an oversize hump on her back. Daisy was barefoot. Her long brown legs were exposed nearly to the crotch in cutoff jeans — legs that were beginning to look less like sticks and more like a woman's, he noted. Emily came out the door after her, turned backward as if to fuss with something behind her.

Two pretty, dark, young women, one tall, one short: his daughters. He got out of the truck to go and help them. As he started up the walk, he saw Theo emerging from the house behind Emily. The little boy, not yet three, was carrying a brown paper grocery bag by its handles. Something stuck out of it — a pillow? a blanket? He spotted Mark and smiled. Now Emily took Theo's hand to help him down the wide porch

3

stairs. He paused on each one, and the bag plopped slowly from step to step behind him as he descended.

Mark met them on the walk. 'Hey,' he said. He kissed each girl on her head. They smelled identical, a ladylike herbal perfume: shared shampoo. He took Daisy's sleeping bag from her. 'Theo!' he said, and extended his hand down to him. 'To what do we owe this pleasure?'

'I'll explain it all to you,' Emily called back. She had moved ahead of them down the walk, between the orderly gray-green procession of rosemary plants. She was tossing her stuff into the open back of the truck.

'So he's supposed to spend the night too?' Mark asked Daisy. Theo was not his son. Theo was his ex-wife's son, by her second marriage. He liked Theo. He was, in fact, charmed by him — he knew him well from various extended-family events — but he had never before been asked to babysit for him. And actually, no one had even asked.

Daisy shrugged. She looked, as she often did, sullen. Or evasive. Her face was narrower than Emily's, her nose still slightly too big on it — she was fourteen — her eyebrows darker and thick. She had shot up within the last two years, and now she was only a few inches shorter than Mark. She carried it badly, trying to hide it. Mark had worried when she was younger that she would be plain, which seemed to him an almost unbearably sad thing: a plain woman. Within the last six months or so, though, her face had changed and strengthened, and he saw that

4

that wouldn't be the case. That she might, in fact, be better-looking than Emily in the end, more striking. It had made him easier around her, he realized.

They had caught up to Emily, who said again, 'I'll explain it *later.*' She sounded irritated, as though she were the adult and he a nagging child. She took Theo's hand and led him to the door of the truck's cab.

Mark went around to the driver's side. He opened his door and stood there looking across the cab's wide seat, waiting for Emily to look back at him. She wouldn't. Or she didn't. First she was helping the little boy clamber into the truck; now she climbed up herself and was busy buckling him in. When she finally raised her eyes and met her father's, he was ready. He lifted his hands. 'Hey, Em,' he said. 'You will admit — '

'Daddy, it's an emergency. A real emergency.' Her eyes, he noted now, were red-rimmed, their lids swollen.

Theo looked over at him and nodded. 'It's a mergency,' he said, and inserted his thumb into his mouth with an air of finality.

Daisy squeezed in next to Emily, and Mark got in and started the truck. He pulled into the street. After nearly a full minute had passed, he asked, 'So, the nature of this emergency is . . . ?'

He could feel Emily's gaze on him, and he looked at her. She was frowning — her dark eyebrows made fierce lines. She shook her head. 'We can't . . . we shouldn't . . . talk about it now.' She gestured at Theo, sitting between them, watching them soberly.

Mark nodded. After another long moment he said, 'But at some point it will be revealed.'

'Yeah,' she said. She turned away, and when he looked over again, he saw that she and Daisy were holding hands. What the hell was going on? Daisy's mouth hung open stupidly, as though she'd been sucker punched.

They drove in near-total silence the whole way to his house. Everyone's eyes stayed devoutly on the road, as though the familiar scenes rolling past — the valley as it widened out and spread the fall colors of its vineyards before them, the deep green of the hills riding along above it all — were some new and fascinating nature movie. Once Daisy said in a near-whisper, 'Are those pills supposed to knock her out or something?' and Emily shrugged. That was it.

Knock *who* out? *Not Eva*, he thought. He imagined her, his ex-wife — small, dark, quick moving, graceful. Her sudden sexy smile. Not Eva.

Above Calistoga, he turned in at the unmarked dirt road to his house. There were sparse, newly planted vineyards on either side of it. He had to swerve and dance the truck to avoid the ruts. He could feel Theo's weight swing against his side. After about a quarter of a mile, he pulled into his driveway and then up onto the cement pad where one day he planned to build a garage.

As soon as he cut the engine, they could hear the dogs barking in the house. The children started to unbuckle their seat belts, and he swung himself out of the truck. He began to gather their possessions from the back. They came and stood behind him — silent, oddly passive, waiting for their things to be put into their hands.

He led the way. When he opened the back door, the dogs shot out and started jumping around, abruptly quieted by their joy in being released. Their heavy tails whacked everyone.

Theo made a little noise of terror and delight and stepped between Mark's legs, gripping his thighs. Mark put his hands on the boy's narrow shoulders, and was instantly startled.

Why? Why did it feel so strange to touch the little boy?

Perhaps because he had anticipated the way the girls felt when they were Theo's size, when he had loved to touch them, to hold them. Theo's body was wiry and tense, utterly unlike theirs at the same age. It felt hot with energy.

'It's okay, big guy,' Mark said gently. 'They like you. They like kids like you.'

Theo looked up at Mark, wide-eyed and alarmed. 'They would like to *eat* me?' he asked. He was lighter-haired, lighter-skinned than the girls, and this difference somehow struck Mark as sad.

'No, no, no,' Mark said. 'They like to lick you, and play with you. You'll see. They're nice.'

He squatted by Theo and held his own hand out to Fanny to be licked. When Theo imitated him after a moment, Fanny's long, rough tongue came out and stroked the boy's hand too. He snatched his arm back and jigged a little in fear and pleasure, a prancey running in place. He

7

wore miniature red high-top sneakers. His striped socks had slid down almost entirely into them. One of his knees was thickly scabbed.

Emily and Daisy had disappeared immediately into the house, to put their things away, Mark assumed. He stood up. Theo grabbed his hand, and walked right next to Mark, into the kitchen, through it, virtually riding his left leg and talking all the while to the dogs: 'No bite me! Bad dog! Bad, bad dog! No bite!'

Mark was feeling a rising, irritated frustration, which he didn't want to focus on the little boy. He gestured across the living room, toward the back of the house. 'Let's go figure out what everyone's up to, shall we?'

Theo looked up at Mark. 'Yah,' he answered.

Theo shadowed him to the doorway of the back room. The girls' beds nearly filled its narrow space. It was dark and underwatery in here — the one window faced out into an overgrown evergreen shrub, which Mark kept meaning to prune, and hadn't. The light that filtered through it was weak and greenish. Daisy was carefully spreading her unzipped bag out on her bed, as she always did. This was her strategy to avoid making it, a chore she hated. Emily was already lying down, one arm under her head, staring out the window at nothing. Ignoring him, Mark felt.

'A word with you, Em?' he said, his voice carefully neutral.

Both girls looked at him. They seemed startled, like sleepers he'd wakened. He turned to his younger daughter. 'Daze, could you keep an eye on Theo for a minute? He's scared of the dogs.'

She nodded.

'I *not* scared,' Theo was instantly shrilling. 'I a big boy. I not scared.'

As Mark and Emily stepped toward the doorway, Daisy, who had flopped down onto her bed, was starting a game: 'How big *are* you, Theo? Big as a . . . *lion*?'

'Yes!' the boy cried.

As soon as Mark shut the door to his room, Emily sat down heavily at the foot of his rumpled bed and said, 'Oh, Daddy, it's John. John's dead.' Her face twisted, and tears immediately began sliding down it, as though she'd been waiting until this moment to allow herself her full measure of grief.

'What do you mean?' John was Eva's husband, the girls' stepfather. Theo's father.

'He's dead, Daddy.' Her hands came to her face now and covered her opened mouth. She inhaled sharply through her fingers, and then closed her eyes. 'He got hit . . . by a car. A car hit him.'

Mark pictured it. He pictured it wrong, as it turned out, but he saw John then — his large body, bloody, slumped behind the wheel of his ruined car. He saw him dead, though he still didn't believe it.

Mark sat down next to his daughter and held her, and she wept quietly and thoroughly, as he couldn't remember her weeping since he had told her he was moving out — long shuddering inhalations, and then a gentle high keening as

9

her inheld breath came out. From the other bedroom he could hear Theo shrieking, 'Bad! Bad!' and Daisy's voice trying to distract him.

'Sweetheart, it's okay. Cry, cry,' he said. And then he said, 'Shhh.'

Though he was still thinking of John, still trying to take it in, he was also aware of thinking that it felt good, holding Emily. And of wondering when he had last held her, her or Daisy. He couldn't remember.

When she had calmed down a little, he stretched away from her to grab the box of tissues from the stand by the bed. She blew loudly, using several, and wiped her face. His shirt was wet where she had leaned against him.

'How did it happen?' he asked at last, keeping his voice gentle. 'When?'

She seemed stricken again at the question, her eyes swam and grew larger, but she held on and whispered back, 'This afternoon. A car just . . . hit him.'

Mark cleared his throat. 'He was driving?'

'No.' Her hair swung as she shook her head. 'Walking. With Eva and Theo.'

'Jesus. They were *with* him?'

'Yes. In St. Helena, on that busy corner when you come into town. Just . . . I guess the guy was just driving too fast and he didn't see them.'

They sat together. There was a mirror above the wide bureau they were facing, and Mark watched Emily in it, her reversed face somehow older than her seventeen years, foreign to him.

'Your mom is okay, though,' he said after a moment.

10

She nodded. Then stopped. 'Well, she's all doped up actually. Actually that's why we had to come here.' Her voice had gotten practical again. 'She's a mess.'

'But . . . unhurt.'

'Unhurt.' She snorted wetly. 'Yeah,' she said, and then keened again.

'Honey, honey,' he said, rocking her against him.

'How can stuff like this happen, Dad?' she whispered against his chest. 'John . . . John was so good. He was so nice.'

John was good. He was nice. This is what Mark had thought from the first time he'd met him — that Eva had found herself a nice man. He had felt some pain about this, some sense of loss, but also relief. If Eva held on to him, if she married him, it would make everything better. John would take care of her; he would ease everything that was hard in her life. She wouldn't be so angry, so closed away. Things might actually improve between the two of them.

And that's how it had happened. Eva had married John, five years earlier. And a couple years later, she'd gotten pregnant with Theo.

Mark remembered discovering that. He had come by to get the girls one summer day. When he pulled up, Eva was kneeling in the garden, weeding — the basket next to her overflowed with bright green tufts of this and that. She sat back on her haunches when she saw him, and then, laboriously, slowly, she stood up. She had on worn faded denim overalls with a T-shirt underneath, and a large straw hat with a curvy brim, a flowered band around the crown. Her dark hair was tucked up into the hat, but curling strands looped down at her neck, her ears. Her feet were bare, small and tanned and slender. He noticed all this. Then she put her hands on her hips and arched her back slightly. He recognized the gesture instantly from her pregnancies with the girls; and that made him aware, suddenly, of what he hadn't noticed before: the downdrooping heaviness of her belly pulling against the overalls.

The world shifted for him. He knew he'd lost her. He understood that, and only then understood also that he hadn't truly known until now that he would. And while he was registering this, feeling the confusion of these thoughts, he was also aware of the sharp, keen bite of wanting her anew.

He was careful to give no sign of any of this. After only a few seconds' pause, he continued up the walk, and when she smiled, that dazzling, sleepy smile — a mark of pregnancy too: he should have remembered — and asked him how he was, he lied. He told her in his steadiest voice, *Fine, fine*.

'Poor little Theo,' he said now to Emily. 'Does he realize, do you think?'

'I don't think so.' She sat still for a moment, her lips slightly parted, breathing through her mouth. 'Well.' She looked at him. 'Yes. He sorta does. He told me John had gone away, that his daddy was gone, a car hit him.' Her mouth firmed. 'But that doesn't mean he understands anything.'

'No,' he said.

She blew her nose again. They sat together glumly, looking at themselves in the mirror, looking at the closed bedroom door next to it. The dogs were barking again.

'And what about Daze?' he asked. 'She seems pretty lifeless.'

Emily sighed. 'She's just not talking.'

'That's what I mean.'

'Well, that's just the way Daisy *is*, Daddy.'

And he realized, suddenly, that he knew this about his younger daughter. He knew that Daisy sank into torpor, into silence, when she was overwhelmed. Even after the divorce, when she was so little — only five — she'd been that way: too quiet, absent, unresponsive. He'd tried to make a joke of it sometimes, tapping lightly with his knuckles on her head. 'Hello, hello. Anybody home at Daisy's? Anybody in there?'

'So how long will you stay, do you think?' he asked.

'I don't know. Gracie was over and she suggested it, 'cause Mom is like, out of control. She said she'd phone you.'

Gracie was Eva's closest friend, called on to witness every celebration, to help at every tragedy. When he and Eva split up, it was Gracie's presence at their house that let him know it was final. She'd answered the door when he came over hoping to talk to Eva, and when she saw him, she said, 'You! You dim-witted asshole!' and slammed the door, before he could speak.

They were friends again now. They'd even

joked sometimes, before Gracie got married, about getting together themselves — a safe joke, he thought, since neither was even slightly attracted to the other.

'Let's figure this out then,' he said to Emily, hoping to appeal to her organizational strengths. 'Where do you think Theo should sleep?'

'I don't know. He still has a crib at home.'

'Ah!'

'But he can climb out anyway, so he usually sleeps with someone else.'

'Who? Eva?'

'Sometimes. Sometimes John and Eva, sometimes me or Daze.' She shrugged. 'It's like he chooses different people for different reasons at different times.' She made a face. 'Sometimes he sleeps in the hall. On the floor. You have to be careful not to *trip* on him if you get up in the night.'

He had a vision of this suddenly, the little boy asleep with a blanket on the floor. Emily in her nightgown stepping around him. The routine of this, the jokes that would be made in the morning. All that was settled and domestic in his children's lives, all that he hadn't been able to hold on to for their sakes. He said, 'Maybe he should stay in with me. I've got the biggest bed.'

Someone knocked on the door. Daisy called, 'Dad, the dogs are going crazy out here.'

Mark got up. At the door he turned back to Emily. 'You okay for now?'

She seemed better. Less blank, less turned in. She looked away from her own reflection and up at him. She nodded.

'Well, come help me out with this three-ring circus then.'

She stood and sighed, put-upon, as she followed him.

★　★　★

A death in the family. That's what he said when he called Marianne to cancel their evening, feeling that he was somehow using it, falsifying it, even though there was nothing in it that wasn't true.

Her voice changed instantly — falsely too, he felt — to sympathy and concern. 'Oh, Mark, I'm so sorry. Who?'

There was a little pause after he said, 'The children's stepfather,' and he felt he had to explain. He said, 'They were very close to him,' though he realized he didn't really know if this was the case.

They arranged to talk in a couple of days, when things straightened out a little. 'I can't wait to see you, babe,' he said, before he pushed the button to disconnect them.

Mark had taken the telephone into the back hallway, off the kitchen, to make the call. While he talked, he'd been looking out the window at his truck, drained of color in the deepening twilight, at the shadowy shapes of the dogs padding around in the driveway, at the blackened fig tree and the looming, dark shed, the tractors parked beyond it: the familiar elements of the world he'd made for himself when he lost Eva and the girls.

15

When he turned back into the kitchen, Daisy startled him, standing as she was in its bright light between the cooktop and the island, everything about her frozen, observant, as though she'd been there a long time. He smiled at her, but her face didn't change. 'What's up, Daze?' he asked, setting the phone in its cradle.

'I was going to ask you something,' she said.

'Yeah?'

She looked steadily at him. 'But I forgot what it was.'

'Maybe it'll come back to you,' he said.

'Uh-huh,' she said.

★ ★ ★

Gracie called after dinner. The kids were in front of the TV, watching an old video of *Time Bandits* and waiting for a cake they'd made together to finish baking, a project concocted by Emily when things began to seem a little aimless after dinner, when Theo started getting wild. For once Mark had been grateful to her for managing things, for being the adult, for getting Theo — and even somber Daisy — to help her decide what flavors the cake and icing should be, to measure the ingredients out.

'Mark!' Gracie cried. 'I meant to come out when you stopped by to get the kids, but I couldn't right then 'cause of Eva, and then you were gone. How's it going?'

'We're okay,' he said. He stepped again into the little hallway off the kitchen and lowered his voice. 'How *is* Eva?'

16

Her voice lowered in response to his. 'Oh, *God*, what a mess!' she said. 'She's finally asleep, I think, but she's got enough stuff in her to knock out a Clydesdale.'

'She saw it happen, Emily told me.'

'My God, yes. Can you believe that? It's just so unbelievable. The bastard came caroming around the corner and wham! he just sent John sailing, I guess. With Eva and Theo standing *right* there watching.' Her voice changed. 'He hit the light post, you know.'

'No. Emily didn't tell me that.'

'Well, she doesn't know. I figured the girls didn't need to hear every single horrible detail.'

'No,' he said. And then, thinking about it, 'God, no.'

'Precisely,' she said. 'I think he probably died right then.' Her voice had sailed off on these last few words, and she stopped abruptly. Then she whispered, 'Just a sec.' The phone clunked. She stepped away, into a silence. After a minute or two, he heard her walking back, blowing her nose. She came on again. 'Anyway,' she said hoarsely. 'Afterward they still had to play out the sad scene where they *hold* him and the ambulance comes and all that.' Her throat made an odd clicking noise. 'Oh, it's just too horrible, isn't it? You just don't know what to say or do.'

'Gracie,' he said.

'Hold on,' she said. He could hear her blowing her nose again.

When she picked up the phone once more, he said, 'It's easier for me than you. I've got the kids here. I feel useful, in a way, fixing burgers for dinner, something as stupid as that.'

'I envy you.'

'I know. I don't envy you.'

'I'm not complaining, Mark,' she said quickly. 'She needs me. Eva.'

'I know.'

They let a silence gather on the line. Finally he said, 'So you're staying overnight?'

'Oh, at least. You can't believe . . . I mean, I'd always thought, Eva, with the children . . . you know. Well, she was someone who always held it together for the kids.' She sighed. 'Boy! Not this time.'

They arranged to talk again in the morning. He'd get the kids to day care and school. Or maybe he'd let the girls stay home. He'd figure it out, what seemed best. He gave her the number of his car phone. She promised to call if anything changed.

When Mark got off the phone and was extracting the cake from the oven, he was thinking of Eva, weeping, hysterical. He had seen her like that more than a few times in the early days of their marriage, when they fought fiercely about things — about principles, it seemed to him now, recollecting it. She'd been that way for a while around the time of their breakup too. Once when he came to pick the children up for an overnight, he'd gone back to the house after he'd gotten them into the truck. He wanted to remind her of the time he planned to return them. But he stopped still in the doorway, unable to go farther. Somewhere inside, shut behind walls and doors in what she thought was privacy,

18

Eva was wailing, the terrified, abandoned cries of a child, one shriek of pain after another, so loud and desperate that you couldn't imagine how she had enough breath to go on.

And now she was suffering for John. For a moment he let sorrow flood him — a soft, virtuous sorrow that it took him only a few seconds to realize was as much somehow for himself as for Eva or John. This seemed so crazy, so wrongheaded — wrong-*hearted* — that he slammed the oven door to stop himself, and after a second Daisy's terrified voice called out from the living room, 'What happened? What was *that?*'

★ ★ ★

In the night, Mark woke. What woke him? Not Theo, who lay sound asleep where he'd wound up — jammed against Mark's headboard, breathing phlegmily, his mouth open. Around the little boy were the stuffed animals he'd pulled out from his paper bag, one of whom, Miss Owl, Mark recognized as having been Daisy's years before.

'That was mighty nice of you,' he'd said to her after he'd put Theo to bed, after they'd all said goodnight to him.

She had shrugged. 'Not really,' she said. 'I like seeing her, actually. She was living in a *box*, before.'

He'd looked at her, tall, gangly, and thought how odd it was that at one moment she could speak like this, as though she were still

19

connected to the child who had believed in the *life* of her toys, and then a moment or two later gesture in a way that made her seem an adult, even sexual.

Before she'd gone to bed, she'd come into the kitchen again and said she'd remembered what she'd forgotten. 'You know, what I wanted to ask you before.'

'Oh, yes. Shoot.'

'Where's John? Where *is* he, now?'

And Mark had answered her wrong, he'd answered the child in her. 'I really don't know, Daze. It depends, I guess, on what you believe. If you believe in an afterlife — '

'No!' she said impatiently, shaking her head. 'I mean where is *he*? Where is his *body*?' And her hand had swept down her own body in a dancer's motion.

He'd stood there a moment, looking at her, fierce and utterly focused in a way he'd hardly ever seen her be. 'I don't know that either, Daze,' he said sadly.

He turned and lay on his back now. He'd left a living room lamp on because Theo was scared of the dark. His bedroom looked somehow disordered and unpleasant in this half-light.

After a few minutes, he became aware that he was timing his breathing with Theo's. This perhaps accounted for the constricted feeling in his chest. But when he consciously regulated himself, when he forced himself to breathe at his own pace once more, he realized the constriction was his alone — that he was thinking of John, hurtling upward, upward, smashing into the post. Of Eva, watching, crying out. He swung his head from side to side on his pillow.

The last time he'd spoken to John had been maybe ten days earlier, an ordinary exchange: how's it going? what have you been up to? John was a large man, big-boned and homely, with sandy hair and whitish eyelashes. He always looked a little sunburned, a little defenseless. When he asked Mark even the most banal question, he seemed honestly to want to know; he would lean forward, frowning, to hear the answer. Mark often found himself responding at too-great length — he'd be bored himself by the time he was done. He was bored this time too, answering John, talking about his business, about the harvest — the crush — about how long his days were right now, about getting the grapes in at the right time, about overextending the crews.

But John had seemed as interested as he always did. He asked Mark more questions, he poured him another glass of wine.

This was on a Sunday in late September. Mark had stopped by to pick the girls up and walked in on a party, a lunch that had apparently gone on and on. It was in its last stages now — the table was littered with crumbs and stained with wine from earlier in the meal: the pale pinkish rings had softly expanded on the white cloth, the droplets were furred. The sun glinted low through the opened door and the air smelled dry and sweet.

Mark was greeted warmly. Another piece of apricot tart was cut for him, John filled his glass, he was introduced to everyone at the table. The

21

girls, who had stood around for the first few minutes after he arrived, disappeared again once they realized he was staying awhile. After some minutes, you could hear the bass of their music thumping somewhere upstairs.

The conversation had resumed. The topic was books, literature, as it usually was at Eva and John's house. One of the guests was a writer, someone who taught too, apparently. They were trying to ascertain how many of them had read Proust. Only two hands went up, Mark was relieved to see, since he hadn't. One was John's and one was the woman's named Cynthia, the writer's wife. And then, looking around, she said, 'Well, *partway*, I must confess.'

Her husband asked if she would have confessed if everyone else *had* read it.

She laughed. She was attractive, Mark thought, in a nervous-looking, over-made-up way. 'That's for me to know and you to find out,' she said. 'Or not.'

They wondered what it meant that so few of them had read Proust. They were fairly literate as a group. How many could there be, in the wide world of readers, if in this population so few had? They joked about it. Maybe seven? 'Maybe *everyone* is a liar,' Eva said.

And so Mark had ended up, as he often did, talking to John. John, who seemed fully interested in Mark's description of the variability in timing of the grapes' ripening, of the possibility of cutting it too close. Of the problems of having too few workers now and too many around at other times. How could you know whether John even cared? You couldn't. He was too nice.

A nice man. What had Eva said when Mark had used this word about him? When he'd said, after the first time he'd met John, 'He seems genuinely nice'?

She hadn't been looking at him, she was kneeling on the floor in front of Daisy, helping wedge her feet into red boots that were almost too small to go on over her shoes. 'Yes, I thought I'd try *nice* this time,' she said. 'I thought maybe I deserved it.'

Mark was standing above her. All he could see of her was the back of her head and the knobbed vulnerable curve of the white nape of her neck where her hair fell forward off it. But he knew by her voice, weighted with harsh accusation against him, how her face would have looked, and he hadn't answered her.

He tried now to imagine John after the accident. Was his face damaged? His head? It must have been. How could it not? He imagined Eva kneeling, holding him. Eva, streaked with blood. He imagined himself, how he would have looked, lying there; and then Eva bending over him, wailing.

He was feeling, he recognized with a pinch of shame, an oddly intense interest in this scene, even a yearning for it, for the drama of it, for Eva's panicked love. He lay there a long time, listening to his own uneven breathing, and under it Theo's — steady, apparently dreamless, thick.

23

2

It wasn't until months later that Eva could bear to think of it as a *process*, her grief. When people suggested it to her in the days and weeks after John's death — *New Agey, sloppy people. Hateful people*, she thought — she was sometimes speechless in her sense of affront at the notion, as though they had unexpectedly slapped her. She wouldn't, couldn't think of this roil of pain that swept in and out of her life as having either a predictable shape or an end point. It seemed to her a monster she'd bedded, one she'd come to love in some way. When it was gone, when it decided on some days — whimsically, it seemed to her — not to be there, not to torment her, then she was tormented by that, by its very absence.

Sometimes in those early days of October and November she felt amazed that life could happen around it: the things of life, the things that had always meant life. The children woke, and their waking woke her — their voices downstairs in the house, their bare feet thudding on the old wood floors. She got up; she urinated and felt the familiar physical sense of pleasurable relief at that, her body's work. That it should work, that she should go on feeling anything because of that, seemed preposterous to her. She brushed her teeth, she made the children's breakfast and got them launched into their day. She went to the bookstore she owned, though the two women who worked for her often sent her home those first weeks after John died if it wasn't a busy day in the office. She came home. She went to see Daisy play basketball, to see Emily cheerleading at a football game. She bought groceries, she picked up Theo at day care, she made dinner.

But anywhere, anywhere in all of this, the monster could arrive and literally take her breath away. Sometimes she felt so overwhelmed when it happened that she squatted or knelt where she was. Once Daisy had found her in the kitchen, crouched on the floor, holding a partly peeled carrot in her hand.

'What, Mom?' she cried. She had stopped in the doorway, confused and frightened. 'What happened?'

And with that it was gone, as though Daisy had broken a spell cast upon her. Eva felt only embarrassed. She stood up, and found the scraper she'd set down so hurriedly. 'It's nothing,' she said, turning her back to Daisy. And because that was so blatantly a lie, she added, 'I just felt a little dizzy.'

Another time she sat weeping through an entire parent conference at Theo's day-care center. The woman talking with her was so young, so unfamiliar with the possibility of this scale of grief, that she took Eva at her word when she said that *it was all right, really, it sometimes just happened, please ignore it if you can*; she went carefully and thoroughly through her notes — tidy writing in black ink on five-by-eight cards — while tears and clear mucus streamed steadily down Eva's face. When she'd finished, the teacher looked quickly and with some embarrassment over at Eva and asked if she had any questions. 'No,' Eva whispered. 'None.'

Sometimes in the first months after John's death, she woke in the night and staggered into the bathroom and threw up, threw up even when there was nothing more there. She thought of it as her whole body's grieving, as a form of clenched and useless weeping.

It was the most ordinary kind of memory that set her off. Once, just after she'd lain down to sleep, she thought of a night when she'd waked at the touch of John's foot on her calf — the bottom of his foot, a soft pad. She remembered that before she had even registered what it was, she had had a sense of it as so intensely dear, so charged for her with love — that light, steady contact, that connection with him — that she had turned to him in the dark and begun to stroke his shoulders slowly and tenderly, bringing him back from sleep to her. Thinking of this as she lay there alone — his dear foot, his body awakening and turning over to her, his big shape in the dark rocking above her — she'd begun to weep, softly at first, and then so loudly that, to her shame, Emily had to come in to quiet her so she wouldn't scare Theo.

And then there were all the small things, the signs of how much she lived elsewhere. The time they were stopped at a light on the way to Gracie's, and when it turned green she had to ask the children where they were going — she simply had no idea, no memory. ('Jesus, Mom,' Daisy said. 'Are you going crazy on us now?') The two times at breakfast when she'd poured orange juice instead of milk into her coffee, to Theo's loud delight.

It was like being in love, she thought — grief. It was like the way you were stunned with love when you were young. She remembered performing the orange juice trick when she'd been so wildly in love with Mark she couldn't think straight. There was that same sense of having lost yourself, of being taken over by some feeling you weren't in control of. Though of course, in neither case did you really want relief.

But relief came in this case, wanted or not. As the *process* went on, as Eva took the first steps toward recovering from her sense of having lost everything, as she was more able to spend sometimes a whole day without being swept by sorrow, then she began to grieve for her very grief, her letting go of John. She didn't want to let go of him! She didn't want to speak lovingly and in the past tense of him. She didn't want not to be furious at his death, at how he had died, at the memory of holding his ruined head in her arms so Theo wouldn't see it. So no one would see it, not even the EMTs, who had to pry him from her grip when they came for him.

A normal day, a day in which she didn't weep, in which she wasn't felled by rage or sorrow, was like a betrayal of what had happened to him.

But they came, the normal days, more and more of them, and by degrees they stole her grief

27

from her — her last connection to John, she felt then.

And here she is now, six months after John's death, having lived through just such a day, setting the table for what will be, after all, a family dinner. Mark is bringing the girls back at about five — he's had them for the weekend — and he'll stay and eat with all of them as he sometimes does, as he used to do occasionally too when John was alive.

She'll be grateful for the adult company. She's spent the day with Theo, who's been, as he always is with her now, alternately wildly active and wanting her to be active with him; and then silent — withdrawn, it seems to her.

She's worried about him. But then she's worried about all the children.

Well, not Emily, actually. Though she's better now, Emily had seemed the most grief stricken of the three earlier, and grief stricken is what you'd expect. What you'd want, Eva thinks.

Grief stricken is what Daisy and Theo haven't seemed. Though Eva knows that Daisy's withdrawal, her silences, are part of her sorrow, as she knows that in some sense Daisy was the most deeply attached to John of the children. The most in love with him. Emily and Theo relied on John, took John for granted — as, Eva recognized, she had too. Though what did that mean? That she knew he'd always be there? Maybe something as simple as that. But that was a something that meant almost everything to Eva.

Daisy, though, limp unpretty Daisy, with her

horrible posture, her unkempt hair, her *droopiness* — Daisy who probably mostly didn't believe that anyone would always be there — Daisy seemed to have pinned the little hope she held on to in that department on John. The wooing of him! He and Eva had laughed about it occasionally alone in their bedroom at night. Only last year he'd shown her an elaborate card Daisy had made and left on his desk, inviting him to her piano recital. And one night when she was about ten, they found a poem from her pinned to his pillow, a poem that galumphed along to the final line, 'Oh stepfather, man among men!' (Eva had used this as a sexual joke once. She had whispered the line to John as he entered her, and they had laughed; but she felt a kind of sad guilt about Daisy afterward, and she didn't do it again.)

It was Daisy who would go anywhere with John when he leaned in and offered his open, careless invitations: 'I'm heading to the bakery' — to the grocery, to the dry cleaner, to the wine shop. 'Anyone want to come along?' Daisy always put aside what she was doing and volunteered, as though she couldn't bear to think of his being alone.

It's difficult to tell how hard it is for her now, she's so private, but even when Eva is most lost in her own pain, she tries to remind herself that Daisy is suffering too. That the more you can't tell Daisy is suffering, the more she is. Eva hasn't known what to do about it beyond trying to get to all the recitals, the games she can manage. Beyond letting Daisy see her own grief, her tears.

Beyond touching her as much as Daisy will allow, which isn't a lot — she's expert at shrugging away from Eva's hand on her shoulder, at turning out from an attempted embrace by her mother.

But Theo is even harder, because Eva simply has no idea what he feels. Not once has he truly wept. Or even in any real sense acknowledged that John is dead, though Eva has tried often to speak of it with him. Not so much the event of John's death — that would be too terrible, too cruel to discuss. But simply the fact that he is dead, gone. And sometimes it seems Theo does understand that, without being able to talk about it. There are even moments when it seems to Eva that he accepts it, as a premise, an underlying fact of his life.

But then no. Today, for instance, in the car on the way back from swimming in the pool at Gracie's, he said, out of the blue, 'When I get big, I'm going to show my dad how good I swim.'

Eva, who was planning dinner, surveying her open refrigerator in her mind, wondering if she could get by without stopping for groceries, was startled to attentiveness. She looked over at him. He was wrapped in a striped towel, his thick brown hair still dark with dampness, his eyes and nostrils pinked from the chlorine and water.

After a minute, she said, 'I wish you *could* show that to Daddy.' She was considering each word. 'He'd be so proud.'

'I'm *gonna*,' the little boy said fiercely.

Eva felt a heaviness forming in her midsection.

30

She tried to keep her voice mild. 'But you know Daddy is dead, Theo.' He was looking out the passenger window — though he was so low in the car, so small, that surely all he could see were the overhanging trees by the road and the cloudless sky behind them. 'Right?' she said.

Now he turned to her. 'Right. But I mean I'm gonna show him in *heaven*.'

Eva was startled. She had never said to Theo that John was in heaven. She knew Mark or Gracie or Gracie's husband, Duncan, would never say such a thing either. Had someone in day care, hoping to be kind? Would one of the girls have thought this was the right thing to say, the comforting thing?

She knew she should ask him more about this. She knew she should say something to him. But what? That if he were with John in heaven, he'd be dead too?

Hardly that, of course.

That she didn't believe in heaven? That *they* didn't believe in heaven? — since he was part of what she thought and believed.

And then what?

They were driving.

They were driving! How could she instruct him in what death meant, in the horrible enormity of his loss, when they were driving down this sunny highway with the acid yellow of the mustard bright between the rows of pale, greening vines? When she was thinking only seconds ago about whether she should swing into the supermarket for lettuce, a lemon?

What she said to him in the end was, 'I think

31

your dad would be happy that you're such a good swimmer.'

'Yah,' he said, and turned his head back to look up at what was passing above him.

Eva blames herself for part of this. She thinks sending Theo away to Mark for those few days right after the accident, not letting him see her wildest grief, was a bad mistake. She thinks it's made it all unreal to Theo — John's death. That in some way he doesn't accept it, he's fighting off the knowledge of it. No wonder he collapses in on himself, Eva thinks. No wonder he falls silent. Imagine the work involved!

But then she had said, 'You're my absolute hero, Theo.' She gripped the cool small knob of his bare knee. It tensed and jumped under her hand. 'My superhero, not to put too fine a point on it.'

He looked over at her and smiled vaguely. '*I know* that,' he said.

*   *   *

When Mark arrives with Daisy and Emily, he calls from the front hall and Eva emerges from the kitchen, drying her hands. The girls greet Eva distractedly and disappear upstairs to check their phone messages. Theo trails after them. He misses them when they're away. And they miss him. They'll let him hang around them tonight. By tomorrow things will be back to normal. In the kitchen, Eva puts water on to boil in a big pot. Then she goes to the butler's pantry off the hall and pours a glass of wine for herself and

32

Mark from the bottle he's brought; and they go down the hall into the living room, where he's lighted a fire, at her request — the air outside has started to get cool. The fire is popping noisily from time to time, spewing hot orange sparks onto the stone hearth, sparks that slowly dim and turn black. Mark sits in a chair near it, the poker in his hand, and Eva tucks her legs up under her on the couch.

It's odd, she thinks, to sit here with Mark in this big Victorian house, the heavy wood trim painted an elegant creamy white, the furniture so solid and comfortable. Their life together had been such a struggle financially, and the places where they'd lived with each other had always had an improvised air: borrowed and second-hand furniture, threadbare couches covered with Indian spreads, tables made from solid-core doors, bookcases of cinder blocks and planks. And the bookcases themselves filled with paperbacks: hardcover books were an extravagance reserved for birthdays or Christmas. The money came later for both of them. For her, by marrying John; for Mark, as his work was more highly valued. And though they're both well used to it now, it still feels a bit like playing a part to face him surrounded by all this ease.

He has aged well, she thinks. That tall ranginess has filled in, bulked up, but there's still a vaguely animal quality to him: his pale eyes in his long dark face, his slightly feral way of moving — smooth, almost stealthy. Even now, sitting forward to watch the fire, then getting up to put another log on, he conveys a sense of inheld power in everything he does that makes him beautiful.

Maybe she's forgiven him for that, she thinks.

They've lowered their voices slightly to talk about the children. They talk about Emily, about how pleased they are that she's been accepted at Wesleyan, how good it will be for her to be away from the family. They agree again that she has to learn to relax, to let herself be funny, which happens from time to time. They both try to call up funny-Emily stories, and can't, which makes them laugh. 'There you have it,' she says.

And now they move on, feeling generous to each other, expansive. He tells her about his work, about his crew members, about their idiosyncrasies, their jokes. She tells him about a reading series she's arranging. They talk about the shade of blue in the dining room, which she wants to change. 'The problem is I can't stand the names.'

'The names?'

'The paint names. Who thinks them up?'

'Ignore them. They're just words.'

'I can't. I can't ignore them. Words count. If I had a dining room named *seafoam*, I'd think of it every time I stepped in.'

He grins. 'And you'd feel . . . ?'

She shrugs and laughs. 'Wet, I guess.'

All of this is easy and comfortable, as it hadn't been in the years before she married John, when she was still so angry with Mark she didn't like to stay in the same room with him if the children weren't there. She thinks of this, this newly companionable relationship with her

34

ex-husband, as another gift John has given her.

Mark is talking now about how the overgrown land behind his house has been cleared for a vineyard by his neighbor, affording him a startling new view of the mountain. They both speak of the skyrocketing real estate prices in the valley, of how grateful they are to have bought when they did.

And now she's suddenly talking about Theo, the child who doesn't even belong to Mark. She has felt the impulse growing in herself, and in her ease with him this evening, she gives over to it. She explains about the trouble Theo's been having in day care, about how he apparently can't seem to stay long with any one activity. Sometimes he gets angry, he has a tantrum — his caregiver has to give him a *time-out*, an expression Eva detests, and can't say without a mocking emphasis. She tells Mark she thinks this is related to John's death, to Theo's not accepting John's death. 'He never speaks of it,' she says.

'Well, it was pretty awful. He probably doesn't like to think of it.'

'But don't you think he needs somehow — I don't know — to confront it? I know that sounds like psychobabble, but I think . . . I can't help feeling he doesn't really believe John is dead. And it can't be good for him to hang on to that fantasy.'

Mark doesn't answer for a minute. She can't tell what he might be thinking. He's turned away, looking at the fire. But now he looks over at her and smiles. 'I'm sure he'll be all right, Eva.

I know he will.' Somehow, for no good reason, this reassures her, her spirits feel lighter.

When they go back into the kitchen so Eva can pull the meal together, the kids hear them and come downstairs, and there's the pleasant sense of milling around that has happened only occasionally since John's death. Mark is showing Theo a trick where they hold hands and the little boy walks up Mark's body until Mark flips him over. Emily is talking to Eva about the college catalogue she's gotten in the mail from Wesleyan, and one of the courses she's thinking of taking next year — and Daisy is sitting on the counter, listening. Emily stands next to Eva while she talks, more or less leaning on her. Eva finds this odd, this impulse to physical proximity. She can't imagine having wanted such a thing from her own mother. But when Emily talks to Eva, she often touches her, idly rearranging her mother's hair, straightening her collar. And now that both girls are taller than she is, Eva sometimes feels swamped by them — by Emily's impulse to tell her everything, by Daisy's presence and the needfulness she feels in it, by being touched in this idle way whose meaning she doesn't truly understand.

Now she pokes Daisy off the counter and hands her a bowl of salad to take to the table. Then they are all trailing her, picking up the dishes and glasses she asks them to bring.

As Mark comes into the dining room with their wineglasses and the bottle, he asks Eva where she wants him. She's setting Theo into his booster chair, pushing him in. 'There,' she says,

36

pointing. 'At the head of the table, please.'

Theo frowns; he looks over at Mark. After a moment he says, 'Why is Mark's place called the *head* of the table, Mumma?'

Eva is moving to her place, sitting down. 'Hmmm,' she says. 'I suppose the idea is that you're supposed to think of the table as being like a person. Imagine it standing up, imagine if we just tilted it. It would make a big, rectangular body.' Her hands mimic the shape. 'Over there, on top,' her finger makes a circle in the air, 'is the head. So Mark is at the head.'

After a long beat, Theo's frowning face opens, and he cries, 'And me and Daze are the arms!'

'Right,' Mark says.

Eva drinks a little wine, the wine Mark has brought as a gift.

'And *I* am the leg,' says Emily grandly, her hand rising to her small bosom. 'The only leg. This happens to be a one-legged table.'

Theo picks up his glass of milk, and is just taking a swallow when Mark says, 'A *peg leg*.'

Theo's milk shoots out of his mouth, splattering the table and his plate. 'A peg leg?' he yells, delighted.

'Oh, Theo!' Eva is up, in two steps at Theo's place, wiping up in front of him with her napkin.

'Well, he said *peg leg*, Mumma. That was *funny*!' He turns. 'That was funny, wasn't it, Mark?'

'Wipe your face, sweetie. Use your napkin.' She is picking up his plate to get at the milk underneath it. 'It *was* funny.'

'You know me,' Mark says. 'Famous wit.'

Theo rubs his face thoroughly, extravagantly, and as he finishes, he begins to call out, 'Peg leg! peg leg! peggy-leggy! leggy-peggy!'

Eva sits down as the chant goes on. 'Enough!' she says. 'Enough, Theo. We get it.'

He falls silent, and everyone begins to eat, passing the bowls around. Theo is looking at Eva now. She watches as an idea visibly dawns. With the delighted emphasis he reserves for bottoms, for sexual body parts, for bathroom functions, he announces, '*Mumma* is the table's *butt*!'

Eva makes a face across at Mark.

'Right, Theo,' Daisy says in a world-weary voice, a voice meant to suggest, *Grow up, why don't you?*

Theo turns to Mark and says it again. 'My mom is the table's butt!'

Eva can see that Mark doesn't know what to say. He's not used to this *boyness*. She leans forward toward Theo. 'Hey, mister,' she says. 'Listen up. I'm going to tell you a story.'

Theo turns to her with his wicked grin. 'A story about a *butt*!' he says.

'No, because we're all heartily sick of hearing about butts. This is a story about a little boy.' She has a sip of wine. 'A *big* boy, I mean. A big boy, who . . . Let's see. Got *lost* one day. Lost in the forest.'

He is suddenly attentive, the smile gone. 'Was there a wolf?'

'There was *not* a wolf,' Eva says firmly. 'It was not that kind of forest. But night was coming on and the woods were getting dark, and the big boy was far, far away from home.' She taps her wineglass. 'This is very nice, Mark,' she says. 'Made from some of your grapes?'

'Tell!' Theo says. 'Tell it!'

Eva smiles slyly. 'Oh, Emily knows what happens next. Don't you, Emily?'

'Me!' Emily says. 'Thanks a lot, Mom.' But she's used to this game, one they often played when John was alive. He had invented it to keep Theo sitting peacefully at the table through a long meal. Emily stops and thinks, and then she carries on. 'Okay. Well. The boy was very scared, but he didn't cry. He knew he had to be brave, because . . . he was all by himself, and no one else could rescue him. It was his own fault he was lost, too, because everyone had told him not to go into that forest, they told him over and over that it was dangerous in there, but he went anyway, because what he liked to do best of all was stuff that people told him not to do.'

'He was *bad*.'

'He was not bad exactly, but he was really naughty. But all of a sudden the boy heard . . . ' Emily raises her eyebrows, opens her mouth in mock surprise. 'Guess! Guess what he heard.'

'What?'

Her smile is open and teasing. She doesn't answer him.

'What? What? What? What?' Theo is rocking his body with each cry.

'Daisy knows,' she says. 'Ask Daisy.'

Daisy shakes her head, biting her lip.

'What?' Theo says to Daisy. '*What* he heard?'

'Come on, Daze,' Eva says.

Daisy meets her eye with a face so pained that Eva is startled.

But then she looks away from her mother, across the table at Theo. After a moment, she starts, hesitantly: 'He heard . . . hoofbeats.' She is unsmiling. 'And then he saw it: a beautiful white horse, running toward him. Even in the pitch-dark he could see it, it was so white. And it said . . . '

She gestures rapidly, erasing herself. 'Well, it didn't say anything, because horses can't talk, but it trotted in circles around him in the woods, and the boy knew that he should follow the horse, that special white horse.'

Daisy's voice is soft and rhythmic and compelling, and Theo claps his hands eagerly.

'So he did, he followed. He could see the horse ahead of him, he could see the white legs going in and out of the dark trees, and the horse, tossing its mane. And sometimes it whinnied, and he knew it was calling to him, and sometimes, when he almost couldn't see it anymore, then he *would* see it, waiting for him to catch up, and he'd know which way to go. And then . . . '

'What?'

'And *the-en* . . . ' She pauses. It's time to pass the story on, this is the way they do it. She looks at her father. The back of her head is to Eva, the long, carelessly gathered fall of thick dark hair. 'Then, Mark knows the end,' she says.

Eva can see Mark's surprise. And Daisy must see it too, because her voice is uncertain as she says, 'Right, Dad?'

40

She has remembered, as Eva has — maybe they've all remembered — how much this was John's game. How much it is not Mark's. Daisy has picked the wrong father.

'Unh . . . ' Mark meets Eva's gaze and frowns. 'Yeah.'

Eva watches him trying to recall the way they went, the stories she used to tell the girls, to read to them. She feels her body tense.

'Yeah,' he says again.

'So?' Emily says, openly teasing him now. 'Come on, Dad.'

'So.' There's a long pause. 'He followed that horse.' He drinks some wine. 'Up hill and down dale.'

'Excellent, Mark!' Eva says.

He smiles at her and continues. 'Until he saw ahead of him a clearing.' He turns to Theo, and as he goes on, his voice becomes more comfortable in the narrative. 'And when he came to it, he saw it was where the woods ended. Below him were the lights of his town. And he looked around to thank the horse, but it wasn't there; it was gone. Did I imagine it? he thought. Who *was* that white horse, anyway?'

Eva laughs.

'But he didn't have time to figure it out. He ran as fast as he could down the path to his village, through the streets of the town to his own front door, and there was his whole family waiting for him, and he hugged them, and they lived happily ever after.'

At these words, although she'd known they had to come, Eva feels a strange shift, it seems in

41

her heart. Or maybe it's just relief — couldn't it be relief? — that everyone's managed this without John. That the awkward few seconds when she and Daisy, anyway, felt his absence, and Mark's *not-John-ness*, is over.

That they're done.

Now Theo shouts triumphantly, 'The! End!' and everyone laughs. Eva doesn't think anyone has noticed her moment of pain.

★   ★   ★

When she says goodnight to Mark, he kisses her on the cheek, holding her for what seems to Eva a moment too long. A moment that fills her with yearning, in spite of herself. But yearning for *being held* itself, she thinks. For John. Not, she is certain, for Mark.

As she's getting ready for bed, though, she thinks of Mark and the way it was in the orange juice days when they first met, when it seemed they couldn't get enough of each other. Even when they were angriest at each other — and they fought often and hard: tears, yelling, slamming doors, things tossed around — even then they could find each other again through sex, through the way their bodies worked together.

One night when he was driving them home from someplace, they started arguing about something. Eva got so mad at him that she turned to open the car door, her impulse simply a desperation to get *away*. Mark reached over to grab her, and the car shot off the road, rocketing violently into a deep ditch. When they came to a stop, they sat still for a moment, panting. Then they turned to each other. They touched each other to be sure the other was whole, all right. They wept together in fear and relief. They laughed and compared the bruises that were already emerging. And before they got out to look at the damage, to see if they could push the car, they made love on the front seat, hidden by the hard slope of the shoulder from the headlights that occasionally strobed by on the road. Eva remembers the sound of a rushing river somewhere in the dark below them, and the way it felt to be riding Mark like a jockey, the steering wheel bonking her knee with every thrust forward.

She remembers it. It, and other times. Once when she was menstruating heavily and he had her on the kitchen counter, so that when he stood up to come into her, his face was violently smeared with blood. The first time they were able to do it after the long wait for the stitches from Emily's birth to heal. Times in the shower, times when they'd leave a party early and barely be in the door before they'd begin. Times that had once made her hungry for him when she called them up.

After they separated, she'd been able to recast all of these times. Or rather, they'd recast themselves. They came to seem repugnant to her — ugly, forced, extreme. Symptomatic of some inability between them to make themselves happy, even sexually, in a daily way, an ordinary way.

43

She's agitated now, more wakeful than when she came upstairs. She's angry with herself for thinking of fucking Mark. She pulls her bathrobe on and goes down the wide stairs to the first floor.

As she passes back to the kitchen, she sees that Emily and Daisy are at the dining room table. Their faces turn to her, it seems guiltily. Books and papers are spread out around each of them. She steps forward into the room and speaks sharply to them: Why are they still up? Didn't they do any homework at *all* at their father's? Why can't they organize their weekends better?

She watches as their faces close over with dislike for her, with anger. Emily answers her patiently and condescendingly. She's wearing too much eye makeup, Eva thinks. She looks like a raccoon. Eva would like to say this. She would like to tell Emily how cheap and ridiculous she looks.

Ah! she's cruel. They are right to hate her. Who wouldn't? 'An hour, then,' she says.

Daisy protests.

'One hour. That's it. If it's not done, it's just not done.'

As she crosses the hall to the kitchen she can hear them begin their low murmurs of contempt for her. She turns on the overhead light and winces at the reflected sight of herself in the glass of the French doors — her dark hair frazzling gray, her face white and pouchy.

She opens the refrigerator and stands in its exhalation of cool, slightly rotted-smelling air. After a moment, she reaches for a half-full bottle of wine. This is not what she wants — she doesn't know what she wants — but she pours herself a glass. She's full of anger — at herself, at the girls, at Mark. Standing at the kitchen counter, she drinks.

The wine is too cold, too sharp.

It was a nice day until just now, she thinks. She's trying to calm herself. She makes herself remember Theo, swimming, his little body working so hard to get across Gracie's pool. She thinks of the game they played at dinner, the fairy tale and the white horse.

Happily ever after, she thinks.

And for the first time on this ordinary day, it comes to her: her sorrow, her sweet, sad familiar. Almost gratefully she bends under it, tears thicken in her throat. Leaning her upper body over the counter for support, she begins at last to weep.

3

Mark had an affair; that was the simple way to explain what went wrong in his marriage to Eva. The girls were small then, six and three, his dark-haired daughters. Daisy still had the stubby fat fingers of babyhood. He adored these fingers. In fact, sometimes Mark felt nearly dizzy with the intensity of his love for both of his daughters, with his consuming adoration of their physical beings, his fascination with every phrase that fell from their lips. With their lips themselves, delicate, perfect, framing the words.

But he'd forgotten his love for Eva. Or rather, he'd misplaced it. He knew it was still there somewhere, but for the moment, he didn't know how to get to those feelings.

The problem, it seemed to him, was that she'd sunk so heavily into motherhood, into *managing* all their lives. He'd barely be in the door at night before she would start rattling off her list — what needed to be done to get supper on the table, what had broken in the house that he'd have to fix, soon! what one or the other of the girls had taken to doing that he'd have to help her deal with. Oh! and had he picked up milk? (or Pampers, or dog food) on the way home? And why was he so late? and since he was so late, how come he couldn't have called?

It seemed to him that what she wanted — without ever articulating it and maybe

46

without even understanding it — was for him to have had to live through her day, to be as stuck, as mired, as she was. This is what made her angry and cold. He felt too that there was a kind of squalor to their life at home that couldn't help but feed both their misery. Dishes always sat undone in the sink. The children's projects — spilled paints, scissors and scraps of colored paper, dried-up playdough, toys — were always spread on the dining room table, on the floor. Books, dolls, blankies, dress-ups were every-where. You couldn't sit down without first having to pick up whatever child's toy you might have sat on. Sometimes, coming into the house, he felt he couldn't stand it. Once, within a few minutes of arriving home, he had filled the sink with soapy water and started to wash all the leftover dishes, to wipe the smeared and crumb-scattered counters. When Eva came into the kitchen and saw what he was doing, she charged him.

'Oh, stop it!' she cried out. 'Just fucking stop it, stop it, stop it!'

He thought at first she just wanted to hit him, to pull him away from the sink. Then he realized she was tugging at the apron he'd put on, trying to tear it from him. He yanked it over his own head and threw it on the floor, and Eva burst into tears.

She let him hold her that time. 'I just can't *do* it,' she sobbed, while he said to her, over and over, 'I only wanted to help. I was just trying to help you, Eva.'

He saw how it had happened. They were living out in the country, she was too much alone, she

47

had to manage the house and the girls and the shopping and the meals. There was the house itself, with its tilting floors and the doors that didn't quite shut, the faucets that dribbled water. It took half an hour to draw a bath. There was the long rainy season to endure, the girls cooped up, fussy, wanting to be entertained and read to. There was the dry, hot summer and the dust that coated everything. He understood much later that she'd been depressed and overwhelmed. At the time, though, he mostly hadn't cared to understand, because her anger at him made him angry at her. He had simply turned away from her. He sought comfort first in the life of the girls' world, the intense love for them that was like a shield against Eva's sorrow, a blameless weapon against the anger he felt coming from her. When he arrived home, they were the ones he greeted with love, the ones he touched, the ones he smiled at.

And then he turned to Amy.

Their affair lasted just under a year, starting with a relaxed flirtation in the cantina where Amy was a bartender and he sometimes stopped in to talk with friends, to have a few more moments of ease before heading home to face Eva's pinched-in rage.

Mark liked to flirt — he liked women generally — and in some sense flirting was part of Amy's job. When she had a male customer who seemed receptive to it, she gave a special spin to the opener, 'What can I do for *you*?' Mark had laughed out loud the first time she asked him that.

When he stopped by, they talked, brokenly but easily, between her serving other customers. The third or fourth night he was in, Amy told him that she knew who he was, that she lived in a tiny bungalow at the edge of one of the small vineyards he managed. That she'd seen him there.

Yeah, he'd noticed it, he said.

He'd envied it, in fact. He'd seen her too, on the little deck at the back of the house, a woman alone, sunbathing and reading, and he'd imagined how simple, how easy it would be to live like that in such a place.

He should come by for coffee some morning and check it out, she said. She had a towel slung over one shoulder. She always had a towel slung over one shoulder, and he pointed this out to her. She tilted her head and grinned. She was pulling a tall glass of ale, slowly. 'Just looking for a guy with a bar of soap,' she said.

He did go to her house, one rainy morning when there was nothing much doing in the vineyards. And after that they began to meet several times a week, for coffee, for sex, for the easy conversation that followed it in a house where there were no children, no chores he was responsible for. It was all so simple, so without blame and resentment. Sometimes he managed to get away on a weekend afternoon, and they'd fuck and sleep, and then wake to fuck some more. In the summer Eva took the girls to her parents' place in Martha's Vineyard for a week, their more-or-less annual visit. Mark waited for Amy outside the cantina in his truck nearly every night and followed the red taillights of her old Volkswagen Beetle down the dark, empty road to her house.

But over the long, rainy months of that next winter, she began to want something more from him. Because he couldn't give it, because he couldn't imagine inflicting the pain it would take to extricate himself from Eva and Emily and Daisy — couldn't, in those rare moments he allowed himself to think honestly about it, imagine making any kind of life with Amy that he'd want — she gradually came to be angry with him too. More and more she insisted on her terms: if they were going to continue, he needed to get a divorce, they needed to get married. But even while she spoke of this, of their coming together permanently, she seemed increasingly to dislike him — even to despise him. In the end he couldn't talk about a book or a movie, he couldn't have an *idea*, without inviting her contempt for his critical faculties. He could see, long before they got there, where they were heading.

Still, when she broke it off, he was crazy with the desire to hold on, to keep it going. The most graphic images of their lovemaking occupied every idle moment of his day — at work, at home, driving around in his truck. He nearly cried out sometimes with the anguished hunger that would flood him thinking of her powerful long legs, opening, of himself kneeling above her, entering her. How she straddled him, how she pulled at him with her mouth, her teeth. A few times he had to stop the truck, torn between rage

50

and jerking off. Once he hit the steering wheel so hard he carried the bruises on the curved outer flesh of his palm for a week.

But he came out of it; he recovered. And as he became himself again, Eva came back to him, she emerged from the dark spell she'd been under.

What did it? Mark was never sure. Maybe it was the sex, which had, oddly, gotten better and more frequent through the affair with Amy — at first because he had wanted to ensure that Eva didn't guess he was involved with someone else, and later out of the appetite and sexual energy that had come to seem generalized in him, that occupied him constantly.

But of course other things had changed in their lives by then too. The girls were a year older, and Eva had found care for them. His business was doing so well that they finally had what seemed like enough money. Eva had gotten a part-time job she loved, in a bookstore this time. In any case, it was like being rewarded for giving up an indulgence, getting his old, dear friend back. Rewarded with interest: the thought of her began to preoccupy him through the days as thoughts of Amy had at the height of their passion. As those thoughts still could, if he were honest, from time to time.

But he felt it differently; he saw it differently. With Amy it had been, almost embarrassingly so, *parts* of her body that compelled him: her long, muscled calves and thighs, the wide dark triangle of her bush, the light clicking sound her sex made when his hand opened her legs. With Eva,

51

he thought, it was the whole of her, as it had been from the start: the way she gestured and frowned when she spoke, her odd turns of phrase, her smallness, which made him feel powerful and protective. Even the way the house smelled when she was cooking, which seemed to him, somehow, to emanate from her, to be part of who she was. All of this made him, simply, happy.

Summer began. The evenings were long. The girls were old enough now, they played well enough together, that Mark and Eva could resume their old habit of a glass of wine before supper. They sat together out on the terrace she'd painstakingly made from used bricks the year before. They sat in the shadows of the western mountains and looked over at the sun still laying a golden blanket over the eastern ones, and talked the way they had in the early days, but more calmly, more sweetly, he would have said. Eva had her own news to report now — eccentric, interesting customers who'd stopped in and the funny things they said: what books were doing well, which had unexpectedly bombed; the visits from sales reps; the balancing of accounts — and so Mark felt he could at last speak openly of his own concerns: it wouldn't be the occasion for her feeling the more resentful, the more deprived of a life in the world. They talked of the seemingly whimsical popularity of certain grapes, of how the valley was changing, of the exponential growth of the vineyards, of the problems of worker housing and the moral responsibility for it. They talked of foolish things

52

too: whether Diane Keaton was actually acting in *Annie Hall*, or just being her ditzy self. Whether people on the East Coast, where Eva was from, had a stronger sense of irony than those in the West.

They were sitting there one night in July when he told her about Amy. What he had come to feel as they drew closer together was that the secret of Amy was an impediment to their new openness, an impediment he couldn't live with. He wanted there to be no separation between them. He felt it as he would have a sexual necessity: the need for Eva to take in and understand — no, to *love*, that's what he wanted — even the part of him that had betrayed her.

During the long silence that fell after he'd said it, before she said, in a voice gone cold and distant, 'How long?,' they could hear Emily inside talking to Daisy, imitating Eva's voice at her most playful and affectionate: 'Know what, my silly girl? You are the funniest bunny *ever*.' In the difference between the two voices — Eva's, the little girl's playing at being Eva — Mark could hear what he'd already lost. Instantly he understood, of course, that he should never have told her. He saw, just those few moments too late, that it was worse than cruel: it was uselessly cruel.

And he hadn't bargained on Eva's own capacity to be cruel. Or, at any rate, to be unforgiving. He should have remembered from all their arguments that she saw these things — these moral issues, he supposed — in a clear, hard light. There was black and white. There was before, and there was after, for Eva.

It was over, she told him. Well, what she said was, 'Okay.' She stood up, carefully setting her wineglass down. 'That's it, then.' Her voice was hoarse, strained.

She went back into the house. He sat in the cool shade looking over at the warm hill opposite for a few minutes. He could hear her in the kitchen. She was slamming pots and pans around as though she were about to cook for hundreds.

'Get out,' she shrilled when he followed her, when he began to plead. 'I want you out.' Her hands made frantic crisscross, waving gestures, her neck was corded with rage. 'Gone! Take your . . . ridiculous penis, and . . . just go!'

His ridiculous penis?

The girls had come to stand in the doorway now, wearing strange dress-up costumes, old clothes of Eva's that drooped on their chest and showed their tiny nipples, that puddled on the floor around their feet. Their round mouths were dropped open at the sound of their mother's rage — they looked like dopey cartoon fish out of water. They shouldn't have been there. They shouldn't have had to see this, or hear it. But there was no one to rescue them. Mark couldn't. He had to get through to Eva somehow. He could hear his own voice speaking Eva's name, trying to make his case.

'Do you think I could ever want you again?' she was shrieking. 'When every time we made love I'd be thinking of your . . . fat ass pumping up and down over that . . . weaselly woman!'

54

His fat ass? His ass wasn't fat.

She stopped now, and looked at him. She was panting. She'd backed up as far away from him as she could get, to the kitchen counter. She was resting against it, she was bent slightly forward from the waist. She started to laugh.

Mark heard the hysterical note, but the little girls didn't, and in their relief — oh, this was all a joke! a game! — they imitated her, laughing falsely, much too loud, much too shrill. He looked at them. The fear was still in their eyes, but the kitchen was full of laughter, a raucous accusatory sound: nightmare gaiety.

Mark couldn't stand it. He left.

He left. As he was shutting the front door, he thought he heard Eva's laughter become weeping, but he didn't stop to be sure. He just kept going, across the yard, into his truck, then down the long curving drive in the dusk of the overhanging trees to the road that led to town.

Later, when he tried to call up the words he'd used to tell her, he couldn't imagine what they might have been. 'Eva, there's something you should know'? 'Eva, I need to tell you about something I've been keeping to myself'? 'Eva, I want to tell you something bad about me, something terrible, and then I want you to rise above it'? How could he have thought it would work? How could he have thought there were any words he could speak about his affair that she could stand to hear? Yet he must have said something like one of those phrases.

He *did* remember the sense he'd had just before he spoke: the excitement — excitement, that's what he'd felt! — of beginning a new adventure.

★ ★ ★

Mark and Eva had met at a wedding, Mark's third wedding in as many weeks. He was depressed by this one, as he had been by them all — by the sense of purpose swimming all around him in these friends of his, by the fearless, touching commitment they were undertaking that was so unlike anything he could imagine for himself. To each couple he'd given the same thing — thick glass beer mugs. He liked beer. Either they did or they didn't. The hell with it. The hell with them. The hell with everything.

Mark was twenty-five. It had taken him six years to get through two and a half years of college — he was dyslexic — and he'd only recently decided to stop, to quit. He could do it — he could have done it — he was sure of that. But that would have been the point, the only point: proving that to himself. It didn't seem worth it. Everyone else he knew was moving on, entering life, thinking about work, about what came next — getting married — and Mark figured it'd be two or three more years anyway at the rate he was going before he even got a degree. A degree that would equip him to do nothing in particular.

He was drinking too much. It was the way he'd gotten through all of the weddings. This one was of a woman he'd dated several years earlier. They'd since become 'good friends,' and when she bent to enter the getaway car in her pale suit and he saw her long, nicely shaped legs, legs he'd once pushed this way and that with the ease of sexual ownership, he felt somehow abandoned. *Damaged goods*, he thought. Unexpected tears of self-pity sprang to his eyes.

Eva was in bad shape because she'd just graduated, and her graduation meant the end of her year-long affair with one of her English professors. She hadn't quite believed in this ahead of time. She'd thought it was possible they'd continue to meet. She'd thought it was possible he might end his marriage and join himself to her forever.

But he'd said he mustn't stand in her way. Those were the words he'd used. He'd sat down behind his wide desk, a desk on which they'd made love more than once, using it now like a barrier between them. He'd said, not unkindly, that she must move on.

Move on? To where? To whom?

As the car pulled out, as the other, lucky couple turned to wave together out the rear window — like royalty: the pretty tilting back and forth of one hand of each — she felt herself begin to cry. She reached into her shoulder bag for a plastic packet of tissues and began to extract one. When the car pulled out onto the country road at the end of the driveway, Eva stepped blindly back and bumped into Mark. They turned and faced each other in the crowd of happy people, two weepy wedding guests. 'Got an extra one of those?' Mark asked, and Eva handed over a tissue. As one, they blew their noses. Then, looking at each other, each still holding the tissue to his face like a kind of mask, they began to laugh.

'There's just nothing like a good honk, is there?' Mark asked after a minute.

'I've always said so,' she answered.

And they walked slowly back to the tent together, where they ordered coffee and didn't move again until, in the gathering dusk, a young woman on the catering staff asked for the folding chairs they sat on.

They'd stumbled into each other, Mark liked to say, and he often described the early years of their marriage as 'further stumbling.' Neither knew what he wanted, what she'd be good at. Eva taught high school English in San Francisco and hated it. Mark did construction, got a union card. They moved north, out of the city. Eva waited tables and hated it. Mark worked on a housing development at the edge of Napa, a crummy development using the cheapest possible materials. Eva got a job in a stationery store, first selling, then running it.

At night she sometimes read to him, books he'd never read himself, or struggled so hard just to get through that he hadn't been able to think about them. She read him Conrad, and they talked about honor, and when it became too costly — a foolish, expensive notion. She read Chekhov, who amazed them both by the way he turned his stories around with just a phrase or two at the end and made you wonder what in them was meant to be taken as true. They took long walks. They made love, they argued about

58

life, about where they were headed, what they wanted to do. About what one *should* do. They argued fiercely, dramatically, in a way that Mark realized only later that he loved, that made him feel alive.

Then Mark was hired by some friends who had bought land outside Calistoga with family money and were going to plant a vineyard, doing the work themselves. He spent the next year and a half with them. It felt like a new life starting, a door opening. The land was rocky and uncultivated, but it was level, on the valley floor. They cleared it, they pulled out trees and the biggest rocks. They ripped the soil. He came home every night dirty and exhausted, having pushed himself all day long to the edge of what he was capable of. If they hadn't been the age they all were then, they could never have done it.

One of the others had been a vineyard manager for a big winery, had gone to UC Davis before that. But all of them had read up on the valley and its long story, and they knew a great deal that he didn't — how the land had been formed in prehistory, what chemicals and nutrients the different soils in the valley contained, what the differences were in temperature and rainfall from north to south, from hillside to valley, what kinds of grapes would be best suited to the land they'd purchased, and what they would need to do to those grapes to make them flourish.

They started the vineyard in the spring, driving stakes into the still-rocky soil. In the fall, they planted their rootstock, irrigating it by hand with water hauled in a truck from a nearby stream. That winter, when the work slowed, Mark went back to construction, but the next spring and summer, he came back to help dig a pond and install an irrigation system.

They made mistakes, and they certainly did everything the hard way. But neighbors were generous, once they saw they were going to stick with it. They offered advice and equipment, and the work got done. Those long days were the ones that cemented Mark's relationship with the place, the land. He felt he'd found a home. This was exactly the work he wanted to be doing, exactly the person he wanted to be.

Eva got pregnant with Emily that year, and they rented the house on the hill with the little vineyard of their own. She quit her job, and Emily was born. They didn't argue so much. Eva ran the house and grew vegetables and baked, and played with Emily. Mark started his own business, managing a few small vineyards using what he'd learned. They were, he would have said — he did say — happy. His business expanded slowly but steadily as wine and winemaking became chic, as people in the money descended on the valley, people who wanted vineyards of their own; as the number of vineyards exploded — now twenty-five, now forty, now one hundred. They made love, it is true, with less frequency than early in the marriage, but with a comfortable ease, a knowledge of each other's body and pleasure that only occasionally seemed too practiced.

They had Daisy. They had talked about

wanting a boy, but when the doctor held the baby's slicked body up above Eva's knees and Mark saw the deep cleft between her incurving helpless legs, he felt flooded with a loving relief, with gladness. He realized that he'd been frightened all along of a boy. He didn't want him — a dyslexic, wild boy, like himself.

But it was after this that things began to seem too much, that Eva became withdrawn, angry. That Mark turned away from their dreamy stumbling and made a mistake, fucked Amy for eleven months. That Eva got so mad at him that she threw him out. And then settled for a nice man — older, calm, devoted.

Was that it, was that what had happened?

That was it, Mark felt. She'd *settled* for John. And it seemed to have worked, it seemed to have made her happy. She and John moved into the derelict old house in town and fixed it up. John bought the bookstore for her. She had Theo. She seemed at peace. When Mark dropped by to get the girls, when he came over for birthday parties or holiday celebrations, he could feel the calm and the sense of order that surrounded her. It had to do with money, of course. But it had to do also with John, with his steadiness, his *niceness*.

Sometimes though, watching Eva move so efficiently across her big, expensive kitchen, watching her turn her slow, lovely, slightly gap-toothed smile on one guest or another, Mark would catch himself wondering if she didn't miss their old life too, their questions, their passionate talk, the fights, the times they woke in the night

61

afterward and wordlessly, wildly, began to make love. As much as anything, he felt, it was his betrayal that had made her available for a man like John. His fault.

★ ★ ★

It wasn't until about eight months or so after John died, on a hot day in May, that Mark understood what he was doing, what he'd been feeling all along. That he realized he was wooing Eva. That he saw that he was trying to reclaim her, to reclaim her through the children.

It hadn't started that way. Early on, when Eva was so miserable, taking the girls more often had just felt the necessary, the right thing to do. Anything, to help. But it probably shifted, something shifted in Mark, when he'd started sometimes to take Theo too, along with the girls.

This had happened for the first time in early December, two months after John's death, when Theo appeared at the top of the stairs with his backpack just as Mark was leaving. Daisy and Emily were already outside, and he was standing in the hall talking to Eva.

They heard Theo on the stairs at the same time, and they both turned and looked up, watching his slow descent in silence.

Mark broke it as Theo reached the bottom. 'What's up, big guy? Whatcha doing?'

'I got my stuff.'

'I see you got your stuff. Where are you taking it?'

'To Mark's house. To you,' Theo said.

'Oh, sweetie,' Eva said, squatting to be at Theo's height. Her dress fell in a circle around her on the floor. It was made of a fabric printed with tiny sprigs of flowers everywhere. *Sprigs.* Mark would have liked to offer her the word.

'See, honey, just the girls are going to Mark's this time,' she said.

'Why?' he asked.

'Why,' she said. She turned her face up to Mark. She looked stricken.

'Because I'm their father,' Mark said. 'Because Emily and Daisy are my girls, so I like to have them come stay with me.'

Theo had looked from one of them to the other. 'That's no fair,' he said.

No one answered him.

He sat on the bottom step. 'It's not *fair*,' he said again. And then he started to cry.

Mark had looked at Eva. It seemed to him that she was about to cry too, for life's unfairness, for Theo's pain. For her aloneness. For everything.

'I sure don't mind taking him, if you think it's okay,' he'd said.

He watched as her face lifted to him again and changed — opened in relief.

'Would you, Mark?' she said.

After that, it had become an easy, comfortable thing. If Theo wanted to come, if Eva hadn't planned something special to do with him in the girls' absence, Mark brought him home too. He told himself he was doing it for Eva, but he also truly liked the little boy — for his enthusiasm, for his sweet, vulnerable presence lying in bed at night next to Mark, for his wiry physical energy, so like what Mark remembered of himself as a kid. Sometimes, when he rocked Theo at night, or kissed him as he put him down to sleep, he had a sense of loving himself, of healing some part of himself — a sense that he couldn't have explained clearly to anyone else.

He had rationalized all this, he had told himself that the girls didn't need him anymore. When they were at his house, they spent hours in their room with the door shut. He could hear them talking, or Emily on the phone. Sometimes they did each other's hair. Emily often went out, with friends, on dates. Daisy stayed in their room. As he moved around the house, he could see her there reading, or working on something at the desk, or lying on the bed listening to music on her Walkman. If he were honest, he would have to say he didn't know them anymore. And they didn't seem to care to know him.

No, it was Theo who was interested in Mark, who wanted to do the activities he planned for the weekends — so that when Mark bought a picture puzzle the girl in the shop said was age appropriate for a three-and-a-half-year-old, when he helped Theo set up an elaborate marble chute with blocks that stretched from the living room into the dining room, when he knelt next to the tub and reached over to soap the little boy's smooth, soft skin, singing him the bathtub songs he'd sung to the girls, it seemed to him that he was just responding to the situation — that it took nothing away from Emily and Daisy, who had moved on anyway.

But then on that day in May, because both

girls turned him down, he took Theo alone out for an afternoon of fishing. After they'd returned, Daisy sulked around the kitchen while he fixed dinner, not so much helping as getting in the way. At one point, when Mark asked her to pass him a colander, he addressed her as *Miss Grumps*. This was a mistake. She burst into tears. She accused him of loving Theo more than he loved her, she said she didn't know why he even bothered to have her over.

Mark was so pained for her he couldn't answer, he just reached out his arms and pulled her in.

It was at this moment, actually, holding his grieving daughter, feeling a pang of deep sorrow at misunderstanding her — ungainly Daisy, so tall she had to bend her head slightly to rest it on his shoulder — that he realized why he was doing it, all of it. That he understood he was trying to earn his way back to Eva's love through the children. Most of all, through Theo. The sense of recognition he felt, the quick jolt of shame, lasted only a moment. He was holding Daisy. He would do better by her. He did love her.

He loved her and Emily, and he had come to love Theo too. There was nothing false about any of it. It had happened because he loved Eva. He still loved her, and loving the children, all of them, was a way of coming back to that.

He stood in his kitchen and stroked his daughter's hair and whispered, 'Sweetheart, of course I love you'; and what he had moved on to thinking was that he could do it, he could make it happen. He knew he could. He just needed to be slow and patient. He would approach this the way he had approached college, he thought, with the conviction that though it might take him longer than it would take someone else, there was no reason he couldn't do it. None.

4

Sometimes when they were younger, Daisy and Emily would talk about which of their fathers seemed more like a *real* father. This was in the early days in the house in town, on Kearney Street, when it was still being renovated, before they moved into separate rooms. When, as Daisy remembered it, they were still friends. (As Emily remembered it, they were always friends, but in this, of course, she was wrong.) It was before Emily went into seventh grade; it was when they still walked to school together every day, when they still lay down at night in the two beds only a few feet apart and talked on and on, long after their bedtime — talked until Eva came to the foot of the stairs and yelled, 'If I have to come up there, someone's going to be very sorry.' In those days, they often spoke together openly and clearly about the central complexity in their lives: having two fathers. Lying next to each other, their disembodied voices rising in the dark, they would list all the ways in which each one — Mark or John — was unconvincing. *Fake*, they called it.

Mark was too young, they said, though they knew he was only about five years younger than John. But John was much more grown up. *Realer*.

Daisy couldn't have said what she meant by this. It had to do with a quality she later understood as a kind of attentiveness John had, a focus — on you, on what you said, on what you thought. Daisy knew, even then, that she loved John, that she loved him more than she loved Eva, maybe more than she loved Emily. She wasn't sure about Mark.

What Emily meant — what she said she meant — was that Mark didn't have the right clothes for a father, or the right car, that he let them get away with stuff, that he took them out to dinner too much when they were at his house. He was disorganized where they were concerned, Emily said. All these things were *fake*.

Her voice in the dark sounded strict, sounded *correct* to Daisy, as it always did. At this stage in their lives together, Emily made the rules for Daisy, and Daisy believed she was incapable of error.

They both agreed, on the other hand, that John was too polite to them. He spoiled them; he bought them too much stuff — whatever they wanted, almost. That was fake too, wasn't it?

Daisy wasn't convinced of this, because she loved John and she loved these things about him. Emily was harder-hearted. It *was* fake.

But what was real? They weren't sure. Eva was, they knew that. Maybe one real parent was enough. That's what Emily decided she thought, in the end.

Not Daisy. Daisy wanted two — a mother and a father. And the father she chose was John, partly because at around this time Mark more or less disappeared from their lives anyway. He had started dating someone, 'dating hard,' Eva had said to them, smiling in a mean way. He canceled weekends, he didn't show up sometimes to pick up one or the other of the girls after school. When they did go to his house, Erika was often there, and he seemed sometimes hardly to notice that they were too. Or maybe he just didn't care anymore. But it didn't matter to Daisy, because John had stepped forward and become the center of her life.

Emily had moved into her own room by now, and that and her entering high school had changed things between them. And they seemed to be headed in different directions anyway. Daisy had grown taller and taller and more and more awkward as she turned eleven, and then twelve. By now she towered over everyone in her class, boy or girl. Emily was small, like Eva, and pretty and popular. Within two months of entering high school, she had a boyfriend, a junior, Noah Weiss, a diver on the swim team. (When Daisy thought of Noah, she remembered being at some meet with Emily and seeing him for the first time. Even years later she could recall the amplified, echoing noise the cheering voices made in the tiled pool room, the heavy humidity of the air, the clean, bleachy smell of the water, and the way Noah looked, standing with his toes gripping the end of the board, his chest wide and hairless, the pouch in his Speedo prominent and, to Daisy, embarrassing. She had tried to ask Emily something about this afterward, about whether she didn't think of it when she looked at him, think it was *funny*, really, as Daisy did, but Emily said she was juvenile — 'God, you are so juvenile, Daze.')

Theo had been born that year too — the year Emily entered high school — so Eva was lost to them all, lost in a world of breast-feeding and naps and changing diapers. She was always tired, she always said she'd do stuff *later*.

But Daisy had chosen John, and John seemed comfortable, maybe even glad to be chosen. When she talked about it years later in therapy, trying to reconstruct it from John's point of view, Daisy wondered if it hadn't been deliberated, his kindness to her. Maybe, she said to her doctor, he and Eva saw that she was too solitary, too shy. Maybe they discussed it together, how now that Eva was so busy with Theo, and Emily had moved off into the life of high school, Daisy needed extra attention. But what she concluded was that even if it *was* calculated in that sense — an act of *parenting*, that weird gerund — it didn't matter. It had been done lovingly. It had changed things for her. She had a friend, an ally. Whatever Daisy asked him to do, John did. In return, she went with him — on errands, on hikes, on bicycle rides. And whatever they were doing, John would talk to Daisy. Or rather, he'd ask Daisy to talk to him.

At one time or another over the years that he was her stepfather, John asked Daisy how she would describe herself to someone else; he asked her how she imagined music when she dreamed: as notes? or maybe just as waves of sound or feeling?; he asked her whether she thought the way a language was structured — she had just finished reciting a poem she'd memorized for

70

French — made a difference in the way people thought; he asked her whether she thought she would be a different person if she'd grown up somewhere else geographically — New York, say, or Beirut; he asked her whether she would have preferred to be the older or the younger child in the family, instead of the one in the middle, and what difference she thought that would make.

He never seemed to anticipate or to want a particular answer. He was just interested in what she thought.

Once he asked her how her life was different from the way she would have liked it to be. Daisy didn't even need to think to answer this. She told him she wished her parents hadn't gotten divorced and that they still lived in the house up in the hills.

John was taking her to a doctor's appointment that time, driving. It was raining and the windshield wipers were slapping out their steady beat. John seemed concentrated on that, or on the road — in any case, you couldn't have told from his expression that she'd said anything important. She watched his face and thought about her answer, about how hurtful it might be to him. Stupid! she thought. She said, 'But then I wouldn't have you and Theo, so I don't know. It's hard to know.'

'It is, isn't it?' He had looked over at her quickly and smiled. 'Hard to know.'

Only a few months before he died, he'd asked her a question about Emily. 'What do you think of this business of having a beautiful older sister,

71

Daisy?' he'd said. 'Would it be a good idea if we bumped her off?'

Daisy had burst into laughter at this, but then, because John had been the one to say it, she allowed herself to realize, maybe for the first time, that there was a part of her that would have liked Emily to disappear forever — though simultaneously she understood that she would have felt bereft if that happened, that she would have felt that there was no one to instruct her in the way she should enter the world each day.

She was riding bikes with John on Bennett Lane when he asked her this. She had to raise her voice a little to answer him — he was behind her. She told him that sometimes she did feel that way next to Emily — ugly and angry. He caught up to her and was pedaling along beside her, frowning in concentration on what she was saying. She said, 'But I really love Emily too. Sometimes I even feel sorry for her.'

'Sorry? For our Emily?' he asked. 'How come?'

Daisy looked over at her stepfather. He was wearing his yellow bike helmet and an old T-shirt that said ARS(e). He had on shorts, and his legs were white and hairy. He was a nerd. Daisy knew this. He was big and freckled and nowhere near as handsome as her real father. She thought about what she had said. She hadn't known this before — that she could feel sorry for Emily.

'Because,' she said. 'Because Emily always has to do everything the right way, you know?' *Was* that what she felt? Or was she just making this up, to hold John's attention? She wasn't sure, actually. 'Or maybe because she never gets to be, just, ignored.'

John had bicycled silently next to her for a while.

Daisy felt the wind — it lifted her hair and pushed against her skin. It was dry and smelled of dirt from the vineyards.

'Ignored is good, then?' he finally said.

'Well, then you can do whatever you want. Nobody cares. You can think about things for yourself.'

He dropped back and rode behind her again.

In the fields Daisy could see clusters of workers between the rows of vines. The harvest was just starting, and the Mexicans were suddenly everywhere — working in the fields, walking in groups down the sidewalks in town, sleeping at night in cars pulled off at the sides of quiet lanes. As you passed them on the street, as you walked by the park where they gathered in the hot afternoons, you could hear their melding voices, the different rhythm of their speech, their laughter. It was as though they brought their own world with them, she thought, and when she saw them or heard them, she felt her ordinary world was changed for the moment, made somehow exotic and magical.

John's voice came from behind her now. 'But you know that *we* care, don't you?'

'Yeah,' she called back. 'But I mean, nobody in the *world*.'

'Ah! Well.' John had laughed then. 'Yes.'

★   ★   ★

The fall that John died was beautiful. Daisy couldn't recall ever having thought such a thing before, ever having noticed a *season*. Years later, calling it up as an adult, talking about it with Dr. Gerard, trying to figure out what she had been thinking and doing then, she would still be able to remember it sharply — the sound of Spanish, the sense of the work of the harvest, the gondolas and trucks driving past full of grapes, the smell of fermentation you'd suddenly get walking past someone's shed, the color of the leaves, the cooler nights. The world around her. She remembered that she had the sense of awakening to it, to the world. She was full of hope.

She had started at the high school, and because John encouraged her to, she had applied to the literary magazine; she had signed up for chorus; she had gone to the preliminary tryouts for JV basketball, and was assured a place on the team. These were choices she knew were geeky — Emily, who was a senior now, confirmed this for her ('Can't you choose just one kind of normal activity?'), but they were what she was good at, what she was interested in. And if the other kids who were interested in those things were also nerdy and geeky, they were kids Daisy felt she understood, kids she had a chance with. She realized that her life in high school was going to be different from Emily's, but John made her feel all right about this. Made her feel she might be happy.

When John died, Daisy felt it was wrong that they were sent to Mark's house. She had wanted to stay at home, where John was being mourned

74

by Eva; where, she felt, he might still in some sense be *present*. They were at Mark's only two nights and the day between before Eva called and wanted them back, but Daisy felt it as a kind of exile, an exile where they were not supposed to talk about what had just happened — she supposed because of Theo. An exile where life seemed to have rolled on, right over John's death, where it seemed they were supposed to pretend everything was unchanged.

Who had decided this? It seemed to have been Emily, but it must have been Mark too, somehow. He was the grown-up, after all.

The night John died, Daisy had heard Mark talking to his girlfriend on the phone, she had heard him call her 'babe.' She had never heard anyone use this endearment except in rock songs. It seemed cheesy to her. It seemed, she recognized suddenly, sexual. Standing in Mark's kitchen, overhearing this, Daisy had understood what her father's relations with this woman were. He was having sex with her. He was sorry he wouldn't be having sex with her tonight. That's what John's death had interrupted for him. What did he care about John?

He didn't. It was wrong that they had to be there, with him.

They had made a cake that night — Emily's idea, as Daisy remembered it — and Theo had licked the frosting bowl. Daisy sat across from him at Mark's dining room table and watched him methodically scrape out every bit of the chocolately goop. He had a little clot of it in his hair; his face was smeared.

75

His piggy eagerness, his animal forgetting, revolted her. She wanted to hit him, to take a little of the soft, pretty flesh of his arm and twist it, hard.

How mean! How mean could you be! *He* was the one who had lost his father. Daisy knew that she was wrong, that her feelings were unjustifiable. She'd left the room abruptly and gone to lie on her sleeping bag in the dark, until Mark came to the door and asked her to say goodnight to Theo. Full of remorse, she'd pounced on Theo in Mark's bed and given him gobbling kisses that made him laugh and yell her name.

But afterward, lying on her own bed again, thinking about it, even *that* made her feel uncomfortable. To laugh! To play! When John was lying alone, dead somewhere. She got up to find Mark, to ask him a question that had occurred to her earlier too, about what had happened to John's body, about where he was.

But Mark didn't know. He didn't even care, she could tell.

It was Daisy who answered the phone when Eva called to summon them home. Her mother's voice sounded exhausted but peaceful, slowed. And that's how she looked when they drove up an hour or so later and Daisy saw her, standing on the porch waiting for them — as though she'd newly recovered from a long illness. She had always been thin, but suddenly she looked very much too thin. Her eyes were so shadowed that they seemed sunken in her head and darkly bruised. It didn't make her less pretty though. In fact, to Daisy she seemed even more beautiful than usual — small and vulnerable and suffering. Suffering so hard that everyone could see that, and love her more.

When they got out of the truck, Eva started down the porch steps to them. She crouched on the cement walk and hungrily pulled them in around her.

Daisy felt awkward. She was too big for this embrace. It was meant for someone the size of Theo. She stood looking down at her mother's head, at the white waxy skin of her scalp at the part in her hair; and then, because this seemed somehow too naked, too exposed, she looked over at Mark, who was watching them. His eyes met Daisy's. He seemed almost frightened.

Then his gaze shifted, his hand came up, and Daisy turned. Gracie was standing above them in the open doorway on the porch.

Eva released them and stood up, and Daisy turned and went up the stairs. She stepped into Gracie's open arms — perfumed, bosomy Gracie. 'Sweetie,' Gracie said. Daisy had the sudden notion that she wanted to stay in this embrace forever. Gracie rocked her for a few seconds. Then she stepped back and touched Daisy's hair. And now everyone was on the porch, at the door, and Gracie was hugging Emily in just the same way.

'Come in, Mark,' Eva said. Daisy turned. Her father was still on the walk, alone, looking up at all of them. Eva blew her nose. 'Come in for a minute, why don't you? Have something to drink.' Her voice sounded hollow.

Daisy watched him come up the steps and

approach her mother. His arms lifted and came around Eva, and she disappeared against his chest. He held her. Watching them, Daisy remembered abruptly the way they had looked when they were still married, when they held each other then — how they *went with* each other, somehow, in a way John and Eva hadn't. They stood there together a long time. The others had drifted away, into the house, but Daisy stood and watched. When Mark was done, when he let Eva go, he was still touching her shoulder. 'Eva,' he said. 'I'm . . . so sorry.'

'Don't . . . don't make me cry again, Mark,' she said. 'But, thanks. I know. I know you are. But come on in. Come in.' She gestured vaguely, expansively, and he walked into the house, past Daisy, still standing there like a lump in the doorway, past Theo, who'd knelt a few feet into the hall and dumped out his bag of toys and bedding so they all had to make their way around them.

Now Emily's voice rang from the kitchen. 'God, look at this food, at this huge amount of food. Is all this food for us?'

As if in response to her, everyone moved to the kitchen doorway. Eva stepped just inside it. 'People have been so kind,' she said hoarsely, almost apologetically. The wide island in the kitchen was covered with dishes — casseroles, bowls, aluminum pans shiny with plastic wrap, fruits in ribboned baskets. There were little labels on some of them.

'Look at this.' Emily began to read: 'Blueberry

78

muffins. Heat twenty minutes at three hundred fifty degrees.'

'I *want* blueberry muffins,' Theo said. The top of his head was at the level of the island's surface, and he stood beside Emily on tiptoes trying to see.

'Or how 'bout, listen to this! Sesame chicken wings. Hey! Also three hundred fifty for twenty minutes.'

'Don't like sesame,' Theo said.

'But I do,' Emily said, and bonked him lightly on the head.

Daisy said, 'It's chicken, Theo. Like fried chicken. You like that.'

'Do you, sweetie pie?' Gracie asked. 'Maybe we should make a feast then. Eva?' she said, raising her voice a little as though Daisy's mother were hard of hearing, or a child. 'Would you have some lunch now? Shall we use up a little of this stuff?'

Eva was like a sleepwalker — amiable, absent. 'Of course,' she said mildly. She turned to Daisy's father. 'Mark, you'll stay, won't you? We have more than enough.' Her arm rose. 'Funeral meats,' she said.

Mark said he would, he would stay.

Gracie bossed them all around, and gradually they found napkins and silverware and plates. They set the table, they got out different drinks for everyone, arranged the serving dishes they were using on trivets and hot pads. Eva moved slowly, robotically, and Daisy wondered if that was something the medicine had done to her.

'Oh, my darling,' she said after they'd sat

79

down, and then nothing more. Her face was blank. She was looking into some middle distance.

They all avoided one another's eyes, no one willing to answer her, and their knives and forks clinked loudly in the silence.

*   *   *

Daisy had felt herself stop inside after John died. For months, it was simply as if she were frozen. She compared herself to the others and saw that there was a way to do this, this grieving, that she couldn't somehow *get to*. Eva wept often. You would come upon her in the living room, in the kitchen, with tears streaming down her face, and she would blow her nose quickly and sometimes apologize. You could hear her at night, crying or wandering the house.

Emily was tearful for the first few weeks too.

Daisy knew that she should weep, but she didn't, she couldn't. She understood that everyone thought that Emily was doing it right. That even here, mourning John — whom Daisy had loved the best! — her older sister was doing a better job of things. As the weeks went by — November, December — she could feel too that her parents were worried about her, even irritated at her for her silence. For her *nothingness*. And because they thought she must have a sadness she wasn't showing, they kept at her. They asked her questions. They wanted her to talk.

She overheard them discussing her once in the

kitchen when Mark had come to get them. He was asking about everyone, how they were doing, and when he came to her at last, he just said, 'Daze?'

There was a silence, and Daisy knew her mother would be answering with a gesture, a face, a rolling of her eyes.

'Yeah,' Mark said. 'Well: Daisy.' What would he be doing? Shaking his head?

Daisy was sitting on the back stairs, which came off the kitchen at a sharp angle. They were narrow and steep. She had stopped where she was, partway down, when she heard Mark come in and call to her mother, whose voice had answered from just below Daisy. The walls here had been stripped and left unpainted, and Daisy was moving her hand slowly over the cool, bumpy surface of the old plaster as she listened.

'I'm at a complete loss,' Eva said. Things clunked — cooking things.

'Have you asked her directly, *'How are you doing, Daisy?''* *His voice exaggerated each syllable.*

'Pretty much. And the answer is 'Okay, fine, sure, whatever.' ' She sighed and did something. She said, 'It's like waiting for a baby to begin to talk — waiting for him to figure out that all this *noise* everyone around him is making *means* something — that's exactly how I feel waiting for Daisy to understand that having feelings is the way most people experience life. Like it's some code she hasn't cracked.'

After a moment, Mark said, 'The thing is, Daisy has plenty of feelings.'

'Oh, I know, I know. I just wish she'd let us *at* them, that she'd figure out how to say something about them.'

'That she'd learn to talk,' Mark said.

'Yes!' Eva said passionately.

Daisy knew they were right. That she should talk about it. But what could she say to them? 'Why didn't *you* die?' 'I don't need *you*.' She knew it wasn't fair to be angry at Eva, at Mark. But she was.

As the winter rains began and deepened, the grief of the others began to ease. Eva often moved at her old familiar speed through the days. Sometimes you could hear her laughing when she talked on the phone in the evenings. Oh, she still turned in on herself when she was alone with Daisy, or with Daisy and any of the others — at home or in the car. Then everything about her dimmed and quieted; she had nothing to say. But in the world, more and more she was herself: bright, lively.

Emily, who'd sobbed at the service for John so brokenheartedly that Daisy knew her own silence, her stillness must seem, by comparison, cold and unfeeling, was once more caught up in the world of her friends — in holiday parties, in deadlines for applying to colleges, in writing those essays, in going off with Noah, who was home from college. In sleeping with him, *fucking* him.

Daisy knew this because Emily had talked about it with her. And though it was nothing Daisy wanted to hear, she was incapable of not listening to the details: where they did it (in the car mostly), how it felt (exciting beforehand, sort of boring during). Emily told her what he said, what she said, who knew about it, who else was doing it too, who else was doing other things — hand jobs, blow jobs — and on and on, Daisy taking it all in and not knowing what to say in response, or even what she thought about it.

She felt a thickening of her aloneness and anger at the others. She remembered that Theo, who had worn new, hard shoes to the service, shoes he didn't like, had kicked at the wooden back of the pew in front of him, had kicked so fiercely and relentlessly, despite Eva's hand on his legs and her tearful, whispered admonitions, that Gracie had finally carried him outside and they had sat in the sun on the front steps of the church until it was all over and the others came out and found them there. Gracie was singing to him when they arrived, the simple, repetitive songs that always worked with Theo.

Daisy thought that kicking was exactly what she felt like doing. Kicking, hard.

Kicking whom?

Eva, for one. Eva, for laughing, for getting excited about taking some writer out for dinner. Emily, for sailing off into her own life. Mark, for his obliviousness, for bringing Theo around all the time. Even Theo, for forgetting John, for acting as though Mark were his, as though he would make a perfectly good new father.

Sometimes things would seem all right for a few days. Mark would come over for supper, they would all hang out together, it would feel natural and familiar and Daisy would forget that Mark shouldn't even be there. That John should.

Or Daisy would be at basketball practice and lose track of everything except how her body felt moving forward, lifting for a layup. There were nights doing homework with Emily at the dining room table when she could experience a near physical pleasure at finishing a geometric proof; at the slow untangling of a sentence in Latin; at the way the overhead light fell over the contours of Emily's face, a face as familiar to Daisy as her own. At those times it seemed possible that the minutes, the hours would carry her forward in some safe way.

But then everything would shift and go wrong again.

Early in January she jammed her thumb in the car door. She watched this happen as if in slow motion, knowing in the half second before the pain began that it was coming and that it would be bad.

A bone had cracked. It swelled up. Of course she couldn't play basketball. For a few days she went to practice anyway and sat on the bench, watching the other girls go through the drills, looking at the splint on her hand, feeling that her body itself had betrayed her. And then, unable to stand that, she quit the team, despite the coach's assurance that he would hold her spot, that she could come back and play as soon as her hand healed.

It was raining one afternoon when she came out of school, one of the lashing rains of winter, which she'd watched arriving from inside her science classroom. Mrs. Pagels had had to turn the lights on, it grew so dark outside, and everything in the room had suddenly looked cheap and worn. Daisy knew that she shouldn't ride her bike home, that she wouldn't be able see well or to use the brakes, so she left it in the rack and walked.

The next day when she passed the rack on the way in to school, her bike was gone — stolen. Daisy felt such a sense of shocked betrayal that tears came to her eyes.

They had to write an essay for English describing something in their lives that had made them happy. 'There's a house up in the hills beyond St. Helena where I don't live anymore,' Daisy wrote. 'And in it there's a man waiting who isn't alive anymore.' She turned these two sentences in and got a D, and her English teacher asked to see her during study hour. When Daisy arrived outside the classroom, Miss Gaines was still talking to someone else, a boy Daisy didn't know. The door was shut, but Daisy could hear their voices rise and fall. She watched them through the glass pane. The boy's face was friendly and animated.

When it was Daisy's turn, she knew her face was nothing like that. She knew the empty, sour way she looked, but she couldn't help it.

Miss Gaines was young and pretty, though her nose was too big. She had a British accent. She wore black clothes most of the time, the only teacher Daisy knew — the only *person* Daisy knew — who did. Her face opened in kindness to Daisy as she spoke of the paper. She told Daisy that, though she had all the sympathy in the world for her (*in the world*, Daisy thought, and smirked), Daisy still had to respond to the terms of the assignment, and the assignment had been an essay. Did she understand? Yes, said Daisy, feeling a raw, empty rage that would last for days. 'I understand perfectly.'

That same night, Eva had tried to talk to her about her silence, her unpleasantness to others in the house. Why? What was wrong? She wanted to help.

Daisy hated her mother's face when she spoke like this, her frowning, sympathetic eyes, the sad lines pulling the corners of her mouth down. There was nothing wrong, Daisy said. 'If you broke your thumb and had your bike stolen, you'd feel the same way I feel.'

'Which is?'

'Which is, like a piece of shit.' She turned away, she pretended to be concentrating on her homework, the long passage in Latin in front of her.

Eva was sitting across from her at the dining room table. Emily, apparently, had been clued in that this conversation was coming — she'd disappeared up to her room to study. Eva was watching Daisy steadily. She cleared her throat. 'If you won't talk to me about what's wrong, Daze,' she said, 'how can I help you?'

'You can't help me anyway.' She flipped the page, seeing nothing.

'I could try.'

'How? How can you help me?' Daisy looked up. She was furious, suddenly. She slammed her book shut. Eva started slightly. 'Everything in my life is ruined.' Her voice nearly cracked.

Eva didn't answer. She looked away, but Daisy could see that her mother's eyes were filled with tears. This infuriated her. It seemed like a request, a demand for something from her, and Daisy couldn't, she wouldn't, respond. She grabbed her Latin book and the dictionary and left the dining room. She took the stairs two at a time. She slammed the door to her room behind her.

It was on account of all of this that she was going to have to work in the store, her mother's bookstore, for the entire summer. Emily was going to France on some program in which she would live with a French family and come back fluent, but Daisy had to work. They were trying to make it seem as though it wasn't a punishment, a punishment for being who she was, for feeling how she felt, but it was. They wanted to keep an eye on her, to keep her doing something useful. And in truth, they'd offered her other options and she'd turned them all down, so it could be said — she'd heard her mother say it, actually — that she'd *chosen* to work in the bookstore. But that was a lie.

She thought of the question as no one had posed it to her. As John would have asked it: *What is it, do you think, that you'd like to do with yourself this summer?*

She thought of John, the last time she'd seen him, the morning of the day he died. She had been the last one to leave the house, which had suddenly fallen silent once the others were gone. When she carried her bike down from the back porch, John came out of the garage, which they'd made into an office for his business. He was wearing a light blue shirt, frayed wildly at the collar, and baggy khaki pants. His big white feet were bare. With his long, sloping jaw, his strawlike lashes, he seemed like a large, homely boy.

'Biking it again,' he said.

'Yes.'

'How come you don't walk with Emily and her crew, you think?'

She had shrugged.

He came over and stood by the porch. 'They're nice enough to you, aren't they?'

'They're okay. They kind of ignore me, I guess. But I can't talk about any of the stuff they're into anyway, so that's fine. The thing is, I'd rather just be alone.'

'You don't want to be too alone, though.'

'I'm not, *too* alone.' At that point, this was true. She stayed late almost every day for one activity or another, and she was beginning to have a sense of who might be possible as a friend.

Suddenly John grinned. 'Of course, you're talking to a guy who spends his entire day by himself, buried in books. Which isn't *quite* alone, but some would say, Daisy, that it looks like it. Looks suspiciously like it.' He tapped her handlebars with his freckled hand and stepped back. 'Anyway, see you tonight,' he said. And Daisy pushed off and rode down the driveway.

She thought of the fact that she hadn't looked back. She wished she had looked back. Though she knew it made no sense, she felt as though she had missed some signal, some private message he might have had for her that would have helped her through all this.

And, of course, the thought came to her from time to time that if she *had* looked back, if she'd called to him, if she'd taken up just a few more seconds of his time that morning, everything else in his day would have been off by just that much, and he wouldn't have stepped into Main Street at the exact moment the car came around the corner.

She thought of her mother those few days later when they'd come back from Mark's house, how everyone was so careful and loving around her, the way she'd said, 'Oh my darling,' when they sat down to eat, as if John were still alive, as if he were there in the room but visible only to her.

What would she like to do with herself this summer?

Nothing. Zero. Nothing.

5

Eva sits in the car for a few minutes after she's turned the engine off. It's early evening, but it's a mid-June evening, so the sun is still high above the hills around her, even at this hour. The face the mountains present is deeply shadowed though — almost black here and there where the pines are thickest. Something in the car ticks lightly, dying. Eva is looking at the house, *her* house — substantial, Victorian, every bit of ornate trim restored by her and John after they moved in, and the clapboard siding painted an historic pale pink. Its front windows are shuttered against the light, and it has a blind, blankened air.

She's been gone from it for more than a week, taking Emily to visit her parents and then to the orientation that is to precede her trip to France. And though Eva started the trip eagerly, wanting to get away, she has finished it almost desperate to be home. At times during these eight days, she has yearned for home as you might yearn for the touch of a lover's body.

Now that she's here, though, looking up at the house from the car, she feels reluctant even to go in. She has the odd sense that this was not what she meant. Not *this* home.

But what other home is there?

The car is heating up slowly now, so she opens the driver's-side door and steps out into the dry evening air. She retrieves her bag from the backseat and goes up the walk, surveying the plants and the lawn. Everything looks fine, except for the hose lying uncoiled in the front yard. She knows when she lifts it, the grass will be yellowed in a bright, serpentine line where the hose has lain. She mounts the porch stairs, the bag on its wheels banging up behind her.

When the front door swings open and she steps inside, she's hit by the mustiness, the stale heat. She doesn't want the air conditioner, though — she hates its hum, its sealed-in feeling — so she moves around quickly, opening the windows at the front and sides of the house. As she walks back and forth, she is almost overcome by the sense she has of seeing things anew — a sense that surprises her, her absence has been so short.

She thinks of the versions of itself the house contains in her memory, of her history with John in these spaces, all the changes they'd lived through. The house was a wreck when they bought it, and they had inhabited it through its messy transformation — the pulling down of the cheap, lowered ceiling panels; the rewiring and replumbing; the stripping of layers of old wallpaper; the replacing of windows; the renovating of the kitchen; the sanding and painting. They had come to know intimately all the possible varieties of dust, which inevitably made their way around the plastic sheeting they hung to keep them out, under the doors they sealed to block them in. They had lived, for months, in odd rooms of the house while other rooms were being worked on.

For a time, this room, the living room, was their bedroom. Standing in it now, she thinks of how it felt, waking on the mattress on the floor next to John, the sun pouring in — of course they had no shutters yet — the light grit that had settled in the night palpable on the mattress when she turned to see if he was awake too.

It is hard to connect that past to this room. It's orderly and lovely. The ceilings are high, and the casings around the windows and doors and baseboards all have four or five curves articulating and reversing themselves where a newer house would have one, or two. Or none. The furniture, though some of it is old, has been re-covered with pale fabrics — California colors, as Eva thinks of them. On the walls are the contemporary paintings John collected, and a large N. C. Wyeth oil, an illustration for *Treasure Island* — two men fighting in a ship's cabin under the light of a swinging lantern. Books are stacked here and there, some of them the books John was reading, or about to read, or just finished with at the time he died. She hasn't been able to bring herself to remove these last reminders of what he loved, how he thought — though she's packed his clothes in boxes and donated them to Goodwill, though she's boxed his papers and stored them in the attic.

A breeze wafts through, smelling of rosemary, of jasmine.

She goes into the lavatory under the stairs and pees, then washes her hands and face. Lifting her head from the water, she looks at herself, hard.

The eight days traveling have taken their toll. Her eyes are puffy; her face seems a little swollen. Even her clothes — the white blouse, the black linen slacks — seem tired, wrinkled, and stretched out of shape.

She leaves the blouse hanging out over the slacks and goes back to the kitchen to open the windows there, surveying the backyard as she does this — Theo's expensive climbing structure over in the corner and the paving stones marking John's path out to the garage. In front of the garage is the basketball net he and Daisy used to horse around at. She thinks of the noise of the ball on the cement, its reverberation on the backboard, the running commentary John kept up as they played. The way all of that drifted into the kitchen in the late afternoons and made her feel safe, encircled.

She sits down at the kitchen island. She can't remember when she last came home to an empty house. To no one. Theo is at Gracie's — he has been staying with her while Eva has been away, though of course he went to day care as usual. Daisy is with Mark. She's been in charge of herself through Mark's long workdays, but she will have been busy. She has started a job in the bookstore this summer, and she is supposed to have gone in daily to be trained by Eva's assistant Callie. Eva had also asked her to stop by the house each day, to water the plants and take the mail in. These chores she has clearly done, though not with any grace — there was the hose left uncoiled on the grass outside, and here's the mail, more or less thrown onto the kitchen island. Eva starts to sort through it. Catalogues. Bills. A reminder that her subscription to *The New Yorker* is about to expire.

After a few minutes, she stops. The cross breeze shifts the few envelopes she's torn, the pages of a catalogue or two. She doesn't want to do this now. She gets a glass of water and stands at the sink, looking out, drinking. Each window here has six panes. In the lower three are the yard, and the trees hiding her neighbor's yard. Above them, in the upper panes, the sky is turning a richer blue. 'Cerulean,' she says out loud, and her voice startles her.

She goes back to the front hall and lugs her bag upstairs. Before she unpacks, she moves around opening the windows up here too, first in her own bedroom, next in Theo and Daisy's rooms, then in Emily's. She stands for a moment and looks around at Emily's domain — Emily, off to meet the world this summer. The room is as neat and well organized as Emily is. The firstborn, Eva thinks. Like some nursery rhyme she can't remember. Like herself. Emily has a bulletin board she'd requested, and on it is hung a calendar with the departure for France six days from now inscribed in thick red ink, three exclamation points after it.

Eva had said goodbye to her daughter this morning on the prep-school campus where she was having her weeklong orientation for the trip. She had driven slowly back through the lovely New England countryside to the interstate. There was no rush — she had ample time to catch her plane home. She had a little headache.

94

They'd spent the night before in a New England country hotel nearby, one of those inns with rockers set out in a row all across the front porch. Sitting opposite Emily at dinner in the old-fashioned dining room, listening to her talk about going to college in the fall, about the plans she had, Eva felt old, and she drank too much. It was a feeling that had gathered, she realized, over the course of the trip. There'd been a culminating moment, near the end of it, sitting in the room with the other parents before their own orientation about their children's trip abroad, when she looked around at all of them — respectable, well-dressed people in their forties. There was a man opposite her, leafing through the informational material they'd left out. Eva was fascinated by him, in a perverse way — he was so archetypical. He was wearing one of those expensive polo shirts and madras pants. Loafers with tassels. His face was broad, and dark with summer color, a nearly mahogany hue. A boat maybe, or hours and hours of tennis and golf. He was a man she might have married, she thought, if she'd stayed in the East, if she'd stayed an easterner. She'd had a flash of gratitude for her life — for the chance decisions that had taken her west, that had made her, if not a westerner, at least not someone who was recognizable, categorizable, in the way this man was. She thought of her marriages to two men, neither of whom gave off this self-satisfaction.

He turned to his wife now, a blonde in a pale pink sleeveless dress. She was reading a brochure. He touched her knee, and she looked up. It seemed a sweet gesture to Eva. It made her think of how she must look to him, to them — herself middle-aged, in her loose-fitting California clothes, her frazzled hair. How he must think of her: post-hippie, New Agey, a ditz.

And the thing was — here was her revelation — that it didn't matter anyway. *They* didn't matter. They were all just who they were, the backdrop to the lives about to be changed by the trip they were waiting to be educated about. They were the *drivers*, for God's sake. The signers of checks. The wage earners. She had a sense, abruptly, of all of them — and now she looked around the room and took the others in too — of all of them as being simply in the service of the young.

Two nights earlier, at her parents' house outside Hartford, the house she'd grown up in, she sat and listened at dinner while her parents, gracious to a fault as ever, had quizzed Emily about the colleges she'd looked at and why she'd chosen Wesleyan, about what the summer held for her, and what she could guess at or know about the life she wanted. She listened as Emily talked on and on, as though there were no reason why everyone should not be fascinated by her plans — and she realized that she, Eva, had no plans, no more ideas for herself.

She had tried to speak of this to her mother after Emily had excused herself, after her wisp of a father had withdrawn. They were sitting in the living room, by the empty fireplace. Everything was dark — the woodwork, the furniture, the old carpets. The house smelled old around them,

96

and things had the threadbare air of the formerly elegant.

Skinny, flinty Martha Bennett had misunderstood her. She was drinking sherry, and she set her glass down sharply on the scarred coffee table. 'For me the moment occurred when my mother died,' she said. She pronounced it *muhthah*. 'I suppose I was about ten years older than you are now when that happened, and what I felt was that I'd arrived at the head of the line — that those ahead of me had stepped aside and now I could see clearly what was coming.' Her eyes swam, magnified to an odd intensity behind her thick glasses.

'No, but this is different,' Eva said. 'It's not about death. It's about these younger lives. About their having so much . . . I suppose, adventure, ahead of them.'

Martha looked at her, hard. She smiled, not ungenerously. 'As I said, dear. Death.'

But it *wasn't* about death, Eva thinks now. She felt that after John died, that death was all that waited for her. But now she wants to go on. She knows that. That is something, surely. She does want to go on. She wants life. More. More of something. She doesn't know what.

Sitting on Emily's bed, she reminds herself — consciously makes herself remember — the way she felt after things had ended with Mark. It was worse, she tells herself. It was so much worse then. She had been young and broke and still helplessly, ragefully, in love with Mark. All she wanted was her own irretrievable past, was what he'd smashed up.

She was working for peanuts then, and living way up on that godforsaken hill. And every piece of furniture, every room, every picture on the wall reminded her of Mark. The bed she slept in alone, the sheets she used. Dishes they'd scrimped to buy together or found secondhand at yard sales. Her own clothes reminded her of Mark. A dress she had to wear regularly to work — since it was one of the few reasonable things she owned — was a dress he had loved because of the long row of tiny buttons down the front, the slow unfastening of which had become part of a teasing start to sex. There were nightgowns he'd given her, a blouse he liked her in because of its primness, because it made what he knew of her sexually such a secret between them.

Gracie was still working as a nurse then, and she'd often stop by after her shift, still wearing her work clothes, her thick white nurse's shoes. Sometimes she spent the night, and they sat up late, drinking and talking about their lives, about men, telling stories from their past. Gracie thought Eva just needed to meet someone, needed to start going out, needed to begin to feel that something else, someone else was going to be possible. She wanted Eva to let herself be fixed up. Gracie was a person who liked to prescribe. Eva thought it came from her work. Or maybe she had chosen her work because she liked to prescribe.

Eva remembers that she'd pointed out Gracie's own solitary life to her. She'd asked Gracie why it should be that *she* needed someone when Gracie didn't.

'I'm different,' Gracie had said. They were in the living room, sitting opposite each other in the old, splayed chairs Eva and Mark had bought secondhand. The girls were long since in bed, though they'd had a dancing party for them before that, twirling them recklessly to an old Jerry Lee Lewis LP on the shiny wood floor that Mark had refinished himself the first summer they moved in.

'Why? You're a woman. You're alone too.'

Gracie had shrugged. She'd unpinned her hair when she arrived, and it fell over her shoulders, a thick blonde tumble that shifted now in the light when she moved. 'I'm tougher than you are. And I don't want to love anyone, and you do.'

This had struck Eva as true about herself. It silenced her. She wanted love. To love.

'Besides that,' Gracie said after a moment, 'I *have* guys. Dozens of them.' She made an expansive gesture with her hand, suggesting an array of men standing before her.

Eva drank some of her cheap wine. 'Not that you love,' she said, as she set her glass down. 'Not that you even date.'

'Well, but I touch them. I hold them. I'm well acquainted with their rigs.' Gracie's grin was lopsided. 'I joke around with guys all the time, sometimes while I'm holding on to their penises.' Her head tilted quizzically. 'Their peni?' She laughed. 'Anyway, it's part of my job description.'

'But not *a* guy. Not a penis.'

'But I don't want *a* guy. I want six. That's the difference between us.'

Eva remembers too that on one of those nights, she'd felt suddenly ashamed for whining about her life. She'd apologized to Gracie for talking as though her lot was so hard. She knew it was nothing like the kind of *hard* Gracie had lived through in Vietnam: she had no right to complain.

Gracie looked startled. 'That wasn't hard.' She shook her head. 'Those were the best times of my life.' Something in her friend's face made Eva reach forward across the table where they were sitting to touch Gracie's arm.

'No, really,' Gracie said. She smiled sadly. 'I've never been as happy, as thrilled on a daily basis, as I was in Vietnam. I'll never get over it really. What could come up to that?'

'For what?' Eva had asked.

'For . . . excitement. For drama.' Gracie's big face seemed to light from within, recalling it. 'For feeling utterly *used up*. For sex, for love.' She looked at Eva and frowned. 'I wanted it never to stop. I should be ashamed.'

'*Don't* be ashamed,' Eva said.

'I'm not. But I should be.' She ran her finger around the top of her glass slowly. 'But it did stop,' she said. 'It did. And now I have the rest of life to get through. One ordinary day after another.'

There was a little smear of blood on the front of Gracie's tunic. Eva thought of how different her ordinary day was from Gracie's ordinary day. How extraordinary Gracie's ordinary day would be for her.

She gets up now and goes into John's study.

100

She opens the windows there too, a row of them behind his desk overlooking the street. She's thinking, oddly, of the woman she'd sat next to on the plane, a woman who was returning from a five-day stay at a spa. She was coiffed, manicured, done up. She was about sixty, Eva thought, but with that careful grooming and elegantly dyed hair that makes a woman look at once much older and much younger than she is. This woman had explained reflexology to Eva.

'And you believe in that?' Eva had asked.

'Of course I do,' the woman said. 'It works; I'm the living testimony. Why wouldn't I believe in it?'

Because it's a lot of crap, Eva wanted to say. Because it makes no sense. Because you're an adult in a post-enlightenment world. What she said was, 'You do look fabulous.'

It had occurred to her then that maybe some of her problem was that she didn't believe in anything. She stands now looking out onto the front yard, the quiet street. Of course, that isn't quite true. She had believed that she and John would grow old together, that he would always be faithful to her.

But then she'd believed that of Mark too, she reminds herself. She'd believed that she brought some access to the world to Mark, that he needed her, that he'd never do anything to threaten that. She remembers now how moved she was the first time he'd asked her to read aloud to him the book she was holding. The sense of sorrow and simultaneous power.

What power?

Something that had to do with the words on the page and the sense of herself as their conduit for him. Or even their translator. Later, hearing Mark talk about a book, using words that they'd exchanged, repeating ideas about it that weren't exclusively hers, but weren't really his own either, she would sometimes feel constricted by this connection with him. And wasn't that a sort of infidelity on her part? A betrayal of what might have been the deepest part of their relationship for him, as his sleeping with someone else had been for her?

But this is the way it was between people, wasn't it? That there is always, a little bit, the sense of being imprisoned by what we love. She thinks of the wait by the luggage carousel for her bag to appear today, when she had watched a family with two small children as they assembled their car seats, their backpacks, their carryalls, their collapsible stroller. There was something exhausted in the young parents — they didn't speak to each other except to divide responsibilities. When they left, the mother had a baby slung across her front as she pushed the luggage cart, and the father had the older child in the stroller, a pack on his back. She had remembered it then — the visceral sense of confinement and burden when the children were small. As she remembered the same sense with Mark of being *bound* to him somehow, being responsible for him. Tied down to him, with him, even though she loved him so deeply.

With John it had been different. Their worlds overlapped, they enriched each other. No

102

translation was necessary, no taking of responsibility — at least on her part. And sexually too, there was a greater comfort and ease. It was not that it was less passionate, she thinks, but that the passion was quieter, was based in affection. And though she occasionally missed what had seemed so hungry, so driven, in Mark, she also thought of it as something inherent in him, something transferable. Something he could have, and then *had*, easily taken elsewhere.

What happened between her and John sexually seemed born of, seemed part of, what happened between them otherwise.

Though thinking of it now she remembers that he had felt differently. She remembers that she asked him one night, early on in their relationship, what attracted him to her. They were lying in bed in his house. The girls were home with a sitter in the house on the hill.

'The absolute usual,' he said.

'By which you mean?'

'Your fuckability. The sense I had of you as delicious.'

'What a nice answer,' she said, turning on her side to him. It was a hot night, and they were both naked, his thick penis fallen to the side. He had reached over and run his hand down her body, over the curve of her hip. She was actually startled to hear him say this, to have him use this language, her polite new lover. Startled, and then pleased. 'So much better than, 'Your lovely mind, your wit, your charm.'' His hair was oddly mussed, and he looked untended, silly. She reached up and stroked it back into place.

He grinned at her. 'And then, of course, all that — your wit, your charm — which is what made me love you.'

Eva had rolled over on her back again. The streetlight fell in on them. She couldn't get used to this, in town — the lights. It was so dark on the hill. Here, they could always see each other. After a minute, she said, 'So you think being delicious to someone else is step number one.'

'God, yes. Don't you?'

She wasn't sure what to answer. John hadn't been delicious to her, not in that sense, not at first. Not in the way Mark had, for instance, when she sat talking with him in the tent at the wedding that first day, nervously trying to hold his interest so they could stay together long enough that sleeping with him — sleeping with him that very night — might be a possibility. Talking and talking about nothing at all and attending only to the desire that quivered like music between them.

With John, her attention had turned to him only slowly the night they met, drawn by the persistence and intelligence of his interest in her.

'I suppose so,' she said. 'Yes. Delicious.' And she'd reached over and touched him again, moving her hand down to encircle his cock.

★ ★ ★

The night they had met, it was Eva's plan to fall in love with one of John's authors, a man named John Doyle. It was Eva who had read Doyle's book in the galleys that came to the bookstore.

104

She had loved it; she had suggested more than once to the woman who owned the bookstore that they bring him in to do a reading. He lived in San Francisco — easy to get him, then — and John Albermarle, his publisher, ran a tiny publishing house in the valley. It would be politic to support the local effort.

In the galleys it had been the novel itself, the writing, that had compelled Eva. But when the real book arrived with its elegant jacket and the author photograph, she saw that Doyle was darkly, mysteriously good-looking. There was no mention of a family in the brief biography, no hint in the dedication — 'To Ethan and Seth' — of a wife or lover. Of course he might be gay. But the text itself argued against that in its enthusiastic heterosexuality.

She had dressed carefully, elegantly, that night — the dress with all the tiny buttons, and a lacy shawl. She had arrived early — she was in charge of things. Of the chairs, to be unfolded in rows in a semicircle. Of the flowers — daisies tonight from her own garden, set on the counter in a vase next to the music stand John Doyle would read from. She was in charge of the wine and sparkling water and cookies laid out on a table pushed back against the shelves. Of the books, stacked on the signing table near the door.

Frances, the woman who owned the store, would act as hostess and introducer, a role she loved, so she would have most of the interaction with Doyle. But there was to be a dinner afterward in a restaurant a half block away, and Eva was invited to come along for that — she'd go back to the store later to pick up.

Dinner then. That would be her chance.

The reading went well. Two-thirds of the chairs were filled, and Eva sold perhaps twenty-five books. John Doyle was a good reader — an actor, really — giving even the pauses a full dramatic weight, making his face, his voice, anguished, then jubilant, then angry. After he'd finished reading, he responded enthusiastically to the questions asked him by the mostly female audience. Oh, perhaps he lingered a little too long, a little too self-importantly on the nuances of what his work routines were and how he approached his material, but after all, Eva thought, he *had* been asked.

As they stood waiting for their table in the restaurant, Frances introduced Eva as the person in the store who'd championed the book. John Doyle and John Albermarle — the two Johns, one beautiful, one not — beamed down at her. When they were finally seated, she was placed between them at the circular table. Frances presided. Her husband, Roger, famously uninterested in anything that smacked of the literary, was also there. He liked to choose the wine, because he liked to drink it. Lots of it. A different bottle with each course. He liked Eva too, probably because she was young, as he saw it, and pretty. Tonight, before the wine relieved him of feeling the burden of social interaction, he talked to her. Talked her ear off, she would say to the girls later, and motion with her hand its falling from her head to the floor. He talked about wine, about the food and the chef, whose cooking he'd experienced years before in Boston. He talked about Boston, that dull, morally superior town.

Frances had a loud, plummy voice — she practically rolled her r's — and Eva, listening between bits of Roger's commentary to John Doyle talking to her boss, slowly realized he was mocking Frances, repeating her eccentric phrasing, her elaborate constructions, in a dry, sarcastic voice. Though Frances didn't seem to notice — or care anyway.

Eva did. It pissed her off. She felt possessively hurt for Frances, *her* Frances. Sweet, smart Frances, who loved books, who read avidly and widely — Atwood, Musil, Brodsky, Grass, Amis — but who sounded elderly, prissy, unless you actually listened to her. Dismissable. In this case, she was being dismissed.

Nearly simultaneously Eva realized that the other John, John Albermarle, had been plying her with questions off and on all evening — odd questions, which he would spring on her suddenly and which she hadn't taken the time to answer seriously.

And here he was with another, leaning forward toward her just as she was having this revelation about Frances and the other John, beckoning her with his posture: Ahem, ahem: he wondered, did she think a person drawn to books was seeking a kind of experience not available in ordinary life?

'What?' she said. Maybe this was the first question she'd really paid attention to. At any rate, it occurred to her now to wonder how she had answered his other questions. *Hmm? Could be? Who knows?*

'I mean . . . ' He smiled, almost apologetically. 'Do we, are we, looking for something we don't find,' his hand smacked the table lightly, 'here?'

Now Eva leaned back in her chair and turned her body toward him, away from John Doyle, the meanie. She was a little drunk. Her mind swam. What kind of question was this, anyway? Did he intend her to take it seriously? After a moment, she said, 'Well, why did *you* become a publisher?'

He laughed. 'I suppose in some sense because I could.'

'What does that mean?'

When he lifted his hands she saw how enormous they were. Mitts. They had freckles on their backs. 'I had inherited some money. Enough so that I could ask myself what I'd like to do, without also having to ask myself whether I could support myself at it.'

'Unimaginable,' she said.

She was about to turn back to the other John, when John Albermarle said, 'But don't you think there could be a kind of apology for that privilege in my choosing work which steadily loses money?'

'Well, will you end up impoverished?' Eva asked pointedly. 'The resident of a poor farm?'

'It's not likely.'

'Then you're not sorry enough,' she said.

'You're very strict, aren't you?'

'I steadily lose money too, only I have none. I'm poor. I'm embittered.'

'Embittered! You don't seem embittered.'

108

'Oh, I'm not.' Eva sipped her wine. It was excellent. Thank you, Roger. 'I'm not. I love my work.'

'And is that because, do you think, *you're seeking through books an escape from ordinary life?*' His voice made fun of the question, of himself asking it, but he clearly wanted an answer, too.

'No, I love ordinary life.' She leaned toward him and lowered her voice. 'But I'm actually very angry at books right now. I've been tricked by books. Particularly by the book our friend here wrote.' She gestured vaguely in John Doyle's direction. 'Oh, I expected so much more of him. He's disappointing, isn't he?' John's mouth opened, but Eva went on. 'And this is your book too, of course. I'm angry at you too.'

He smiled. 'No you're not. It's a wonderful book. It shouldn't matter to you who wrote it.' Somehow, though he was implicitly repudiating John Doyle, it didn't seem a betrayal to Eva.

Eva leaned very close to him. The air near him felt warm. 'I'm sorry I met him though,' she said. 'I've learned a lesson here: I should have settled for just the book. I shouldn't have come tonight.'

'Oh yes, you had to be here tonight.'

'We needed young *blood!*' Roger asserted surprisingly — who knew he was still able to take anything in? He was leaning forward on the other side of John. He took another great gulp of wine.

At the end of the meal, after John Doyle had left, after Frances had paid the bill and they'd all said goodnight at the door of the restaurant,

John Albermarle offered to drive Eva home.

When she said she had her own car, he offered to walk her to it. When she said she had to pick up at the store first, he told her he'd help.

John did the chairs, folding them, carrying them by twos in his enormous paws to the closet in the back hall. Eva retrieved the empty glasses from where they'd been set down all over the store — on shelves; under seats; on *books*, she was appalled to see. She picked up napkins and wiped up spills and stains. John asked her about the store, about Frances, about her own preferences in books. There came a point when Eva realized the embarrassing imbalance of their exchanges, when politeness demanded that she ask him a question or two also.

Hers were less speculative than his, and more rude. Where had the money come from for the publishing venture?

Land, he said. His family had been in the valley a long time.

And where did his interest in publishing come from?

Well, he supposed from his wish — didn't she think this was all too human? — to impose his taste on others. The chairs clattered and clanged as he folded them.

And where, she asked, did the confidence in his own taste, his taste in books, come from?

'Why, from the *Lord*,' he said, bent over a resistant chair.

Eva laughed out loud, and clapped her hands together.

John stopped and lifted his face to her, his

110

hands on the back of the chair — the prince of chairs: big, freckled John Albermarle.

She should love *him*, she thought.

He was smiling. She could see he was infatuated with her, maybe even charmed by her childish gesture — her clapping — though she hadn't intended it as charming, it was just the moment's delighted response to what he'd said.

Now he asked her if she'd like to get coffee.

No, she didn't think so.

He went down the hall with the last two chairs. When he returned, Eva had set her purse on the counter, she was wrapping herself in her shawl.

'Why not?' he asked.

She told him she had to get back and take the sitter home.

She had children? His face seemed to mask over, all smoothness.

'Yes, two.'

It wasn't possible. How long had she been married?

She watched his long face open again when she said she was divorced. (This is part of what she would come to love about him, the openness of his face, the way it registered every shift in feeling without his seeming to know that about himself.)

'Well, maybe I should follow you back and take the sitter home for you. You must have to leave the children alone for a while when you take the sitter home.'

Would any other man in the universe have stopped to figure this out? she wondered. Even one? But she shook her head. 'I couldn't let you do that,' she said.

He started to protest: it was no imposition.

'No, I mean I don't *know* you. I couldn't ask the sitter to go home alone with you when I don't know you.'

'Well, I could stay with your children, then, while *you* take the sitter home.'

Eva laughed. 'If I wouldn't let you take the sitter home, why would I let you stay with my kids?' She turned away from him — they were at the door now — and flicked the lights off. The light from the streetlamp fell in on them, white, cold. When she turned back to John again, his face in chiaroscuro seemed harder.

He stepped up to Eva. He pulled her shawl tighter around her and knotted it at her bosom, pinning her arms inside it. He kissed her. As it happened, he was also standing on her feet when he did this, but Eva ignored that for the moment. John was holding her head in his hands as though it were a beautiful, fragile object. The Golden Bowl, she thought. She felt golden. His kiss was as soft, as tender, as those she gave the girls at bedtime. After a long moment, she said, 'Ouch,' and moved her feet under his.

★   ★   ★

Now she turns from the windows in John's study, she stands a moment behind John's desk, then sits in his desk chair and swivels it around. The trouble is, she thinks, that coming home now is like returning to her grief, to her own

112

emptiness. Home. What does it mean to her anymore, without John? She has a sudden vision of his face surprised in death, of the terrible moment when he sailed up backward away from her into the air. Then the sound his skull made, hitting the post. She will never forget it. She feels a moment of such bitterness and anger that it shortens her breath. She looks at her hands lying on his blotter, their torn and ripped cuticles, the bitten-down nails.

She had cleared his papers from his desk after he died, but she'd left the framed photographs he'd chosen to look at each day, and now her gaze moves from one of these to another. She picks each one up and stares at it, as though it could connect her somehow with him to see these as he did. There's one of all three children together on the front porch stairs when Theo was about one, beautiful and chubby, and the girls were still the same height, slim dark twins — though Daisy is looking off to the side in this picture, and her profile seems strangely adult. There are two of Eva, one in the bookstore, looking up, startled, from behind the counter with her glasses on. She has never understood why John liked it. The other one was taken on their honeymoon in Greece, and her face in it looks woozy to Eva — John had shot it just after they'd finished making love. There's also one of her, stunned with relief and joy, holding newborn Theo, asleep in his jaunty nursery cap, in the hospital.

She wants her children, Eva thinks.

No, that's not right; the one she wants is Theo.

Not Daisy, she realizes. Thinking of her daughter, Eva feels the *no* in herself, the defeat. Enormous Daisy. Sullen. Needy. Sullen because needy. She reaches for the phone and punches in Gracie's number.

She put Theo down a little while ago, Gracie says. 'But I bet he's still awake. If he is, I'll be right over with him. So here's the deal: if you don't hear from me within a few minutes, I'm on my way. And I'll call back if he's konked out.'

While she waits, Eva goes into her own room, her and John's room, and changes her clothes, unpacks her bag. She takes her toiletries into their bathroom and spreads them out. How much space she has, without John's things! She is tired of space.

She is down in the kitchen, seeing what there is in the refrigerator, when the front door opens and Gracie halloos.

By the time Eva steps across the tiled floor to the hallway door, Theo is there, running toward her in bare feet. She bends down and scoops him up, feels his legs circle her waist, his short arms twine her neck. He smells of an unfamiliar soap. She rains kisses on his face, and swings their bodies together from side to side. Gracie is beaming at them from down the hall.

When she finally sets Theo down, he jumps up and down a few times, in excitement. He's wearing short seersucker pajamas printed with football helmets. He says, 'What did you *bring* me, Mumma?'

Ah! Nothing!

She's brought him nothing!

And she has a sense of herself suddenly, as the child, the one who has grabbed at him, wanted something from him, while offering him only her hungry self in return. She feels ashamed. Everyone knows about the gift after the trip away. She knows about it. She knows better.

But when she says they're going to get something special tomorrow, he doesn't protest, and she turns to thank Gracie, who's still standing in the hallway by the opened front door.

Once Gracie has left, she carries Theo upstairs to bed. She sits next to him and sings softly until he falls asleep, suddenly and deeply, poleaxed by fatigue. She sits a long time after that, watching his still face, which seems almost returned to infancy, softened as it is in sleep, his eyelids and mouth slightly opened.

She remembers one night when John was still alive, after Theo had climbed into bed with them, his waking her by saying aloud in his sleep, 'Where I put it? Where that goddam piggie is?' The phrase was so incongruous, so sweetly childish in its focus, and casually, profanely adult in its language, that she had felt a complicated series of emotions in response — surprise, amusement, joy; and then sorrow, sorrow at the thought of his adulthood, its inevitability and the loss it would bring.

She had intended to sleep next to Theo tonight — that was in her mind, she realizes now, when she called Gracie: curling up with his thin wiry body, hearing him mutter and breathe in the night.

Why, then, has she carried him to his own bed? Why does she go back down the hall to her room now, and start to undress there, to get ready to lie down alone?

It's something about not having brought him a present, she thinks, about seeing herself as so in need of him, as so like a greedy child herself in that. She had felt exposed in front of Gracie at that moment, and ashamed of herself.

She can't go on using Theo for comfort, she tells herself. She needs to let go of him, to have a life — more of a life anyway — in the world.

★ ★ ★

Two days later, with the sense of doing something self-prescribed as being good for herself, something almost medicinally necessary, Eva goes upstairs after the dishes are loaded in the dishwasher and calls a man she barely knows, Elliott McCauley, a man whom Gracie has suggested will be *good company*. Eva asks him if he'd like to meet for dinner sometime in the next few weeks, and he says yes, yes he would.

6

The Valley bookstore is on Main Street in St. Helena, three doors down from the grocery. It's in essence one large open room, with a comfortable office and a lavatory down a little hallway at the back. There are posters on the walls, enlargements of famous photographs of famous writers, a few more women than men: Colette looking up from her desk with her steel-wool hair, her black mouth prissed. Toni Morrison, mammoth and fierce in an elegant dress and graying dreadlocks. A blurry portrait of an unexpectedly tentative-looking Willa Cather. And perhaps a dozen or so more, including the dramatically lighted Hemingway by Karsh, and a smiling photo of Saul Bellow as a younger man, wearing a rakish hat.

The register where Daisy presides is a U-shaped counter that bumps out from the wall into the room halfway back in this space. It's slightly elevated, and Daisy thinks of it as being like a throne, or a pulpit. From here she can't see everywhere in the store — the arrangement of the shelves makes what Eva calls 'reading nooks,' in which she's placed comfortable chairs — but even so Daisy can always tell when someone is there because the weathered, unfinished floorboards creak loudly at the lightest step.

Daisy is alone for the next two hours, the end-of-afternoon hours. Eva has gone to pick

Theo up and to get dinner organized, and Callie, one of the women who works in the store, left at three. This is part of the deal, part of the reason Daisy was hired for the summer — to give Callie more time to be with her kids. But it's okay, because Daisy likes Callie. Callie was the one who trained her while Eva was away taking Emily to her exchange program, and Daisy liked the sense of being an equal that Callie seemed to allow her. She liked Callie's patience in explaining the procedures and routine. And she liked it when Callie occasionally seemed to include her in her little asides at Eva's expense: 'Now this isn't quite the way your mom likes it done when she's around, but she runs what you might call a really tight ship. The rest of us mere mortals find this works just as well.'

These late-afternoon hours — the hours Daisy works alone until Eva comes with Theo to close up and take her home — are usually slow ones. Most of the tourists have cleared out, driving back to the city or returning to hotels in the valley to rest and get ready for dinner. The locals usually come in in the morning to buy books, when there's a chance to gossip; but in any case, by this time of day, they are doing what Eva is doing — picking up kids, shopping, cooking.

Eva has posted a list of chores by the cash register, chores Daisy can do if there's time on her hands, and Daisy has actually done one of them this afternoon — rearranging all the special-order cards by distributor so they can find the books easily when deliveries come in and quickly call the customers who want them.

118

But she finished that a half an hour ago, and now she's just sitting on the stool behind the counter, her feet resting on the top shelf under it where there are boxes of desk supplies. She's alternately watching the pedestrians stroll past the plate-glass window — moving slowly in the searing heat — and tearing at her cuticles, pulling the hard little edges off across the bottom of her nails, sometimes causing a bright drop of blood to rise.

Suddenly she hears voices from the street, loud, braying voices: kids! She looks up. It's a group of boys, older boys, moving in a staggering group, punching at one another as they pass. Then they're gone. One thing Daisy is grateful for is that kids her age don't come into the bookstore. That at least there isn't that possibility for embarrassment: that she almost certainly will never have to wait on someone she recognizes from high school.

From the back, in the children's section, she can hear the only customers in the shop, a mother reading a book to the two little girls she brought in with her. Daisy knows this woman — she's come in three or four times already during Daisy's shift. She won't buy anything. She just likes to bring her kids in and read to them. She's young and pretty and nice to her kids, though sometimes she talks too loudly, too enthusiastically, in that stupid, fake way grown-ups have of interacting with their children: 'Wow! The steam shovel book! That's just about your favorite book in the whole world, isn't it?!'

But reading, her voice is steady and low. Daisy

listens to its murmur. It makes her remember the way Eva read to them, to Emily and her, when they were little. She remembers too the way the room felt around them in the house in the vineyards up on the hill, remembers the shiny floor, the couch with the old blue bedspread flung over it, the piney, dry smell of the air coming in the open windows. She can call up the way it was to lean against Eva, to smell her Eva-smell, to feel her arm tense as she got ready to turn the page, and then move under you, so you'd have to shift your weight a little each time. Sometimes if Mark were there, he'd stop and listen too, with a dreamy look on his face, as though he were seeing the things Eva was reading about. As though he were just a kid, like them.

It seems astonishing to her that all that could be gone. That whole life. That Mark is gone, and John too. That she's here, alone, that these are her hands, her legs — she leans forward and rubs her legs — with this little bit of blackish stubble.

She has shaved her legs for the first time this summer, using Eva's razor. It was one of the June days when Eva was gone off with Emily back east. Daisy had walked the few blocks over to the house to water the lawn and the plants in the front yard. She didn't mind this chore. There was something pleasurable in the arc of water in the sun, the way the earth darkened and glistened momentarily under its flow, and then drank and emerged dry again. Daisy even liked the leak from the nozzle, the way the cold water dripped back over her arm, her clothes.

When she was done, she took the mail in and left it on the kitchen island. She went upstairs and wandered through the rooms there, dark because all the shutters were closed. Everything was still and airless and hot, and Daisy was aware of the perspiration wetting her underarms, rolling down her back. She went into Eva's room and lay on her bed awhile, smelling the light perfume Eva always wore.

She sat up and went to Eva's dressing table. There were three mirrors facing her, and set on the surface in front of them, a fourth, on a brass base, which magnified her face several times. Daisy looked at her skin closely in the mirror, poked it, squeezed a few whiteheads. Her nostrils seemed immense and hairy. Ugh. She opened Eva's makeup drawer and tried the black eyeliner. Some gray shadow. Blush.

In the mirror, three dramatic Daisies looked back, darkly glamorous. Pretty!

She could look this way. She could put this makeup on for school this fall and look like this and everyone would notice.

And suddenly, with this notion — the kids at school (when she thought of them she pictured certain pretty girls in her class, girls who *ran* her class) — the face looking back at her in the mirror looked different. She seemed grotesque to herself, *painted*, though she was wearing, she knew, no more makeup than all those girls did. Probably less.

She got up and went into the bathroom. She washed her face. The rinse water in the basin was faintly gray, then pink. While she was drying herself with one of the big white towels, she noticed Eva's razor in a cup on the sink's wide lip. She opened the medicine chest. There was a tube of something called Rosemary Mint Shaving Cream. Daisy slung a leg up into the sink and ran the water, splashed it on herself. She soaped up with the shaving cream and slowly, carefully, shaved off the fine hairs on her legs. Then she took off her blouse and brassiere and shaved her underarms too. And then, because she hated the way it looked, she decided to shave the dark hair between her legs. She had to chop at it with a scissors first, it was so long. She put the little handfuls of disgusting crinkly hair into the toilet and flushed it away. When she had cut off as much as she could, she shaved down to smooth flesh, the way it had been before, when she was a little girl.

Now she looks out at the store window again and then slides her hand under the waistband of her shorts and feels down there. It's stubbly too, like her legs — harshly scratchy against her finger-tips, and then soft and warm in the middle.

The floorboards creak. The children are getting up, talking. Daisy sits up, begins to stand and reach to put away the special-order cards.

But the mother is carrying a book this time — she's going to buy it. They all come toward Daisy, their faces shy and lifted, as though she might be proud of them for making this purchase. She says what she's supposed to, 'May I help you with that?,' and the mother hands it over. It's a book Daisy doesn't know, a book of lavishly illustrated nursery rhymes. Nothing Eva ever read to them, nothing John had read to Theo — for it was John who read aloud in their new family, sitting in the living room with Theo after supper, while Daisy and Emily did their homework on the dining room table. At first he read just picture books, naming books ('What do we see on this page?'); and then he did the simple stories — goodnight stories or the adventures of machines: trains, steam shovels, little cars. Then he read some baby fairy tales; and he and Theo were just beginning *Winnie-the-Pooh* — though Eva said Theo was too young for *Winnie-the-Pooh* — when John was killed.

Daisy rings up the book and takes the woman's credit card. She lays it in the machine and slides the bar across it. The woman signs the bill and Daisy separates the sheets, staples the receipt to the woman's copy. She asks if they want a bag. No, the older girl says shyly. 'You want to carry it, Adrienne?' the mother asks. The girl nods. Daisy hands the book to the little girl, and then the receipt to the mother. The mother puts it into the big straw bag slung from her shoulder.

Daisy watches them leave, the way they move together, the way the girls bump against their mother, the way she leans out over them as she opens the door. They pass almost ceremonially under the arch of her body. The door shuts. Daisy is alone.

She rings the cash register open again to put away the credit card receipt. The drawer slides out. The bills lie in their trays, pinned down under their hinged bars. Daisy lifts the tray, sets the receipt in under it, sets it down again. She stands looking at the denominations for a moment, and then she reaches in and takes a ten and, after a moment's hesitation, a five. She folds them together and slides them into the pocket of her shorts. Then she shuts the cash drawer and sits down again on her stool to listen to her heart thudding, and to wait for her mother and Theo to come and get her.

★ ★ ★

Daisy is a thief — why doesn't it make her feel bad? Why doesn't it make her feel guilty? It just doesn't. The money that she took, that she's continued to take over the hot, dragging weeks of summer, feels somehow hers by right, as though it's making up for something done to her, some injury.

'Caused by Eva?' her shrink asked. (This was many years later, long after all these events took place, when Daisy was looking back on the things that happened in the year and a half or so after John died and trying to figure out what in all of it was wrong, what was right, trying to figure out why she'd gotten as lost as she had. And what part of being lost was perhaps necessary to finding herself. Or had she found herself? Maybe she'd been rescued from a dangerous fate. She knew most people would think so. She knew in some ways that she ought to think so. That she didn't was part of what

124

confused her, part of what she was talking about with Dr. Gerard, part of what she was seeking to understand.

'Maybe not exactly *caused* by Eva,' she said, trying to remember how that earlier Daisy had felt. 'But certainly connected to her. *She* got to weep, she got to be the widow, she got the sympathy.' There was a long silence during which Daisy was looking at the floor, at an elaborate rug that nearly filled the office and was made of every color you could imagine. 'And then she seemed to be trying to move on.'

'To live her life,' the shrink said.

After a moment's pause, Daisy laughed. 'Well, yes,' she said. 'Unforgivable, wasn't it?')

In her bank account, Daisy has her real money, money she's earned, the money Eva has paid her. But in a box on the floor of her closet, behind a jumble of shoes and possessions she hardly bothers with anymore, she has a shoebox of cash, the cash she's stolen — small bills, but they add up to just over a hundred dollars. Every week or so she puts more in, and nearly every time she does this, she sits on the floor of her closet and counts it with an exacting and murderous pleasure, feeling her sense of isolation and anger increase with each oily bill she adds to the pile. All those years later she could still remember how justified it all felt to her at the time, how somehow *earned* the money seemed.

So much so that when Theo, who has suddenly become obsessed with money, gets caught pilfering change, Daisy feels no connection to the drama, no pang of recognition or guilt. He took the coins from the purses they always leave lying around, because, as he says, they have so many coins and he doesn't have enough. Like Daisy, he has hidden his stash, but he hasn't been as inventive. He has simply put it in the drawer by his bed, where Eva easily found it.

On this July evening, Eva is making him return everything, and Daisy sits, unmoved by his grief, as he tearfully counts out the six quarters and three dimes he stole from her. He has the hiccups, because he's been crying so hard.

'Now say you're sorry to your sister,' Eva says. She's standing in the doorway to Daisy's room, supervising this punishment. Daisy can tell by her face that she is amused, maybe even charmed, by Theo's innocent guilt — that this forced confession and compensation are pure theatrics, a ritual Eva must feel is important for Theo's proper development or something. Daisy's angry that she's been forced to be part of it.

You would think that her own thievery, and maybe even her resentment of Eva, would make her capable of saying something kind, something that lets Theo know she doesn't really care, that he hasn't done anything so terrible. But something else is at work in Daisy too. Something that makes her mean to Theo. So she waits with an exacting, hard-hearted distance as he says, 'I'm very sorry, Daisy.'

After a moment she answers, 'Yeah, well. Don't do it again, is all.'

'He won't,' Eva says. 'Will you, my *poupée?*'

She holds her hand out to him, and he crosses to her and takes it, shaking his head sadly, remorsefully.

★ ★ ★

Three more times in August Daisy steals from the register, waiting for a moment when no one is around. The last time Eva is actually in the store, but working in the office with the door closed.

Just as Daisy shuts the cash drawer, she sees him: Duncan, Gracie's husband. He steps forward from behind the shelves where he's apparently been standing, watching her.

For how long?

You can't tell from his face. It's perfectly pleasant, in the mannered way he has of looking pleasant. He's a medium-sized man, gray-haired and handsome in a tight, almost forbidding way. He has a high forehead and dark, blank eyes. His skin is unusually pale. He doesn't look like a Californian. He always dresses elegantly, even Daisy has noticed that, and he's always sarcastic. Even to Daisy. Even to *Theo*.

He has a terrible limp — some accident he was in. Daisy doesn't like him.

'Eva here?' he asks amiably.

Daisy lifts her chin toward the back of the store. 'She's in the office.'

He's smiling at her, his lips slightly parted. Why didn't she hear him? The creaky floor, his limp. He lurches up to the counter now. He leans on it. He gestures at her body, her hip, where she

127

has shoved the money into her pocket. He says, 'I think you should share that with me.'

Daisy feels breathless. She looks away quickly. Then back. She shakes her head.

'No?' he says, and smiles at her.

She doesn't smile back. She's watching him. Everything he does seems somehow false. Constructed.

'You sure?' His voice is light, entirely friendly.

She nods.

'Well then, I guess I better tell.'

Daisy shrugs. A sick feeling, a dizziness, overwhelms her.

Duncan is watching her too. Can he see her fear? Her weakness? He turns, he starts toward the back of the store.

And stops, three steps away. He turns partway around. She hasn't moved. He smiles again. 'You're tough, aren't you, Daisy? I've always liked tough.'

Daisy watches him. She knows he's toying with her, teasing her. She knows he'll tell in the end — how can he not? — but she decides that she won't let him humiliate her too.

Or she doesn't even decide. Her *will* simply rises to deny him.

He steps forward, close to the counter again, and he speaks more gently. 'You know, if I don't tell, if I keep our little *secret*, it's as though I'd taken your mother's money too. I become an accessory. An accessory *after the fact*.' He pronounces this carefully, but oddly, dramatically, as though there were something funny about it.

128

There's nothing funny. Daisy's heart is slowing. Venom slows it. She hates him.

'That must be worth something to you. My . . . complicity. For your sake.'

Daisy watches him.

He picks up a pen. He is fiddling with a pad on the counter, a stack of sheets gummed together that Eva and Callie write notes on. On its side it says, 'Freudian Slips: now you can write what's really on your mind.' It strikes her that he's nervous. More nervous than she is. Nervous, or maybe excited. The pen scratches on the pad. Stops. He looks up. His eyes are dark and cold.

'What's it worth, Daisy?' he asks.

After a long moment, she says, 'How much do you want?' Her voice sounds dry and scratchy.

He laughs. 'Daisy,' he says. He sets down the pad. 'I want it all.'

Daisy thinks of it all, all the folded bills in the box at the back of her closet. She knows he isn't referring to that. She knows that he doesn't — that he can't — know about it.

But maybe somehow he does. Maybe he's seen her take the money earlier too. Maybe he's been spying on her for a while? All summer?

Looking at him steadily, she shakes her head.

'No?' He steps back. 'Well, we'll have to think about this, Daisy. I'll think about it. You ponder it.' He nods, a series of smaller and smaller motions of his head. 'I'll get back to you.'

Now he smiles broadly, almost genuinely, and turns to go. She watches him: slide, lurch; slide, lurch. It seems to her he's exaggerating his limp for her benefit. How can she not have heard him? At the door he turns and looks back at her, still smiling. He fans his fingers in an arc at her, like someone lighthearted, like a character in a television sitcom.

When he's gone, she looks down at the pad. On it he's written *yes* three times: yes yes yes. She tears off the top page of the pad. You can still see the press of the words on the next page down, though, so she tears that one off too, and crumples them both and throws them away.

7

In mid-August, almost ten months after John's death, Mark discovered — Gracie told him — that Eva had begun to date 'a little bit' again. They were in a funky antique store in Sonoma, shopping together for Eva's birthday. Her forty-third. Gracie was holding a vase she was thinking of buying. She told him this in an offhand way. Deliberately offhand, he thought.

For a moment he was startled. He turned away from her. But then, standing among the tables laden with china, with linens and baskets and glasses, he thought that if you looked at it in a certain way, it could be said that Eva dated him too, though their times together were unfreighted and family-focused. But they'd had picnics with the children along, they'd gone to stupid movies they could all laugh at, they'd fixed meals together and sat down at opposite ends of Eva's table and talked. Talked until Theo and Daisy got up and drifted away to television or music, until the old clock in Eva's living room struck nine, and then ten.

Still, he was hurt.

It didn't make sense. He understood that. After all, he had been dating all along, himself. Or sleeping with women occasionally anyway. Not anything serious, not anyone he cared about. Just with a sense that it was part of life. His life.

131

Maybe, he thought, that's what Eva had decided too. That she should be going out. That she needed to begin to live again.

But was she sleeping with someone?

He asked, 'What do you mean, a little bit?'

'You cannot be jealous!' Gracie set down the vase and stared openly at him.

What had she heard in his voice? He'd said it casually, he thought. 'Well, I guess I can be whatever I like. But I'd still like to know what you mean by *dating*.'

She made a dismissive gesture. 'Well, it doesn't matter anyway. It's nothing serious.' She moved ahead of him down the aisle, touching this or that.

'How can you tell?' he asked after a minute. He'd stopped looking. He couldn't concentrate.

'It doesn't *matter*. She's not ready for anything serious.'

'Because of John, you mean.'

'Of course, because of John.'

'Because of how he died?'

Gracie looked at him. 'How he died, how he lived. John.' She lifted her hands. 'John the person. The person she loves.'

'Well, she'll still love John when she falls in love with someone else.'

'Now what on earth does that mean?'

Why had he said it? 'I don't know, Gracie,' he answered honestly. 'Just . . . she can love him all she wants, but there's part of her that must want to be . . . actively in love too, to be, in *life*, with her love, with whoever she loves. You know.'

Gracie looked at him oddly. 'Well, that's just

132

kinda sweet, Mark,' she said, drawling widely. And then, after a moment, 'You know,' she grinned, 'maybe you and I *should* have got together.'

He laughed.

'Oh, laugh, cruel man.' She laughed too.

As they were standing at the cash register — she'd found an antique painted wicker basket for Eva — Gracie suddenly said, 'I don't know, Markie-boy, but I don't think you should get your hopes up.'

'Hey, who says I do? Who says I have?'

She shrugged, and then laughed again. 'I don't know. Forget it. Forget I said anything. What do I know?'

Exactly, he thought. She didn't know. She hadn't seen them alone together, hadn't felt the deepening trust between them. Sometimes when he dropped Daisy off in these summer evenings — or Daisy and Theo — and he and Eva sat together talking lazily about their lives, he felt close to their old intimacy, he could imagine that something had already started which was going to go on and on.

★   ★   ★

Mark arrived at Gracie's house for Eva's birthday party, rattling up her long driveway in his truck, light brown dust pluming behind him in the slanted sunlight. Parked in the driveway were the two cars and the truck that Gracie and her husband, Duncan, owned; and the vintage Jaguar that belonged to Eva's old friends

Fletcher and Maria. *The usual crowd was assembled*, he thought. He grabbed the wine he'd brought — three bottles clanking in a paper bag — and his present for Eva, and crossed the gravel yard.

Gracie had come into big money in the mid-eighties, like everyone else along for the ride in Napa. Hers came directly from the source: she became a real estate agent just as the boom times hit, a pure coincidence. She'd been a nurse before then, and after more than fifteen years at it, including one in Vietnam, she had burned out. He could remember her telling him that she knew she'd had it when she actually struck a patient, a drunk with a broken arm who kept trying to smoke in the emergency room, even though she'd explained to him several times why he couldn't. 'I mean, at the moment I was doing it I thought of it as fundamentally therapeutic. You know, he was going to blow the whole place sky high if he lit up near some oxygen tank or something. But later I realized I was just pissed off. I was pissed off and I hit him.' She shook her head. 'Not good nursing, man. I was out of there the next day.'

She still lived in what had been a tiny house on the valley floor — her 'nursing home' she used to call it before she fixed it up; but the house had grown and changed since she came into money, and then changed some more after she married Duncan. The party tonight was to be out in back, where she'd put in a lap pool a few years earlier, and a large stone patio encircled with rosemary and lavender. The added-on French doors to the living room were flung open, front and back, and as he walked up to the house — a pavilion when it was opened up like this — Mark could see directly across into the space behind it, and even into the vineyard beyond that, at the near edge of which Duncan was setting up fireworks.

Eva's birthday was August 21, and Gracie and Duncan threw this party for her every year, complete with fireworks and ritualized games. Gracie organized the games, her own elaborate version of Charades. Duncan was in charge of the fireworks. It was among his many interests, interests that alternately puzzled and intrigued Mark, as Duncan himself puzzled and intrigued him.

Gracie spotted him from the kitchen, off on one side of the living area. 'Sweetie, yummy, come and kiss me,' she called out.

He smiled at her. 'If I must,' he answered.

She was pink with heat and exertion. As he embraced her, he inhaled her scent. She smelled of herbs he couldn't have named, and of her own perfume, and the musky odor of perspiration. Her face glistened. Her heavy, blonde hair was pulled up and held in a clip at the crown of her head, but it showed darkly, damply at her scalp. Her lipstick was gone, and her face seemed to him somehow innocent, generous, without it.

'Oh wine, delicious wine,' she cried when he handed her the bag. She lifted the bottles out and looked at the labels. 'Man, you *shouldn't* have,' she said, grinning. She knew these little wineries because of what they were doing to real estate values in a way that paralleled Mark's knowledge of them for what they were doing to prices in the wine business.

He opened one of his reds to let it breathe, and she poured him a glass of an already opened sauvignon blanc that was sitting in an ice bucket. She took her apron off and followed him outside. She was wearing a loose, flowing sleeveless dress and sandals.

As they stepped out onto the patio in the slanted, warm light, Duncan and Fletcher were returning from the edge of the vineyard. Maria sat at the long wooden table, which was already set for dinner, the tall wine and water glasses turned upside down. When Duncan spotted Mark, he raised his glass — a martini glass, he never had wine before dinner — and called out, 'Ah, the farmer! In the dell, as it happens.'

Mark nodded and raised his glass in return, though he wasn't sure whether or not a kind of joke was being made at his expense. 'Sir,' he said, and drank.

'Now can someone tell me what the heck a dell is, exactly?' Gracie asked.

Was she trying to distract Mark from what he might have found offensive in Duncan's remark? Maybe. Often enough Gracie seemed to want to shelter others from what Duncan said or did that might be uncomfortable.

Eva had once called Duncan 'congenitally ironic.' Did this mean she didn't like him? Mark wasn't sure. Gracie and Duncan had met after Mark and Eva split up, so whatever talking she'd done about Duncan and what she thought of him, she'd done with John, not Mark.

Duncan gestured now. 'A dell: this valley, my dear, from which you extract such a pleasant livelihood, even as you make it less livable for most of the rest of the universe.'

Gracie laughed her big laugh: haw, haw, haw. They had all sat down by now, their chairs pushed back slightly from the set table. The evening was still fully light, the air just beginning to freshen after the day's heat. Mark stretched his legs out. He was aware of a kind of tension in himself. He was just waiting, really, for Eva's arrival.

He listened to the conversation though, to Duncan, who had started to explain the fireworks. He knew a man in San Francisco who designed them, and he was full of technical information. He was talking now about how multibreak shells worked, about how long the fuses had to be to allow a certain height to be reached before the shell burst, about the names of the shapes they'd see tonight — willows and palms and roundels and chrysanthemums — and about how each was packed.

He and Gracie certainly *were* an odd couple, Mark thought, watching them. Gracie was open and voluble. She was attractive, he supposed, but she was also large and blowsy. Horsey, he might have said, if that didn't seem unkind, and also unsexy. Because Gracie was somehow sexy. She gave off a sense of availability, of openness, of animal energy that did that for her. She had the ease and generosity he associated with nurses — a kind of tough-minded sweetness. And then layered over that was the intelligence and shrewdness, the understanding of people that made her successful in real estate — though there was a way, he supposed, in which it would have been hard to be unsuccessful in real estate at the moment she entered the profession in the valley.

But Duncan. Mark looked at him, speaking quietly in his contained, precise way. He was wearing a soft linen shirt of the palest gray. His eyes were small and dark, hooded slightly. His skin was pale, lightly lined, especially around the eyes, and somehow almost luminous. Duncan was a tough nut, Mark thought. There wasn't an interpersonal bet he didn't hedge — with sarcasm, with mockery. Even, sometimes, with a certain facial expression — a slight lifting of his upper lip.

What Mark knew of him, of his life, he knew in bits and pieces from Gracie or Eva. He'd wanted to be an actor when he was young, but had ended up a stuntman for some years — a good one, as it turned out, Gracie had said. She had spoken proudly of this. That he was naturally athletic, utterly fearless. But then he'd been injured in a terrible accident at work. He still limped as a result. He'd spent more than a year in various surgeries and several years after that in pain. He moved always with economy, maybe because it hurt to move. The effect, though, was of control. Steely control, Mark thought, given his lack of expressiveness otherwise. His eyes settled on you, steady, observant, but somehow not connected to you. Cold.

Gracie maintained that the accident wasn't all bad. That the rehabilitation had changed his life in many ways for the good. For one thing, he learned woodworking and slowly became a kind of master furniture maker, which was how he made his living now. And for another, it had given him time to read, widely and deeply. He became an avid reader. This was how he'd met Gracie, actually, four years earlier — at Eva's bookstore, where each of them had taken to dropping in regularly, for different reasons: Gracie to schmooze, to gossip — about neighbors, about the kids and Eva and John and Mark and life; Duncan to talk about books. And to buy them, ten or a dozen at a time. Eva introduced them, and they married a few months later.

What could have drawn them to each other? Watching them, Mark was thinking that he couldn't have answered that question. Gracie was talking now, telling a joke actually, imitating a haughty British accent — Princess Anne on a quiz show. Duncan's eyes were steady on her with no emotion Mark could recognize, except a mild, disinterested amusement. There was something in his constraint, though, his self-containment, that Mark could see would be attractive, might have drawn Gracie. When she got to the punch line, delivered in the fruity voice, 'Oh! I know! It's a horse's cock!' Fletcher and Maria laughed out loud. Nothing changed or shifted in Duncan's face.

Maybe he'd wanted her money. She was quite well off by the time they met. But then Mark

139

remembered that Eva said there'd been a huge settlement after the accident.

But maybe he'd already run through it. Maybe the medical care used it up. He did all right with the furniture he made, more than all right: it was written up in arts magazines, in *Architectural Digest*. But all that kind of work must be a little irregular anyway — steady commissions or purchases for a few years, and then maybe a barren stretch. So money could have been part of it.

Now something did shift in Duncan's face — a sudden sharpened attentiveness. His gaze had moved though, away from Gracie. Looking up to follow it, Mark saw Eva in the opened doorway to the house. Eva, and Daisy and Theo. Gracie must have felt his gaze move too, because she had turned around.

'Eva!' she cried out, getting up. 'Late to your own party, aren't you ashamed. Hey, Daze. Hey, Theo, cutie-pie.'

And then they were all standing, lining up, shifting positions, everyone kissing and embracing Eva and the children. Mark waited his turn. He held Eva first. She was wearing a black backless sundress, and her flesh was cool and silky under his fingers. He hugged Daisy. As he pressed her against himself, he was aware, abruptly, of the push of her breasts against his chest. When had that happened? He had to resist looking at her as she stepped back. Instead he picked up Theo and swirled him around.

But he watched Daisy, particularly a little later, as she helped Gracie and Maria bring the

140

food out. She was wearing a gauzy, billowy shirt, maybe Indian, over baggy khaki shorts with many pockets that reached almost to her knees. You could see her bra through the shirt, a skimpy, mostly symbolic garment. She seemed more self-conscious, more self-aware, than she usually was. Did that come with these changes in her body? Once she looked up to find his eyes on her, and she blushed. Blushing was new for Daisy, he thought.

Earlier, Maria had been asking her what she was up to this summer, and she spoke, shyly it seemed, about her job in Eva's bookstore. They were all attentive, even Duncan, and that seemed to overwhelm her, being the center of attention. Color rose to her cheeks as she answered their questions. He noticed she sank back in what seemed relief when the conversation moved on, when Maria and then Gracie began to talk about their first jobs, Maria's in a drive-in, on roller skates, Gracie's as an au pair in Winnetka for a wealthy family. She'd eaten with the cook, in the kitchen, she said. She'd never understood anything about class in America before. She said, 'I thought my title was *au pére*, actually — for the father.' She raised her eyebrows and grinned. 'I thought this for very good reasons, I'd like you all to know.'

At some point during all this, Mark saw Duncan reach over and turn Daisy's glass right side up, then fill it with wine and push it toward her. It seemed a gracious gesture, a welcoming of her as a quasi-adult, someone with experiences like the ones they could all remember. He was sorry he hadn't thought to do it himself.

They ate, and as they ate, the sky turned gold and pink, and then quickly a darker and darker blue. It became *inky*, he thought. There was a kind of intimacy in the candlelight now, in the way it made a circle of their faces in the surrounding dark.

When they finished the first course, but before Duncan set off the fireworks, there was an elaborate ritual they observed every year: the tranquilizing of the dog, an old spaniel named Miranda — she was terrified of the noise of the explosions. As Gracie held the dog's jaws apart and dropped the pill in, they all raised their glasses and toasted her: 'Miranda! Here's to Miranda!' Mark watched Gracie's sure hands stroke Miranda's throat until she swallowed.

Gracie asked Theo to be in charge of letting them know when Miranda was groggy. He went to sit next to her on the floor by the table, dropping from Mark's view. 'But what is *groggy?*' he asked, his voice floating up.

'Sleepy. Out of it,' Daisy said.

'Loagy,' Duncan offered. He'd put on rimless glasses that reflected the candlelight.

'Thank you, my darling,' said Gracie, 'for offering a uselessly-more-obscure-than-the-original-word synonym.'

'What is *loagy?*' Theo's voice asked, and Mark watched as Eva's slow smile changed her face.

The third or fourth time Theo reported Miranda as groggy, saying the word importantly, Gracie confirmed that this time she was, yes indeed, recognizably *groggy*, and Duncan got up

142

and walked out to the edge of the vineyard. Watching him move away, the laborious heaving up and then falling of each step, Mark thought — he was sure they were all thinking — of the damage done to him. He stepped farther and farther into the night, and finally he was just a pale shape moving around out there.

Suddenly there was the singing of a rising rocket and the sky lighted up — white first, and then in successive falling, expanding sprays, blue, and green, and deep red. Theo leaned back in Eva's lap with his thumb in his mouth, his face turned to heaven. But they were all rapt for five minutes or so as the artificial thunder echoed across the valley floor and the colors radiated in gorgeous, spilling, liquid cascades of light. Miranda lay uncaring and woozy at Gracie's feet, lifting her head occasionally with a slow, rocking, swinging motion, as though it were too heavy for her neck. She looked, as Daisy pointed out, like one of those plaster animals with suspended bobble heads some people set in the rear windows of their cars. The sulphuric smell of the gunpowder floated over the table.

When it was over, they sat for a few minutes. In the silence they heard coyotes howling back and forth across the valley. Duncan had joined them, to applause led by Eva. The talk was more desultory than before. Why fireworks were so magical. Remembered July Fourths. Childhood. Theo's eyes had closed. Daisy's glass was empty, and Mark, this time, reached over and filled it.

After a while, they went inside, into the surprisingly bright domestic light. Eva took Theo to the guest room to put him down to sleep, while the rest of them cleared dishes and cleaned up in the kitchen. When Eva reappeared, Gracie divided them into teams for Charades.

Gracie insisted on this annually, and organized them, though she didn't play herself. She was, as Duncan called her, *the boss*. She even assigned them their words.

Mark and Eva were on the same team, with Fletcher. Their word was *confidence*. They went back into the kitchen to confer on the short skits or scenes they would act out for each syllable, and then for the whole word. As it worked out, all three of them were in the skits for the separate syllables, using costumes and props from a wicker box full of old clothes and junk Gracie kept especially for parties and children's visits. But for the word itself, Eva and Mark stood up alone, side by side.

'Whole word,' Eva announced. Then she turned to him and said, 'I have something to tell you, but you mustn't tell another soul.'

'Last thing on my mind,' he said.

She stood on tiptoes and he bent down. She whispered to him for a few minutes, just nonsense syllables. But her breath was warm on his face, in his ear, and he was suddenly aroused and sad. Still, when she stepped back and said, 'Now, you won't tell anyone, will you?' he answered, as he was supposed to, 'You can trust me, absolutely.' The others got it in two and a half minutes.

Then Mark and Eva and Fletcher sat down, and it was the other team's turn — Duncan and

Daisy and Maria. They gathered in the kitchen, and in the lapses of conversation in the living room, Mark could hear their voices planning their skits. He listened for Daisy. She made only an occasional contribution.

Finally, Duncan and Maria emerged to do the first syllable. They stood, facing each other, and Duncan told Maria a series of knock-knock jokes. After each one, she turned to the audience with a confused look and said, 'I just don't get it.' After a flurry of guesses, Fletcher came up with the answer: 'dumb.'

The second syllable involved Duncan and Maria calling to Daisy, who was offstage in the kitchen, 'Come on, we're late, let's go!' and Daisy answering, 'Just a sec.' They were irritated, clearly parents who had to wait for this daughter often. They called again and Duncan checked his watch. After a few more repeats, when Daisy called out 'Just a sec,' he said, 'This is a lot longer than that. A *lot* longer. Maybe sixty times longer.'

Eva guessed 'minute.'

Maria signaled shorter — shorter word. 'Min!' Eva called, and Duncan nodded. 'Min!' she said. 'Dumb. Min.'

For the whole word, Duncan came out alone and bowed. Something about the way he carried himself made Mark realize how extraordinarily handsome he must have been once. He was still good-looking enough, though the accident and age had harrowed him. He slowly got down on all fours. Daisy and Maria were backstage in the kitchen with the box of props — you could hear

145

them laughing — and with some boots they'd asked for.

'Just a sec,' Daisy called. She laughed. 'Just a sec for *real* this time.' Her voice was lighter, more giddy, than he remembered ever having heard it.

After a few more minutes, she came out. She flung her arms wide. 'Ta-da!' she said. She was wearing an old black bathing suit that must once have been Gracie's. It was too big for her, and she'd held it in at the waist with a tight belt studded with rhinestones. She had on dark red lipstick and the pair of scuffed brown boots Gracie had found for her, which struck her midcalf. Her thighs seemed endless and muscular. Her eyes were ringed with black. She carried a ruler.

She walked over to Duncan and stood behind him. She lifted one leg, set her foot on his back, and smacked the ruler on her own open palm. 'Speak!' she commanded in a guttural, mock-German voice: *schpik!*

Duncan lifted his head and barked several times, mournfully.

'Oh, that's way too easy,' Fletcher said. ''Domination.' Dumb, Min, Nation.'

Daisy smiled and lifted her foot off Duncan, dropping out of character abruptly as she stepped back. Duncan rose up to his knees and lifted his hands in mock resignation.

Mark had looked at Eva when Daisy first walked out. He'd seen that she was as startled as he was by their daughter's appearance. He looked at her again now and saw that her lips

146

were primmed and tight, her nostrils pink. She was angry. But at whom? At Daisy? At Duncan? Somehow Mark felt she might be angry at him, but he couldn't think why.

But now Gracie was standing up and herding them outside again to wait for the cake. Daisy was about to follow them, still in her costume, but Gracie caught her. 'You better change, honey. It's hard on these old geezers to have you wandering around like that.'

'Woof,' said Duncan at the door, grinning at Gracie and Daisy.

Daisy went back to the kitchen, and they trailed out into the darkness, where the candles jumped and flickered in their glass bells on the table. The air was lighter, cooler, than it had been all day.

Mark was behind Eva. She sat down next to Duncan at the table, turned her fierce face to him, and said, 'Whose idea was that?'

Duncan's lips curved slightly. 'Oh my dear, clearly what you mean to say is 'Whose *bad* idea was that?''

'You bet I do.'

There was a silence. Duncan shrugged. 'We were *playing* a *game*,' he explained, his diction as pronounced as though he were speaking to a child.

Eva turned to Maria. 'How could you let her?' she asked.

Maria said, 'I suppose because I had no idea she'd look like that.'

Eva let out a dismissive pffft of air.

'Oh, Eva,' Maria said, cajoling. 'I thought it

was a kind of joke, one we'd get and she wouldn't. No harm done, really.'

Mark said, 'Come on, Eva, don't spoil your party.'

She turned to him. 'You don't think that was distasteful? You don't think it was a betrayal of Daisy, really?'

'You just don't like the idea that she's growing up,' Duncan said. 'That she's sexual. And that's too completely banal, Eva. The budding child, the jealous mom. How unworthy of you.' He was actually smiling, unafraid of Eva's rage.

She turned to Duncan and said, 'You don't know anything about Daisy.'

His lip lifted. 'She's probably got a few secrets from you too, darling.'

Mark looked up and saw his daughter crossing the lighted living room, nearly at the open doorway. 'Daze!' he said, a little too loudly.

The others looked around. She was wearing her gauzy shirt again, and the baggy khaki shorts she'd had on before. But she was barefoot and she hadn't removed the garish lipstick or the black eyeshadow. As she approached the candlelit table, he was actually more startled by her appearance now than he'd been when she was in costume. It was as if she'd not changed back all the way, as if some aspect of the character she'd acted had lingered in her. And in this light, he saw how beautiful she was going to be, with her stern elongated face. As elegant as a Modigliani.

She sat down just as Gracie appeared at the doorway, the glowing cake a warm light under her big generous face as she approached them. She began to sing 'Happy Birthday,' and they joined in. Mark was sitting next to Duncan, and it seemed to him that even singing, the man could imbue his words with sarcasm.

But the singing, the cake, and Gracie's and Daisy's arrivals had moved them on — the ugly moment of Eva's anger was forgotten by the time she blew the candles out. While they ate dessert, Fletcher and Maria were talking about their intention to see *A Fish Called Wanda*, and then they were all speaking of John Cleese — was he the funniest man alive? — and speculating as to which of the Monty Python actors would survive independently the longest.

Mark saw Daisy refill her own wineglass. He leaned over, 'How much have you had to drink, Daze?'

She looked at him, levelly. She'd eaten most of her lipstick off with the ice cream and cake, but he was aware of a changed consciousness about her on his part.

'If you can't tell how much I've had, what does it matter?'

Was it a joke? Was it hostile? Mark couldn't tell. Was it only a question? He looked away, then back. He said, 'You're turning into a real smart-ass, aren't you?'

Something cool and slightly tough happened to her face. She smiled at him and then turned away.

Gracie and Maria had brought Eva's presents outside, and she opened them one by one in the slow, gracious way she had, commenting even on the papers they were wrapped in, the funny or sweet cards. They were mostly kitchen items — everyone knew she liked to cook. A pudding mold, a fancy device for slicing vegetables. But Gracie had given her the painted basket, and Mark had gone back to the same store, alone, and bought her an antique necklace of jet beads. She exclaimed over everything, but it seemed to him she was especially warm about the beads. She put them on immediately at any rate, and turned to the table, her face lifted. 'How do I look?' she asked flirtatiously, and Mark was in the chorus answering, beautiful, wonderful, fabulous. And she did, he thought.

A candle guttered and went out. 'Oh, that's my cue,' Eva said. 'It's late, and I should get Theo home.'

She stood and thanked them all again, thanked Gracie especially. Hugged her. They were all standing now. Maria began to gather Eva's presents. Daisy and Fletcher were clearing. Eva had gone into the house.

She came back into the living room with Theo, his dead weight draped over her upper body and shoulder, his bottom sitting on her arm. He whimpered as she came into the light, and turned his face into her neck.

'I'll put the presents in the car,' Maria said.

'No, let Daisy,' Eva answered. 'I need her anyway. We've got to get going.'

But Daisy was in the kitchen, helping, so Maria and Mark together carried the presents out, along with a big chunk of cake Gracie had wrapped in tin foil for Eva to take home.

When she'd settled Theo in the backseat, Eva got behind the wheel.

Mark shut her door and stood leaning on it, looking down at her. 'Why don't I bring Daisy home in a bit?' he said. 'I'd like the time with her.'

Eva looked at him a moment. Could she tell that he was using Daisy as a way to come to her house? That what he wanted was time with her, Eva, time which might be possible if he brought Daisy home?

'Okay,' she said. Her voice was tired. 'But not too long. We get up at the same old time as usual tomorrow.'

'No, we'll just get the cleanup launched.'

In the truck ten minutes later, Daisy was unusually voluble. She was explaining the Latin roots of the words they'd acted out. Latin-root words were good for Charades because they divided up wonderfully, she was telling him. She loved Latin-root words. 'Even though you're not supposed to.'

'And that would be because . . . ?'

'Oh, they're too long, too elaborate and formal. Simpler words are more elegant. This is what *they say*,' she pronounced, heavily, and her hands lifted, her fingers curved to make quotation marks.

'You got me,' he said. 'Words, turds, in my book.'

'Well, we know about you and books.'

He laughed. 'Ah, Daisy, sad but true.'

'Maybe I'll be a writer,' she said. 'Famous, of course.' She laughed quickly, and then made a face: how absurd, how pretentious.

'I'd read *your* books,' he said. 'Every word.'

'I like to write,' she said, suddenly serious. 'I'm good at it.' A little silence fell between them. Mark was watching the glowing red taillights ahead of him. It made him think of the nights he'd followed Amy home, the slow fever rising in him at the thought of what they would do together, what they were about to do. He remembered catching up with her at the door, slamming into her, carrying her back to the bed. He remembered her legs, their grip around his hips.

He did that while he was married to Eva, while he loved Eva. What a useless fuck he was, finally. There was no chance Eva would take him back. None.

Daisy was talking about writing. About how hard it was most of the time, finding the right words. But how every now and then it felt like a gift, like something that just happened, that she just *knew*. And then it seemed she was reciting a poem about that. Or something ordered and rhythmic that connected to the idea.

When she was silent again, Mark said, 'Is that you? *Your* words?' They'd stopped at the intersection entering St. Helena.

'Pphhhh!' she laughed. 'I *wish*. It's Emily *Dick*inson, Dad.'

'Well, pardon me,' he said. The light changed. 'Still, I like it. Her. Them. Them words.'

After a moment she said, 'But it's true, you know.'

'What?'

152

'That when the words come, it seems easy and natural. *Native*, is what Emily Dickinson says. It seems so native that you forget what a gift it is.'

' 'Native' is a nice word for natural. Native. To me that's like, when I hold a grape, when I taste it, knowing how soon we should pick. I can measure it too — I do measure it — but I also know it by its weight in my hand, by its flavor.' He smiled. He was salivating, thinking of it. 'What is it she said about sipping wine?' he asked.

'I didn't think of that, Dad.' Her face was open, delighted.

'Of what?'

'Of the connection with *wine*! How she's comparing the arrival of the right words with the right wine.' She frowned. 'Well, maybe with a holy wine.'

He thought of Eva, of how he'd like her to be hearing this — Daisy, talking this way. Talking to him. 'Can you write it down for me?' he asked. 'The whole poem?'

'Sure,' she said.

At Eva's house, there was no one downstairs, but Mark could hear her moving around above him, putting Theo down. He and Daisy went into the living room. Daisy sat down in a big armchair. She leaned back, her legs stretched out in front of her. She slowly heeled her sandals off. 'I would hate to be forty-three,' she said abruptly.

He laughed and looked over at her, part woman, part girl. 'Say it this way, Daze: 'I will hate it when I am forty-three.' Because one thing

153

for certain is that the day is going to come when you too will be forty-three. That is for sure.'

'Yeah, well. You may believe that, but I don't.'

Mark was restless, moving around the room, picking things up, examining them — the icons of Eva's life with John. Though some of them he recognized. Some of them she'd had when they were married too: a wooden darning egg, a glass box that held the buttons from the Civil War uniform of a great-great-uncle. He stopped in front of a painting on the wall. It was a small landscape, done with thick luminous smears of paint. You wanted either to eat it or be in it, he thought.

'The oldest I want to get is about twenty-five,' Daisy said.

'But all the good stuff happens after that,' he said distractedly.

'Oh, yeah. Like divorce and betrayal and dying and general wretchedness.'

He looked at her. She had said this casually, sarcastically, but she had said it. Is this what she thought? Is this what his life and Eva's had made her believe? And John's too, he supposed, dying the way he did.

He didn't want to think this. He didn't want her to think it.

'No,' he said. He wanted to correct this vision. 'The *good* stuff. Like marriage and children and getting really skilled at the work you choose. And choosing the work, too.'

She shifted in her chair, watching him. Her hands were laced together across her belly. She shrugged and said, 'Yeah, and *then* divorce and

154

betrayal and all that other stuff.'

'Also,' he said, pretending deep thought, 'it must be that getting *nicer* happens a little later too. Probably after twenty-five. Definitely long, long after fourteen.'

'Very funny, Daddy. And I'm fifteen, for those who don't keep up with these things.'

'Fifteen.'

'Remember? You gave me a bracelet?'

He did remember. Vaguely. He came and sat down across from her. Between them was a low square table with three stacks of books on it. There were also several Matchbox cars. Mark picked one up. A convertible. 'Well, how's fifteen?' he asked.

'You must have noticed, Dad.'

'I guess I haven't. How is it?'

'Fifteen. Fifteen sucks. I hope I'm never fifteen again.'

He set the car down. 'Little fear of that.'

'Thank God.' She sat up a little straighter and scratched her leg. She was frowning. 'But I wonder what work I *will* be good at.'

'Maybe you'll run a bookstore. Eva says you're good at that.'

She made a face. 'That's Mom's thing.'

'Maybe you'll be . . . an actress. You were terrific tonight, playing the dominatrix.'

She looked at him. Her face lit mischievously, her dark brows opening her eyes wide. 'Maybe I'll just be a dominatrix.'

He laughed. Daisy. This was fun, being with her.

When they heard Eva on the stairs, Mark was

watching Daisy's face. It shifted — it closed somehow — and he felt a pang for Eva, for what this meant about her relations with Daisy. Before Eva had stepped in the doorway, Daisy was standing up. She passed her mother as Eva entered the room. 'Night, Mom,' she said.

'Okay, sweetie,' Eva answered. She seemed distracted. She wouldn't have noticed, then.

She came in and sank onto the couch at its opposite end. 'Lord!' she said. Daisy was gone, pounding up the stairs.

'You feeling better?' Mark asked.

'Oh! Yes.' She frowned. 'You mean, about Daisy at the party?'

He nodded.

'Yes. I was just mad at Duncan and Maria, really. I mean, don't *you* think it was distasteful?'

'Honest to God, Eva, I didn't. Daisy seemed really fine with it. She was being funny about it just now.'

'Funny how?'

'Joking about it. But not in any . . . *distasteful* way.'

'You sounded just like Duncan then.'

'Please.' He turned toward her. She was still wearing the necklace. 'Anyway, happy birthday.'

'Yes.' She sounded tired. 'Thanks.' She took a deep breath and let it out slowly. 'It was a nice party, wasn't it?'

'Except for the distasteful parts.'

She laughed, a snorty laugh. Then she sighed. 'Am I such a stuffed shirt? I just want to protect her.'

'From what? No one at the party would hurt

156

Daisy. It's a safe place for her to pretend to be whatever she wants to pretend. And she was pretending. She put it away, with the costume. Just like dress-ups when she was little.'

'You're right. I know it. Maybe I was just pissed off because she seemed ... ' Eva shrugged. 'I don't know. Suddenly to have a life. Beyond my ken, as it were. I felt it with Em too, earlier this summer, schlepping her around. How they'll have these *lives*. They'll go off. They'll fly away, and I seem ... stuck. My life seems ... so set.' She laughed sadly. 'Happy birthday indeed! I. Feel. Old.' Her head swung a little on each word. The necklace glittered.

'Not you, Eva.'

'Well, thanks. You're sweet.'

'No, I mean it. You're still — '

She threw up her hands. ' "*Still!*" ' she cried out, and smiled. 'See? Listen to yourself. *Still. You mean, after all this time. Deep into your old age:* Still.'

'Nah,' he said.

'Nah what?'

'Nah, that's not what I mean.'

'Okay then,' she said. 'I'm sorry. I'm just teasing you, anyway.'

'I mean I want you, Eva.'

Her mouth opened a little. He reached his hand out quickly to cover both of hers, which rested on her lap. He was aware of their warmth, and of his fingertips touching her leg through the loose fabric of her skirt. He slid toward her on the couch. He lifted his other hand to her face and set his palm against her cheek. He heard her

157

sharp intake of breath. She leaned her head against his hand. She closed her eyes.

Under his other hand, her hands turned up, encircled and held his fingers. A tear formed at the outer edge of her eye. He wiped it with his thumb. He leaned forward and kissed her cheek, then set his lips gently on her mouth.

'Aahhh!'

Eva's body jumped, and Mark turned.

Daisy stood in the doorway, seeming to fill its frame. She had on a long T-shirt that said 'Because I Say So.' Her legs and feet were bare. Her face was open in anger and shock. She held a piece of paper in her hand.

No one spoke. Mark and Eva sat about a foot apart from each other on the couch, not touching each other at all now.

'Daze . . . ' he started.

She shook her head. 'Forget it!' she said. 'God! I was bringing you this.' She crumpled the paper and threw it at him. He felt its sharp prick on his face. It fell to the floor, and Daisy was gone.

They sat still for a long moment, not looking at each other. Then Eva got up. 'This is one I'm going to have to deal with right away, I think.' Her face was drawn, suddenly paler.

'Probably so,' he said. 'Yes.'

She started toward the doorway, and then turned. 'You better go, Mark,' she said. 'I need to be just . . . with Daisy. I'm afraid this is going to be complicated.'

'All right,' he said.

She disappeared around the corner, and he heard her slow footsteps going up the stairs. A moment or two later, after he heard Daisy's voice start, accusatory and loud, and Eva's responding in calmer, muted tones, he bent down and picked up the paper his daughter had thrown at him, and he left.

He kept his window open as he drove. The night air was cool against his face. The moon rode high over the mountains to his left. Only the occasional house had lights on, though when he passed the intersection at Calistoga, the Mexicans were still congregated at the drive-in.

On the dirt road to his house, the jackrabbits scattered into the vineyards away from his lights. When he got home, he let the dogs out and left the door open. He pulled the paper Daisy had thrown at him out of his pocket and laid it on the island in the kitchen, smoothing it out. He saw that it was the poem she'd recited for him in the truck, her face lovely and rapt.

> *Your thoughts don't have words every day*
> *They come a single time*
> *Like signal esoteric sips*
> *Of sacramental wine*
>
> *Which while you taste so native seems,*
> *So bounteous, so free,*
> *You cannot comprehend its worth*
> *Nor its infrequency.*

After that, she'd written out another one:

> *If all the griefs I am to have*
> *Would only come today*

159

I am so happy I believe
They'd laugh and run away!

If all the joys I am to have
Would only come today
They could not be so big as this
That happens to me now.

8

Summer ended. Emily returned from France transformed — her hair short and swinging around her face, a clear red lipstick shaping her mouth. She'd lost weight too. Her slight tendency to baby fat was gone. She looked like Eva, it seemed to Daisy: small, perfect, pretty.

She broke up with Noah soon after her return, and Daisy thought briefly that this might mean she and Emily would draw close again, but it didn't happen that way. Instead, it was her girlfriends Emily wanted to see, classmates who were also going off to college in a week or two. She went shopping with them, she made lists with Eva, she packed — and then she was gone.

One night a few days after she'd left, they were having dinner, Eva and Theo and Daisy, when Eva looked around the table and said, 'And now we are three.' Daisy was startled. What did this mean? Eva was smiling, but she didn't seem happy.

Daisy looked away and resumed twirling spaghetti on her fork.

When school started, the leaves were just beginning to turn in the vineyards. Daisy remembered the fall before, when John was alive, when she'd begun high school so full of hope. She had made resolutions and promises to herself in the days just before it all began again this year — that she would start anew, that she

161

would try, that she owed it to him, to herself, at least to try.

And she did, at first. She signed up for chorus; she told the basketball coach she would come out for the varsity team. She submitted a poem to the literary magazine in hopes of making it onto the editorial board. It was one she'd written over the summer, late one night in her room after a day in which Eva had spoken sharply to her in the store about a mistake she'd made, and then later wanted her to be friendly and conversational when someone she knew dropped in. It was titled 'Me.'

Like training a dog to shit in the gutter
You trained me, your good daughter, never
  to utter
A word. Dutiful mute. Me.

When company comes, pull me out of a
  corner,
Jam in your thumb like Little Jack Horner.
A smile. Pull out a plum. Me.

She did make the board, and she went to the first meeting. She went to chorus and got the music handouts. But in the second week of school, a boy, a senior, called her 'Stretch' in the lunch line, and she heard others laughing. She felt the sense of her size, her homeliness, her awkwardness sweep her. She left the line and went outside and sat alone at a table. She resolved to hope for nothing, socially. To expect nothing. It would be work, only work, she

162

decided, that she would think about.

And she did become consumed with her schoolwork in a way she'd never been before. For Latin she often did three translations — one literal, one loose, based on the literal, and one cast in the meter of the original. When she got a C on a geometry quiz — they'd had two problems to solve and she missed one — she hung the grade on the wall by her bed so it would be the first thing she'd see every morning, reminding her to work even harder.

In English they had moved on from Emily Dickinson, they were reading modern poets now, and Daisy was riveted by Sylvia Plath, drawn to her grim fury. 'Daddy, daddy, you bastard, I'm through.' Why should this appeal to Daisy? She didn't know.

She was still working at the store, on weekends and for special events — mostly readings, for which Daisy would arrange chairs and pass books over to the author to be signed. She'd continued to take money, but not as often, and smaller amounts when she did.

She thought about Duncan, about his catching her at it, about his threat to tell. But she thought, too, about her mother's birthday party and the way he'd behaved to her that night, as though he liked her, as though it didn't matter, what she'd done in the store. In any case, the weeks went by and nothing happened, and she figured he'd probably forgotten all about it.

And then one afternoon in mid-October as she was walking down Oak Street on her complicated route home from school — complicated, so

163

no one would fall in beside her or try to speak to her — she became aware of a car moving along parallel to her in the street, at her pace. She looked over. It was Duncan. He was steering with one hand, his body leaned across the front seat toward her. When she turned, he called her name, softly. Immediately she clutched her books even tighter to her chest.

But her first clear thought was that she was sorry she wasn't wearing any lipstick, or a prettier top. And with that response came an unconscious dawning of awareness — awareness of why he was there, and what he was doing, speaking her name, calling her over to him. She couldn't have articulated it, she wasn't sure what any of it meant, but she understood that he'd come on purpose, that he had thought about her and sought her out.

Years later when she tried to explain it to Dr. Gerard, she said that it was as though her unconscious mind knew everything that her conscious mind hadn't a clue about yet; and this was the moment when they began to communicate with each other

All of this might have seemed slow, nearly backward, in another person — a person like Emily, for instance. A person who understood something of her own sexual value, her interest to others. But no one had ever paid any kind of sexual attention to Daisy. She had been a homely girl, an awkward girl, a silent girl, for a long time, and her ability to read that kind of interest in herself was absent. Beyond that, Duncan, of course, was a grown-up, and a difficult, scathingly critical, sarcastic grown-up at that. And he was the husband of Gracie, who was an institution in her family.

But she knew, as soon as she saw him, that he had thought about her over these weeks, these months. She knew that he had planned exactly this, this moment. She walked over to the car and leaned down to the window.

'Get in,' he said. 'I'll give you a ride.' He was bent across the front seat, his face lifted to talk to her. He looked younger than he usually did at this angle.

'But I don't *want* a ride.' How could she be saying this? To a grown-up. To a friend of her mother's.

'Get in anyway,' he said. He sounded unoffended, unsurprised.

Daisy shrugged and straightened up. She opened the door and got into the car. She set her books down on the seat, between them. Her breath was short, her head felt light.

He drove down Main Street and started across the valley, through vineyards.

'Where are we going?' she asked finally.

'I thought I'd show you what I'm working on. My *studio*.' His voice was heavy with his usual sarcasm. It occurred to her abruptly that this sarcasm, maybe much of his sarcasm — which had always frightened her — was directed at himself.

'What if I don't want to see it?'

'I'll show it to you regardless. Because you *should* want to see it. You should be curious about everything. If you're not curious now, you might as well shoot yourself and get it over with. You're dead anyway.' He turned right onto Silverado Road. They drove in silence for a while.

'And then I thought we'd talk about our bargain.' He said this without looking at her.

She looked over at him, though. He was wearing a white shirt, pressed. You could see the creases in the fabric where it had been folded. The cuffs were turned back, and his wrists and hands had light brown hairs that glinted in the sun. 'There is no *bargain*,' she said.

'Well, exactly.' He smiled at her, but his eyes were sober in his pale face. 'The bargain we have yet to strike. The bargain in which I don't report your malfeasance this summer to your *mother* in exchange for something or other.'

'I don't care if you do report it.' She believed this as she said it. She looked out the window at the live oaks, the coppery vines. It would be a relief. Eva would yell at her. She would yell at Eva. It would be over.

What? What would be over?

'Oh yes, you do,' he said. 'You care very much, in fact.' And suddenly she believed this, too. That she cared, that it would be unbearable if Eva found out.

All of this confused Daisy, and fed into the confusion she felt about Duncan and what he might want with her. What she might want with him. She couldn't have explained anything. If someone had asked her, 'Why did you go with him?,' she wouldn't have known. If someone had asked, 'What did you think was going to

166

'happen?,' she couldn't have said.

'What was your feeling?' Dr. Gerard asked.

'My feeling?'

'Yes. Your emotional state, as you drove along.'

'I was excited.'

'And the *kind* of excitement? Fearful?'

'No. Absolutely not.'

'Why not? There was everything to be fearful of, wasn't there? Including the fact that he'd seen you stealing from your mother's store.'

Daisy shook her head. 'None of that mattered. I felt I controlled the situation. From the moment I saw him, even though I didn't know what it was about, really, I felt in charge.'

'And that felt good?'

'Are you kidding? It felt wonderful.'

His studio was off a dirt road near Yountville. It was a huge garage, nearly a barn, behind a small, run-down ranch house. The yard between the house and the garage was full of old vineyard machinery, green or bright orange, but pocked and streaked now with rust, and eviscerated, odd bits torn off to get at other parts, and everything left lying around. As if, Daisy thought, the machines were animals that had been attacked by jackals or wolves, savage creatures who'd been frightened off their prey.

Duncan pulled around to the side of the garage invisible to the house and parked. 'Out,' he said, opening his door.

She got out and followed him to the side door. He unlocked it. He stepped back and she stepped forward, just across the threshold.

After the bright light outside, after the chaos

167

of color and decay in the yard, the vast room seemed muted and still, it seemed to hold a kind of peace and order. It smelled of wood, and thinly, faintly, of something sharp and clean, something chemical. The light fell palely from skylights overhead. The air was cool. She stepped farther in.

In the center of the room was a tall, wooden chest, the drawers missing. It was slightly curved, maybe echoing the shape of a cello, or a woman's body. Its wood was a reddish blonde, with hardly any grain. Tools and unfinished wood were laid out on a long worktable behind it. Along the side wall there was a desk — really just another long table — with papers and drawing instruments on it, and an ergonomic chair rolled up to it. Along the other side wall was a cot. The cement floor was swept clean. At the back of the space were several other pieces of furniture — two tables with curvy legs, an elaborate kind of desk — and behind them, along the back wall, there were partitions from floor to ceiling with pieces of wood leaning this way and that between them.

He was behind her. His hand pressed the small of her back in a way she hadn't been touched before. 'Come into my parlor,' he said.

When she thought of it later, when she talked about it with Dr. Gerard, she couldn't remember how many times they were together in Duncan's studio that fall and winter. Fifteen? Thirty? They blurred together in memory. That first day, though, she always remembered clearly and distinctly.

He showed her his work, it seemed not so much because he wanted her to think it was beautiful — which she did, without caring one way or another: it was, after all, just furniture — but as though he wanted her to see him, to understand him, as someone with a life outside of the circle of family in which she'd known him. He talked about it — the kinds of wood he used, their density and color, the sense he wanted to get of creating something sculptural in the useful pieces. Daisy asked a few questions, but mostly he talked. It was as though he'd rehearsed this. And his voice, talking about his work, changed. It grew younger, she would have said. It was only later, thinking about it, that she realized he had dropped the odd, weighted emphasis, the sarcasm.

While he talked, he filled a kettle at the work sink by the door and put it on a two-burner hot plate that sat on a little table next to his desk. When the kettle sang, he stopped and brewed a pot of tea. He poured her a cup and then sat in his desk chair, swinging it back and forth slightly while he began to ask her about herself. His voice had changed again.

He asked about school: Did she like it? Did she have *friends*?

He said this so contemptuously that it was easy for her to answer truthfully that she didn't. That Emily was the one with friends — thinking of the few times she'd asked someone over after school, or someone had asked her over, and how deliberated, how awkward, their exchanges had been.

He wanted to know whether she'd ever dated anyone, and it was her turn to be contemptuous.

'*Dated?*' she said. 'Is that some word from the middle ages?'

He smiled. 'I suppose you move rather more directly to fucking, then.'

She didn't answer. She was shocked at the word, coming from him.

'*Have* you ever fucked anyone, Daisy?' He had rolled his chair forward; he sat only a few feet away from her.

'It's none of your business.' She was sitting sideways on his cot bed, her back against the wall, the warm mug of tea in her hands.

'Of course it isn't. But I'm curious. More than curious.' He grinned. '*Avid*, I would say, for information thereof.'

She was silent. 'No,' she said finally.

'Ah,' he said. 'So your knowledge of sex is limited.'

'My knowledge isn't, no.'

'But your experience of that great pleasure is.'

She didn't answer. She was thinking of one of the things Emily had said about it, that it wasn't so much fun as you might think. And of Noah, in his Speedo.

'Except, of course, perhaps, for touching yourself. Bringing yourself pleasure.'

Again, she didn't respond, though she thought she could feel herself blushing.

He was watching her, the slightest smile playing on his lips.

She met his eye, and she couldn't help it, she smiled back. Did she like this? talking like this with Duncan? It must be that she did. That she liked his interest in her, she liked the power she felt she had in this situation. And she knew she liked the sense of all of this — whatever it was — as a great and private adventure she was embarking on, something Emily or Eva couldn't imagine, or anyone she knew at school.

'I'm wondering why you took the money, Daisy,' he said.

She felt as shocked as if he'd slapped her. After a moment she was able to say, 'That's *really* none of your business.'

'I agree.' He shrugged and turned his chair slightly to set his mug down on the floor. 'But I happened to see you do it. This is my dilemma, Daisy. That now I have to decide what to do about that. And whatever I do, I want it to help you.' He leaned forward toward her, resting his elbows on his knees. His white shirt was unbuttoned at the neck. She could see where his chest hairs began at the base of his throat. 'It just seems to me that if I understood it, what you were up to, I'd have a better chance at deciding this . . . sympathetically.' He lifted his hands. 'So?'

Daisy thought of John, suddenly, of how he would ask her things just this openly, just this kindly. But Duncan wasn't kind. Was he?

'I don't know,' she said. 'I don't know why I took it.'

'Well, that's fair.'

'I don't know,' she repeated, and then she felt a lump rising in her throat and her eyes filled with tears. She made a stupid noise, a gurgle.

171

'Daisy,' he said. He moved forward and slid next to her on the cot, putting his arm around her, taking her mug of tea and setting it on the floor too. She started to cry, openly. He held her, stroking her back while she wept against his shoulder. She cried for a long time. Later when she tried to explain why, it seemed to her that it was having his attention, it was feeling noticed so particularly. And, of course, it was being held.

Gradually, though, she slowed. She sat hunched against him, looking down at his shirt, his pants, her own hands in her lap, and feeling a growing embarrassment and confusion about how to end this moment, what to say.

And then he lifted her face — she resisted a little, she knew her face was ugly this way, blotchy and smeared — and he was kissing her, so gently at first it seemed just a part of his comforting her, and Daisy relaxed and let him. But then he was licking her! licking her tears, kissing and licking her face, her eyes, and then her mouth again, pulling on her opened lips with his. He tasted of salt, of her salt tears. His mouth was gentle and soft on hers, beckoning hers. Daisy kissed him back.

And then suddenly it felt too hard. Daisy jerked away, and they sat looking at each other. They sat there for a minute or more. Daisy had stopped crying. She was aware of his hand on her back, of the way he smelled, a smell that lingered on her face, of the sound of their twinned breathing in the silent room. When he started kissing her again, gently once more, she responded again. And then she felt his hand

172

move to her legs, grip them, pull them. He pulled her against him, he pulled her down, and they were lying next to each other.

She froze.

'It's all right,' he said. 'Nothing's happening.' His arm was under her head, and slowly she relaxed against it. He stroked her hair, he wiped her face. She closed her eyes. After a while, she curled against him.

He kept his free hand moving, over her hair, lightly on the curves of her ear. He stroked her neck. This felt lovely to Daisy. He turned her face to him, and kissed her again. When she returned the pressure, his hand came up to her lips and his fingers pressed them and stroked them. She opened her mouth and one of his fingers came just slightly onto the inner part of her lower lip, the wet part. She sighed.

'It feels good, doesn't it?'

She nodded, his finger resting against her teeth. She touched his finger with her tongue. His flesh too tasted of salt.

'It's meant to, Daisy. Everything's meant to.' His hand stroked her neck and the hard ridge of bone at the top of her chest. Then he put it on her breast, and his fingers began circling her shirt where her nipple was. Her flesh seemed to thicken, and his touch got lighter. He closed his thumb and forefinger on her, a light pinch, a rolling motion.

'Do you like this, Daisy?'

'Yes,' she said. Her throat was dry.

'Unbutton your blouse,' he said. His voice was flat.

She lay still. 'I can't,' she said finally. She was shaking her head.

'Of course you can, Daisy. Nothing will happen that you don't want to have happen.' He was stroking her nipple again through the shirt. 'You like this,' he said. It was a kind of question, though.

She nodded.

'I want to see you, Daisy. I want to look at my hand doing this to you. I want you to see it, how it looks.' He stopped. 'No?'

He kissed her again, and Daisy, welcoming this shift, kissed him back. When they stopped, they lay for a while, face-to-face. Daisy had never looked at a man's face so closely. She could see the shape of a star in the iris of each of Duncan's eyes.

'Unbutton your blouse, Daisy,' he said.

After a moment, she shook her head.

'Shall I, then?' he said. 'Do you want me to be the one to do it?'

She nodded. This is what she wanted, she understood suddenly. For him to do it all, and for her to be able just to lie here and have him touch her and not have to decide any of it, or be responsible for any of it.

He unbuttoned her blouse, slowly, and pushed the fabric to the sides. Daisy closed her eyes. Her bra was fastened with a clasp in front, and she could feel him fumbling with it. 'Help me, Daisy,' he whispered. After a moment, she reached between her breasts and undid the clasp. He peeled her bra back. She felt the cool air on her breasts.

174

'How lovely, Daisy,' he said, and his warm fingers began their play on her flesh. She felt her nipple harden again as he squeezed it lightly between his fingers. He squeezed harder. It hurt a little, and Daisy made a noise.

He slid down and Daisy felt his mouth, wet and warm on her breast. He kissed her, he licked her, and then his mouth closed over her nipple and he began to suck, gently at first, and then gradually taking her deeper into his mouth with a steady, rocking pull that Daisy felt in her pelvis, her belly. He lay there a long time sucking her, kissing her. Daisy moved her body slightly to his rhythm, it felt so wonderful, she felt it so deeply inside herself. He turned her — or perhaps she turned herself, she wasn't sure — and took her other breast, her other nipple in his mouth. Daisy closed her eyes.

When he stopped, he slid back up, his face by hers, but he was still touching her breasts. His eyes were on his own hands, and she looked down too. His thumbs moved back and forth across her nipples. He pulled them both slowly until they were longer than she would have thought possible and she moaned. He kissed her mouth again, and then moved on top of her. Her body answered his weight. She moved urgently against him.

After a minute or two, he rose on his elbows above her. 'Daisy,' he said, in a conversational voice. She opened her eyes and looked up at him. 'You are so wonderfully good at this.' He was smiling, and she smiled back. 'Would you like me to give you pleasure the way you give yourself pleasure?'

'Yes,' she whispered.

He lifted himself up off her and lay beside her again, propped on one elbow. 'Unbutton your pants,' he said.

Smiling, looking into his eyes, Daisy did nothing.

'Please,' he said.

She cleared her throat. '*Pretty* please,' she said.

'Yes, pretty please.' He licked his finger and touched her nipple again, lightly. She felt it tighten.

She smiled and reached down, and his hand was there, underneath hers, sliding below her fingers as she worked the buttons at her crotch one by one. When she had finished, she opened her legs a little, and his hand found her where she liked to touch herself and began circling her, slowly at first, and then almost right away, feeling her urgency, harder and quicker.

Daisy stiffened her body, she held herself focused under his touch, concentrated on it, only on it; and then crying out, arching up, she came, and as he still circled her, she kept coming, pushing against his fingers, panting.

As she stilled, his hand did too. Together they lay there. Daisy's breathing slowly quieted. She opened her eyes and looked at Duncan's face. He was relaxed, smiling. She smiled back. Then he slid his hand, his fingers, slowly down into the wet flesh between her legs and up again — a caress, down and up.

'That was quick,' he said.

'Yes.'

'*Breathtaking*, really.'

She laughed.

'Do you like this?' he asked. His hand was moving slowly up and down, into her and then back up to her clitoris.

'Yes.'

'You're very wet.'

'Yes.' She was moving a little with him.

'That's for me, you know.'

She frowned and shook her head.

'So I can come into you.' His fingers were in her, a little.

She was silent, suddenly motionless.

'I'm not going to come into you, Daisy. Don't worry.' His hand kept moving, she felt his fingers come into her again, then out.

'Your bush feels odd,' he said conversationally. 'Your hair.'

'I shaved it.'

He stopped moving. 'You shaved it!' He grinned. 'Why?'

'I hated it. I hated how it looked.'

His hand slid down again, to where she was wet. 'You shouldn't hate it.'

'I do.'

'It's beautiful, Daisy.' His fingers were resting in her.

She shook her head.

'It is,' he said. 'There's nothing more beautiful.

'Let me look,' he said. His fingers came out of her, and his hand slid up and away.

She said nothing.

'I'll do it,' he said.

She didn't answer.

'I'll be the one to do it.'

Daisy was frightened now. What of? She believed him, that he wouldn't come into her. Was she frightened of his looking at her? But she wanted it too. It was, she felt at that moment, the thing she wanted most.

He reached across her and eased her jeans down a little on her other hip, then eased them on the side against his own body. Slowly he worked them down to the middle of her hips, and then he got up from her. Her body felt cold. She crossed her arms over her breasts. He was standing at the foot of the cot. He bent forward and pulled her jeans and her underwear down. She heard them flop on the floor.

He knelt at the foot of the bed. He was holding her feet.

'Open your legs, Daisy.' His voice was tensed. She felt pleasure in that — a thrill really. No one had ever spoken to her this way. 'Please,' he said.

She opened them a little way, and he shifted, so that he was kneeling between her feet, touching each one.

She watched his face. She could hear his breath. His eyes were fixed on her. He came forward on his knees between her legs and touched her again. With his hand on her, his fingers again sliding up and down, he looked up at her and smiled. 'You are beautiful, Daisy. Do you know it?'

She lifted her shoulders.

'You do. You do, Daisy.' Now he reached out to her knees and gripped them. He pushed them up, toward her chest. Daisy didn't resist. 'Hold your knees, Daisy,' he said. 'Hold your knees up.'

She did what he said, she gripped her knees.

'Apart,' he said.

She didn't move.

He looked up at her face and smiled again. 'Pretty please.' His voice was harsh.

Daisy pulled her legs open slowly, and felt her own flesh open too.

He put his forefinger on her, and she heard the wet noise she made. 'Feel how lovely you are,' he said.

'Do you?' he asked. 'Do you feel lovely?'

His fingers were circling her again now, much more gently and slowly. Daisy held her knees wide and rocked herself slowly from side to side.

'Do you feel lovely?'

'Yes!' Daisy whispered.

'Open yourself more,' he said. 'Daisy!'

Daisy took longer this time, but it felt wonderful. While she came, he held his fingers still, pushing hard on her as she writhed, and he left his hand there when she was done.

She was panting, she'd dropped her knees. She lay there, splayed open and exhausted.

And then his hands pushed her thighs up again and she felt his mouth on her.

9

The day after her birthday party, Eva had called Mark and arranged to meet him. She thought they ought to talk about what had happened between them, about the kiss — though she wasn't sure what she wanted to say. And she wanted to tell him how things had gone in her talk with Daisy. They agreed on an evening in the following week. She suggested the place: the bar at the Auberge de Soleil. Her thought was that it was so touristy there that they weren't likely to run into anyone they knew.

As soon as she hung up she realized how ridiculous that concern was. Mark had been over at her house so often in the last year, they'd done so many things together, that anyone interested could have made note of all of that long since if he wanted to. There was already plenty to gossip about, if gossip was what you were after.

It occurred to her then that she might have chosen the Auberge for herself — that perhaps *she* wanted a public place. Because this meeting felt different to Eva from all the others — and the reason for this was, of course, that he had kissed her. On the other hand, it certainly wasn't the case that she thought anything was going to happen between them. That was an impossibility, which is what she had assured Daisy the night of the party.

180

Then what, exactly, was different? She didn't know.

She got there first and sat outside, on the balcony that ran around the outside of the circular bar. It had a spectacular view down the wide, darkening valley — this was why the tourists came. Thick stems of an old wisteria vine twined up the posts from the ground below and reached for the roof. From the guest cottages hidden among the trees down the hill, you could hear a party — the voices and music rose muted; there was laughter and the odd loud squawk. Below Eva and to the left in the blue-lighted pool, someone was slowly doing laps.

She ordered wine and sparkling water. She was, she realized, excited to be out, excited to be meeting Mark. This was the difference, she understood abruptly: it was *in her*. And it came, she acknowledged to herself now, because when he had touched her the night of her birthday party, she had been aroused. It had confused her and saddened her at the moment — this arousal — but she'd had to explain it to Daisy just afterward, and as she'd spoken she'd realized she was explaining herself to herself as much as to Daisy; and what she said made sense to her.

She had told Daisy that quite naturally there was an old, deep bond between Mark and her. They had been married, after all. They'd had children together, whom they both loved. (Daisy's face had registered contempt at this. She was backed up into a corner of her bed, hugging a pillow. She hadn't wanted Eva to talk to her, even to come into her room. She'd screamed at her when she knocked, to go away, to leave her alone, but Eva had come in anyway, and Daisy had crawled back quickly across her bed to where her mother couldn't touch her.)

Eva had been sitting at the foot of the bed, not even trying to get closer. Just talking. Below her, she had heard Mark leave the house, and then his truck starting up and pulling away.

She told Daisy that it was natural for Mark to have felt the wish to comfort her, to hold her when she was upset — and here for a moment she knew she was misrepresenting things: her tears, after all, had come *after* he held her. But it seemed that it could have happened as she said. And as she went on, it seemed more and more to Eva that it *had* happened as she said. It seemed reasonable and right that it should have happened that way.

She told Daisy that of course holding her was bound to stir old feelings in Mark. In her too. But that these feelings weren't *real*, they weren't current feelings. They weren't feelings that she and Mark would act on. And most of all, they weren't feelings that had anything to do with John.

Daisy's face changed at that. She seemed startled that Eva would say John's name in this context. She looked, actually, almost frightened, and Eva felt she'd gotten to the heart of what was upsetting the girl: some sort of betrayal of John that she needed reassurance about.

She said Daisy should try to think of her and Mark as old, old friends, if she could. Friends who loved each other dearly, but who weren't

182

lovers. Who wouldn't be lovers, she could promise Daisy that.

Daisy had sat, not looking at Eva now. She was chewing on her knuckles, rocking slightly over the pillow she held.

Eva's finger was tracing the pattern of the crewel work on Daisy's bedspread as she spoke. 'So what you stumbled in on, just now, was . . . residual. Was like an old, leftover part of what we once felt, that emerged out of sympathy, really.' She looked up at her daughter. Daisy's face was turned away, her long, wild hair hid her expression from Eva. 'Can't you see that? Daze? Those feelings — they don't ever completely go away.'

Daisy swung her head lazily, as though the air she was moving it through were thick. She seemed suddenly exhausted. She turned and stretched out, lying down to face the wall. Her body seemed huge, endlessly long to Eva. 'Whatever,' she said at last.

Eva knew better than to touch her. 'Not whatever, Daze. What I said. Exactly what I said. You can take it to the bank.'

The girl looked quickly over her shoulder.

'I mean it, Daisy. It's a kind of promise. Okay?'

There was a rustle, a shift. Daisy sighed.

'Okay, Daze?' Eva resisted the impulse to touch Daisy's leg, which lay close to her now. It was shaved smooth. She hadn't known Daisy had started to shave her legs. This made her sad, somehow, that the girl had managed this transition, this step into womanhood, on her own.

'Yes. Okay.'

'Okay,' Eva said. She made her voice cheerful. 'Okay, then. I'm gone. I'm outta here.' At the door, she stopped and said, 'I love you, honey.'

There was a silence. Then Daisy said, again, *'Okay.'*

Eva left.

She had lied to Daisy, Eva was thinking now. The feeling between her and Mark wasn't residual. Mark had said he wanted her. And when he touched her, she had wanted him.

The sun had set behind the ridge, and lights were coming on in the valley below. The traffic was steady on Silverado Road. Eva sipped her wine, a chardonnay.

But what did it mean, really, to want him? Did she want to have sex with him?

That wasn't what she'd felt.

What she wanted was his touch, his kiss — simply to be held by him. That's what she missed most of all, in her aloneness. Being touched. Being held.

So maybe she hadn't exactly lied to Daisy. She sat back in her chair. In any case, her promise was good. She wouldn't sleep with Mark. That would be a fool's game, the opposite of comfort: a way to open herself to pain again. She thought of him, after all, as incapable of fidelity, of loyalty. She had watched him over the years since they'd split up, she'd seen the flow of women in and out of his life. She heard the stories, from friends, from the girls.

No, *that* way lay disaster.

Though she wouldn't be averse to a flirtation,

if it could be kept away from the children. She wouldn't be averse to using him to comfort herself — as, she thought, he had once used her.

Oh, come on, Eva. That's not what had happened. That was bitterness speaking. He had loved her. She believed he had loved her. He had simply been unable to be faithful, that was all.

She smiled. *That was all*, she thought.

She drank again, letting the wine roll around in her mouth before she swallowed. At the next table, the two couples who'd been comparing hotels moved on to restaurants — Terra, Tra Vigne, Mustards. No one mentioned bookstores. What about bookstores, she wanted to say. She smiled again. The question, of course, would be the answer. What *about* bookstores?

They were middle-aged or older. Moneyed. One of the men balding, the other gray, both in expensive, slouchy, pale sweaters, like the ones Andy Williams used to wear on television. The women wore convincing, subtle color in their hair. They were carefully made up. They had red, red lips. It made Eva think of Daisy in her Charades costume last week at her birthday party, her big dark wound of a mouth. She signaled to the waitress, and pointed to her nearly empty glass for another.

Mark startled her, touching her shoulder. She'd been looking out at the sky, still a light blue high over the dark valley. He sat down, something eager, something open and boyish in his face. When the waitress came, he ordered wine too. Eva watched their exchange, the way the waitress responded to him, just as women always did. After she'd gone, he leaned forward and rested his elbows on the table. He asked her how it had gone the other night with Daisy.

She reported her conversation. She left out her promise never to sleep with Mark, not to get involved with him again.

'That sounds about right,' he said.

'Well. Thank you.'

'And she was really okay with all that? She seemed so pissed off when she . . . when she went upstairs.'

'Oh, you know Daze. She was as *all right* as she'll ever acknowledge being.'

The waitress came with their wine. She watched him swirl his glass, check the liquid out as it slid down its sides, a thoughtless habit by now. They talked a little about Daisy, about his feeling that she had gotten more relaxed around him as she'd gotten more difficult for Eva. They talked about Emily, who was coming home in a few days, who'd written to both of them through the summer — enthusiastic, slightly condescending letters. 'Well, after all,' Eva said, 'what do we know about the world? *Rubes* that we are.' He talked about the ripening of the grapes, the preparation for the crush. They talked about the fatwah against Salman Rushdie, about what his life must be like now. He told her a George Bush joke. They talked about her birthday party, about Gracie and Duncan.

He said, 'It feels like old times, Eva, talking like this.'

He said, 'It's nice to sit like this, across from you.'

It was fully dark. The expensive couples had moved on to one of their restaurants. The only other people left were at the far edge of the balcony.

As they were leaving, he said, 'Shall we do this again? Shall I call you?'

And she didn't say no. She didn't say, 'I don't think so.'

She said, 'I don't know. Let me think about it. Let *me* call you.'

And then, standing by her car in the dark parking lot, she let him hold her and kiss her gently again.

★   ★   ★

She did call him, but she waited more than a month and a half, the month and a half in which Emily had come back from France and then left again for Wesleyan. In which Daisy had started school, and seemed to be trying to make it a better year than the last one — signing up for things, and then actually doing them. Becoming, in fact, *too* busy much of the time, with extra activities. A month and a half in which Mark came by to pick up the girls together once, and then Daisy alone several times, in which he took Theo once, too. In which Emily wrote long letters home, sounding like a different person — older, suddenly. Newly curious. Letters that Eva read out loud at dinner to Daisy and Theo. In which she'd gone out twice more with Elliott, the man she'd been, after a fashion, dating. A month and a half in which she'd allowed Elliott, also, to kiss her, and felt only dutiful. She knew he would take her coolness to be connected to John, and she let him. After all, it *was*, for the most part, connected to John. But she knew too that she had felt differently when Mark held her; and that if Elliott had made her feel that way, the way Mark did, she might have felt free to respond more passionately.

It was mid-October by the time she called Mark again. She had been out the night before with Elliott, and had what she described that morning in the bookstore to Gracie — who'd stopped in before going up the street to open her own office — as 'a perfectly lovely time.'

And it had been. She liked Elliott more each time she saw him. He was soft-spoken and intelligent, with a kind of slow, warm humor. He seemed to delight in human detail in the same way she did — something a child was saying in conversation as you passed him on the street, something one of his patients had told him — he was a psychiatrist. He had grown children, and she liked the way he spoke of them, she liked his pride in them, and what sounded like their adult affection for him. She liked sitting opposite him at a restaurant table with its smooth white cloth and the heavy silverware. She liked the way he looked, slightly avuncular, a little paunchy, almost completely bald, but large, burly, attractive. He had nice hands — nicer, better taken care of, than her own.

Gracie made a face. 'Oh, 'A perfectly lovely time,'' she imitated, in a trilling, elderly voice.

'You sound like some New England dowager. Get *off* it.'

'I am a New England dowager.'

'What horseshit,' Gracie said. She was flipping through a big coffee-table book on home decoration. She looked up at Eva. 'What *is* a dowager, exactly?'

'Oh, it must come from the same root as *endow*. An old woman left with dough. Maybe *dough* comes from that too. *Dough, dow*. I'll look it up.'

'No, don't bother. I don't give a damn what its etymology is. Just don't sound like that no more.'

'But it *is* who I am, Gracie. I'm not like you. I can't do this the way you would.'

'Oh, honey. I don't mean anything, really. If Duncan died, I don't think I'd ever go out again.'

'But Duncan will never die.'

Gracie grinned. 'The bastard. I bet he won't. He's too mean to die.'

After Gracie left, Eva moved through the store, getting ready for the day — neatening shelves, straightening the stacks of books on the display tables. She looked up *dowager*: as she'd thought. Though it most often referred to a queen. A dowager queen. Queen Eva. At ten Callie came in, and Eva went back to her office and started to call the customers whose special orders had come in the day before.

On and off through the day, she thought of Elliott, whom she liked but didn't want, and of Mark, whom she wanted, she supposed, but didn't want to be involved with ever again.

Was that it? Were those her feelings? She didn't know. It seemed to her she ought to know, to be clear about it all. Perhaps she *needed* to see Mark again.

But she knew, even as she was thinking it, that this was suspect. What she wanted was his attention, his wanting her. Why? Because it felt good to be wanted, to be desired. Even if the desire was something he distributed widely, it felt good focused on you. It made her feel alive, flirting with Mark, making him think of her sexually again. Maybe she needed that right now. Maybe it was part of recovering from John's death to feel sexy with someone safe, someone from her past. Someone she wasn't going to sleep with.

Or was she perhaps punishing Mark? Taking some belated revenge, now that she seemed to have some power over him, for the pain he'd caused her years ago?

Maybe she *could* sleep with him. Could she? Images of certain times they'd made love together rose quickly in her mind, and she tried to busy herself with some imbalances she'd noticed in the finances to stop them.

She had lunch with a sales rep who always made her laugh. When she came back, she told Callie three new jokes, one about a talking horse, one about a duck ordering grapes in a bar, one about a forgetful old man in a whorehouse.

At four, Daisy came in. Eva was back in her office, but she could hear her daughter's voice mingling with Callie's and Nancy's as the two older women got ready to leave. She came out to greet Daisy and to say goodbye to the two women.

Daisy was friendly and easy while the others were still there, but as soon as they'd left, the slight coolness that marked their relations now fell between them. Her face stilled and grew sullen, unreadable, as Eva went over with her what she needed to do. 'I'll be in the office if it gets too busy,' she said.

'Yep,' Daisy answered, already slouched on the stool behind the counter. She didn't look at Eva. She was folding and refolding a piece of paper.

Eva sat in the office in front of the computer with the columns of amber figures glowing on the screen. How she hated this business with Daisy! It was as though the girl blamed her for John's death. There was nothing she'd done right since. Not when she was lost in grief. Not when she began to recover a little. Certainly not dating Elliott or that thing she'd seen with Mark. There was never a moment of lightheartedness or ease between them. She couldn't remember the last time Daisy had laughed in her presence.

She got up and went to the door. As she stepped into the corridor, she could see Daisy doing something at the cash register.

'Daze,' she said.

The girl jumped, turning. The drawer clanged shut.

'I didn't mean to startle you,' Eva said, approaching the counter. Daisy was watching her, attentive, alert.

191

'I have two good jokes for you,' Eva said.

'Oh! Cool,' said Daisy, almost breathlessly, it seemed. She sat down again on the stool. She was all attention, smiling — smiling! — as Eva started. And at both punch lines, she laughed out loud.

'Dumb, aren't they?' Eva asked, grinning back at her daughter. How lovely she was, really, when her face opened.

'Dumb is okay,' Daisy said. 'For a joke, anyway.'

'It's true, isn't it? The dumbness is part of the pleasure.' And then, because the moment had made her happy, because she didn't want to push it, she stood straight. 'Back to work,' she said.

But in her office, she was restless, too distracted by the warm surprise of Daisy's response to concentrate.

She called Mark. He was in his truck, she could hear it. His voice softened in response to hers; he said her name.

'I just told our sullen younger daughter not one but two jokes, and she laughed at both of them.'

'Jesus, these are jokes I need to know.'

She asked him if he was free that night. By the hesitation in his voice before he said, 'Sure,' she knew he wasn't.

'You aren't to rearrange anything on my account,' she said. 'How about Monday instead?'

'Either is fine.'

'Monday, then. It's actually better for me. A drink after dinner? as usual?'

Sunday night Daisy came downstairs in a bath towel, full of indignation. There was no hot water.

Eva was reading. She had only recently begun to be able to read again, whole books — this had been impossible for almost a year. Now she looked forward to it. *The book*, waiting in the living room after she got Theo down. Waiting at her bedside. The circle of light falling over the white bedsheets, the subtle smell of the paper, the ink, the arrangement of the words on the page. Wanting just another chapter, and then, perhaps, another. Wanting something she could so easily have. When it had been gone, she hadn't been able to miss it — she was too taken up with grief. But now that it had returned to her, she was grateful to this old love — books, the words — for coming back, for reminding her of the possibility of pleasure, of anticipation. Of being transported out of her own life into others.

She put her finger in her place and looked at Daisy. 'Well, that can happen. This isn't a hotel. It's an old, beat-up house.'

'But can't you fix it?'

'I can, I think, and I will try, if you will speak to me just a little bit less like a servant.'

'Oh, Christ, Mom.'

'And less like that, Daisy, too.'

'All right.' Daisy swung her head, throwing her hair back behind her shoulders. She pulled her face into a new, artificially sweet expression. 'Mother dear, Mommie dearest,' she said, 'could

I ask you please to try to do something about the fact that only cold water is pouring out of the hot-water faucet?'

Eva got up. 'Yes, my darling daughter. But even if I get it turned on again, it'll take a while to heat up, so you should get some clothes or pj's or something on while you wait.'

Eva went into the butler's pantry, off the hall between the living room and kitchen. She found matches and a flashlight in the drawers there. She descended the stairs into the basement. It was unfinished, cobwebby and dank, a place they all avoided. The water heater was in a far corner. She knelt by it and took the cover off the service opening. Bending over, she could see that, yes, the pilot was off. She rested the flashlight so its beam was aimed into the hole. Reaching in, she pressed the gas button and offered up a lighted match. With a little rip of enthusiasm, the pilot went on; and seconds later, more enthusiasm, the gas itself lighted.

Eva recapped the hole and was about to stand up, when she noticed the glue trap behind the tank. It was one of many scattered around the basement, most of them holding only insects and grit. But a mouse had died in this trap — months ago apparently. At any rate, bugs had devoured its flesh long since. Its skeleton lay curled on its side on the clear glue. Eva picked the trap up carefully, avoiding the stickum, and looked closely.

It was perfection — the exquisite miniature bones of its paws, the hollowed-out, belled delicacy of the empty white rib cage, the tiny skull, the teeth smaller than the smallest grains of rice. She was struck — made suddenly tearful actually — by the extravagance, the loss: this much beauty lavished on this tiny dead creature, useless or worse to her. She thought of John, his bones. How they had felt when she scattered them, the odd chunks among the gritty ash, which reminded her of his final fragility, of the way he had so quickly and carelessly been destroyed, the bone that had shielded *who he was* so easily smashed to bits. Exactly such bits as she had thrown off to the sides of the path up Mount St. Helena when she scattered his ashes.

In two weeks he would have been dead a year. Perhaps he and the mouse had died at the same time. She hadn't thought she would mark his death in any way. It seemed morbid to her, grim. Better to remember him alive, every day — as she did, she thought — than to make a fuss about the anniversary of his dying.

But it seemed to her suddenly, holding the little white tray with the dead mouse, that she'd betrayed him. That she'd started down the wrong path, with Mark, with the stirring of feeling for him she'd allowed herself. Even the *way* she'd thought of it, the way she'd limited it in her mind, seemed wrong, seemed disrespect-ful of what she'd had with John.

She imagined carrying the mouse upstairs to John, as she would have done when he was alive, and marveling at it together. A tiny Yorick, she might have said. Yorick-ini. And then John, no doubt, would have recited half the passage from memory.

When she went upstairs, she threw the glue trap away, covering it with paper towels in the trash compactor so Daisy or Theo wouldn't see it and be revolted, or scared. She washed her hands. She went up to John's study and looked up the Yorick passage.

Sitting at his desk, she read, 'Here hung those lips that I have kissed I know not how oft. Where be your gibes now, your gambols, your songs, your flashes of merriment, that were wont to set the table on a roar?' She resisted the tears she felt. Cheap, she thought. Then she read, 'Now get you to my lady's chambers and tell her, let her paint an inch thick, to this favour she must come. Make her laugh at that.'

An image of her mother, her face seamed and embittered by the lines of age, rose in her mind — her mother as she set her sherry glass sharply down and spoke: 'As I said, dear, Death.'

★ ★ ★

By the time she left the house on Monday evening to meet Mark, she didn't want to go. She was sorry she'd called him. She saw it as weak on her part, wrong — the wish to flirt, to be held, to be admired, or, in Mark's fashion, loved. John's memory should be enough for her, she thought. His memory. She had been truly loved. John had loved her. And she had learned how to love from him.

Sitting opposite Mark, she felt herself distant and sad. He looked wonderful. He'd been working flat out with the end of the crush, he

196

said, and she remembered how he had always loved this season, the nonstop pressure, the excitement of it. His hands holding his drink were stained dark.

Their talk was more desultory than it had been before. The energy to be flirtatious, the wish to be found attractive, was flattened in Eva. She found herself thinking about what time it was getting to be, thinking about how much longer she would have to stay, looking forward to arriving home again, to reading for a while, to sleep. *Perchance to dream*, she thought.

Mark asked her for the jokes, and at first she couldn't remember what he was referring to. But then she told them, including the one she hadn't told Daisy, about the old man in the whorehouse.

He laughed. They sat quiet for a long moment. They seemed to have run out of things to say. Eva was about to announce that she needed to get back, she was going to make up some excuse about Daisy's needing homework help, when he said, 'Do you sometimes compare me to other men you know? You know, when you're sitting here with me?'

'Other men I know?'

'The guy you're dating, for instance.'

She made a face. 'My, word certainly gets around.'

He lifted his shoulders. 'Gracie,' he said. 'Our pal.'

Gracie. She nodded. 'Well, I don't know that I'd say I'm *dating*, exactly. That seems to imply a more . . . a bigger commitment of some kind or another than anything I'm thinking of at the moment.' She saw his face relax, some tension ease. 'But I suppose I've thought at one time or another about the differences among various men I've known, you included. That would be human, would it not? I don't think I've done it when I'm with you, if that's what you're asking.'

'No, that's not what I'm asking.'

'What are you asking, then?'

'I don't know.' They were at the inside bar tonight. It was cool and dark out, the tall windows behind him were black. 'I suppose . . . what you want. Why you called me. Why we're here.'

Eva felt ashamed, embarrassed. But he had every right to ask her this, because she hadn't known what she was doing either when she called him. She struggled to frame a reply, an answer, that wouldn't wound him.

'Oh Mark, I don't know,' she said. 'Because I'm human. Because I'm alone and sometimes that's hard.' He started to reach over to touch her, but she went on. 'Because you've been kind and . . . attentive, and I felt I needed that. No simple answers.'

'No.' He watched her face, steadily.

She had forgotten how beautiful he could be, how much pleasure you could take just in looking at him. 'I should go, I think.'

'I wish you wouldn't.' His hands reached across the table and closed over hers.

'No, really, I think I should.' She slid her hands out from under his, and lifted one to signal the waitress.

A silence fell between them. Eva was looking away from him, out the dark window. There were candles on the empty outside tables, flickering. 'I feel I owe you an apology,' she said.

'What for?'

Eva didn't know how to put it. For misunderstanding myself? For using your affection to comfort myself? For using *you*? 'I've been so . . . unstable, I guess. Not myself. Or, I feel actually, I'm only gradually becoming myself again. I've sort of . . . flailed about. I haven't known what I wanted.'

'Well, that seems pretty natural, doesn't it, given the circumstances?'

'I suppose. But it still bothers me to realize it.'

'You're being awfully hard on yourself.'

'Not hard enough, I assure you.'

He smiled at her. 'Eva. You're always too hard on yourself.'

'Well, then, that's how I have to be apparently.'

The waitress set the check down in its leather case. They fumbled, argued, but Eva insisted on paying it. She had, after all, asked him out, she said. And hadn't even been very good company.

She felt an urgency to be gone, almost a physical need. She left too much money for the tip, not wanting to wait for change. She stood up. Without speaking, they walked through the bar, across the foyer with its mammoth bouquet of lilies, and out to the parking lot. Eva was walking just ahead of Mark. She turned at her car to say goodnight. Mark reached for her, and she stepped into his embrace — one last time, she told herself. It felt so familiar, so wonderful,

199

his long, muscled body, his smell. She felt she was holding their youth together, their start, their hopes and then all that had wrecked that. She felt she was holding her past, something she'd already said goodbye to, at great cost, and now unexpectedly had to part with again.

He kissed her, and she kissed him back, but when he pushed harder against her, she pulled away slightly. With her hands still around his neck, she lowered her head, resting her forehead against his chest. His hands moved up and down her back.

'This is all I want, Mark,' she said after a moment, and then she stepped away and bent to open her car.

She didn't look at him as she backed out, as she shifted gears and pulled forward toward the gate at the entrance to the lot. But she couldn't stop herself from looking in her rearview mirror just before she turned out into the driveway, and he was still there, standing where she'd left him, his face and his shirt pale smudges in the dim light.

As she drove slowly down the curving drive, she felt overcome by a sense of loss, a sense that included John, and herself somehow too. It shouldn't have to be so hard, over and over, she thought. It's too hard. She slowed and stopped at the road, and waited, her turn indicator blinking steadily, until she had forced down the tears that welled in her throat and eyes, until her vision cleared and she could start the drive home.

10

Duncan was full of opinions.

(It was only after Duncan, years after Duncan, when Daisy began to have love affairs with people her own age, college students, that she realized how unusual this was. She lay next to one or another new lover and listened to them talk, listened to them tell their stories — about how they ran away from home one summer, about how their brother was killed in a car crash in high school and the family was never the same, about how their mother slipped into heavy drinking and they finally performed a family intervention — and she missed Duncan: the blankness of his past and his endless opinions. *I'm not interested in stories*, she would think. *I could tell you a story. What about your opinions?*)

Duncan thought that the problem with contemporary politicians was that they didn't believe that there was a permanent and deep evil in the world. Therefore they had no capacity to understand and take any dark pleasure in life, no wit. Kennedy was the last president with true wit, he said, and that was because he was Catholic and understood the power of evil.

It was Duncan's opinion that the Napa Valley had become absurd and precious. That it represented all that was bad and would get worse in America about the connection between wealth and race. That eventually everything would get so expensive that no one normal would be able even to afford the wine anymore, and the Mexicans would still be living in cheesy housing and drinking bad beer, and everyone would still be pretending that was just fine because they were a different *kind* of human being from the white folks who grew grapes.

Duncan thought her taste in movies was idiotic. He thought that the only contemporary directors whose films were worth seeing were Robert Altman, Alan Rudolph, the Coen brothers, and occasionally something by Woody Allen. She shouldn't even speak to him of Bergman. (She wouldn't have been able to, never having seen one of his films.) Bergman, he said, *that fraud*, who abused his art to moralize, to moralize simplistically about good and evil.

Duncan thought that computer use wouldn't become widespread until the techies, who were in love with what they'd created, stopped insisting everyone else had to love it too. 'We're Americans,' he said. 'We want something we can turn on, and it goes. Like the car. Like the electric light. We don't want to have to admire the complexity or be involved in it. We don't want to understand *how*. Americans don't care about how. We just want to press the button and be happy.'

It was Duncan's opinion that American girls were insipid. Dull. Because they had no culture, they had no deep sexuality. He had rescued Daisy from this fate. He would be a story she could dine out on.

'Yah, and who in the wide world would I ever tell this particular story to?'

'I promise you, Daisy, you will.' Suddenly, he smiled. ''And when you speak of me,'' — she could tell he was imitating someone, quoting someone — ''Be kind.''

Daisy took in all this and much more over the course of the fall, even as she was learning from Duncan everything about her own body and how it could be brought to pleasure. Because she'd gone on seeing him.

Though she hadn't known, after that first time, that she would. In the car that afternoon on the way back to St. Helena, he had said, 'Well, we're even now, Daze.'

She wasn't sure what he meant. She was stunned with what they'd done, what she'd done.

And now, his saying this. Was it over, so soon? Was that all he'd wanted? Did it end here? Was this the way things worked with grown-up sex?

Of course, she knew it wasn't even really sex at all — he'd never put his penis in her; she hadn't even *seen* his penis — but maybe these were the rules.

She said, in what she hoped was an indifferent tone, 'Okay.' She looked away from him, out the window at the hillside that rose on the eastern side of Silverado Road, at the driveways cutting uphill, the houses you could see through the woods and undergrowth.

'Of course,' he said after a while, 'if you'd like to do this again, have a *spot of tea*, as it were, I'd be willing. What do you think?'

203

She looked over at him. His face was pleasantly blank, unreadable. She shrugged. 'I don't care,' she said.

He grinned then. 'Liar,' he said. *'Pants on fire.'*

She couldn't help smiling slightly. 'So?' she said, after a minute. 'What do *you* think?'

'About what?'

Daisy looked back out the window. 'If we should.'

'I think we should, Daze.'

Her heart thudded heavily.

'Don't you?'

She shrugged again.

'Come on, Daisy. I'll be your slave. Every teenage girl should have a slave, don't you think? I'll put my hands wherever you like. I'll put my mouth wherever you like. I'll look at you and simply adore you. All parts of you.'

She kept her face turned from him, but she could feel herself blushing.

'You liked it, didn't you, Daisy?' His voice was serious, suddenly, and she looked over at him.

'Yes,' she said. 'I loved it.'

'Would you like it again?'

'Yes,' she said, and felt funny, heavy and thick between her legs, in her abdomen.

'Good.' And when she said nothing more for a long moment, he said, 'Is there a problem then?'

She said, 'What about Gracie?'

This wasn't what she meant, not really. Though she would have said she loved Gracie, she didn't truly care about her in relation to what had just happened with Duncan. She

204

meant something else, something about what all the other grown-ups would think, something about how illicit this was. She wanted him to acknowledge this, to make sense of it for her, though she couldn't have found the words to ask for it.

'Well, we won't tell Gracie, I wouldn't think.' She could see his mouth twist a little bit. He looked over at her. 'Just as we won't tell Eva about your *larceny*.'

'That's not what I meant,' she said. And then, 'They're not the same, anyway.'

'But in a sense, they are. You're taking from Eva what belongs to her, because you need to, for your own *private* reasons, and I'm taking from Gracie what belongs to her because, I would say, of my *own* very private reasons. Isn't that the case?'

She didn't answer. You didn't always need to answer Duncan, she was discovering.

'Has Eva even noticed?' he asked.

She shook her head. 'No,' she said reluctantly.

'And I can promise you Gracie won't notice either.'

'But . . . ' She was searching for exactly what it was she wanted to know from him.

'What?'

'Don't you love Gracie?'

'Love,' he said. 'I don't quite believe in *love*. We see where love gets you. 'Love me tender.' 'Love is all you need.'' He looked over at her. 'We don't agree, do we, Daisy? We understand that love is an *idea*, a big fat overblown Western idea. *Culturally imposed*.' His voice mocked his

205

own words. And then he was quoting something, something Daisy would recognize with a start years later, getting ready for an audition for a play. ''Men have died from time to time,'' he said, ''and worms have eaten them, but not for love.''

Daisy waited a moment, and then she said, 'But *do* you love Gracie?' She knew she was really asking him about herself, but this seemed the form the question needed to take.

'Well, of course, I'm *devoted* to Gracie. Gracie is part of my life and who I am forever and ever, till death us do part.'

Daisy felt tearful, suddenly. She bent her head. They were in town now. She lined up her books, her homework, on the seat next to her. She saw them through a blur.

'Of course, the question is, what about *you*, right?'

His voice was surprisingly gentle, but she didn't look at him.

'I adore you, Daisy. I want you. I think about your body and your mouth and your legs all the time. I've thought . . . often. Of doing exactly what we did this afternoon.' They had turned off Main Street now. He drove a half block past Kearney and pulled over. He put the car in neutral and turned toward her. 'Daisy,' he said. 'I'm happy. I'm happy that you liked it so much. That you want to do it again. So now I'll think about how beautiful your crew-cut pussy is, and how you taste, and what it feels like to push my finger into you and to look at you holding yourself open for me. And of how you looked in

206

Gracie's old bathing suit with your mile-long thighs. That was terrific, Daisy. And of how you looked, like a gorgeous giraffe, walking down the street holding your schoolbooks with your hair streaming out behind you. And how you looked thrashing around on my bed.' He reached over and stroked her hair.

She smiled at him.

'Snarls,' he said, and pulled his fingers a little. It hurt.

He dropped his hand. 'Better run, Daze. I bet you're late for dinner.'

She gathered up her books and looked over at him again. 'When?' she said.

'Delicious Daisy.' He smiled. 'Whenever you like. Whenever you can. I'm at your disposal.'

'I can Thursday.'

'Well then, Thursday,' he said. 'I'll find you on the way home after school. We'll have a lovely little rendezvous.'

As she shut the car door behind her, she bent down and looked over at him, hoping for some claim, some sign. He was looking away, but he sensed her. He turned, he snapped his teeth at her.

The next day she put a note in Mrs. Loomis's mailbox, withdrawing from chorus, which met on Thursday afternoons. Her mother needed her, the note said. She started to write something that connected directly with John's death, but as soon as she began it, she felt washed with shame. She scratched out the words and just signed her name.

★ ★ ★

207

Through the next month and a half or so, Daisy managed to see Duncan twice a week usually, sometimes three times if she cut her piano lesson too. She lied to Eva all the time now — she lied about after-school activities, about chorus and music and sports. She lied to Mark about Eva's needing her in the store. She lied to her piano teacher about conflicts, things that had come up. But of course, she said, Eva would pay him anyway.

The world narrowed for her, and Duncan's studio became its center, the place where she felt most alive. She dreamed of it, sexual dreams of the way the light fell in from the skylights, of the order and quiet. In these dreams, sometimes the space opened up to other rooms, other spaces, with a sense of mystery and amplitude that pleased and aroused her.

She felt encircled by Duncan's attentiveness to her body. She loved his absolutism. She loved the way he looked, the dark sober eyes that never seemed to take part in the jokes he made or his sarcasm. She loved the delicate lines that netted his pale skin, the cuffs of his shirts turned back over his tendoned forearms. She loved his soft brown hair, thinning on top, graying by his ears.

She felt he offered her a new version of herself, one she more and more carried with her into her real life. She felt uplifted, in a sense; she felt an elevation over the daily ugliness of high school. She was less afraid, less shy. She saw that she would have a way out. Not that Duncan would be it — she understood that — but that she would be able to escape. How, she could not have said, but she was certain of it.

And she loved the strange sex, which asked so little of her.

★ ★ ★

Get changed,' Eva said.

'Why? I look okay.' She set her books down on the kitchen island and picked up a cheese stick from the blue mug full of them that Eva had set out.

Eva looked at her. Daisy was wearing jeans and a sweater. 'Company's coming,' Eva said. 'Why don't you put a skirt on for a change?'

'Oh shit!' Some writer, she thought. Some book person. Someone boring. 'Who?'

'Gracie and Duncan.'

'Gracie and Duncan?' she said stupidly. She hadn't known. He hadn't said anything. She'd left him fifteen minutes or so before.

'Well, they're still company, Daze. Just . . . something besides jeans anyway. Okay?'

She couldn't believe it. She was furious. She felt tricked. She went up the steep back stairs to the second floor. In her own room, she lay on her bed and let tears leak from her eyes. She put her hand over her face. It smelled of him, of herself. She thought of what they'd been doing, less than an hour earlier. He had sat next to her on the cot, bent away from her, his face between her legs. He had his fingers in her everywhere, and they were pushing in and out as he turned his face slowly from side to side in her wetness, as though he wanted to smear himself with it. She

209

had been dizzy, laughing as she came. And then wanting him, as she more and more did now, to let her touch him, to come into her, something he had said more than once he wouldn't do.

On the drive back, she had finally asked him why not.

He had smiled at her. 'It's not part of the game, Daisy.'

'It's *not* a game.'

'In the sense that it has rules, and it's fun, one might think of it that way.'

'Well, one might think of it that way, but that doesn't make it so.'

He laughed. 'We'll talk about it next time. I'll put it on the *agenda*.'

'If you won't do it to me, I'll tell. I'll tell everyone you seduced me. You took advantage of me. You ruined me.' Daisy was joking, but as she spoke, she felt the anger enter her voice, enter her. But what was she angry at? She didn't know.

'Daisy.' He shook his head. 'You're hardly a nymphet. You tower over me; I tremble in your shadow. *I'll* tell everyone I was scared of you, that you made me do it.'

'Very funny.' She gathered her books and put her fingers on the door handle. She said, 'You know, if you won't, I can find someone else, some high school jerk, who will.' She believed this suddenly — she, who'd never even had a date.

'Idle threats, Daisy. Boring. Beneath you.'

'It's true.' She had slammed the door as hard as she could when she got out.

Daisy didn't go downstairs until she was summoned, long after she heard Gracie yoo-hooing in the front hall, long after they trooped back noisily to the butler's pantry to get drinks, long after they'd settled in the living room. From upstairs, she listened to the interplay of their voices, Duncan's only occasionally audible against the two women's. Theo's rose from time to time, strident in some claim for attention.

She felt a calm descend on her as she moved around. She did change her clothes, pulling on a straight skirt and a sweater Eva had given her, a pale blue sweater with a V-neck. She put on eye makeup too, and a bright red lipstick she got from Emily's room. And, at the last moment, panty hose and heels. She never wore heels ordinarily because they made her so tall. The last time she'd had them on had been for John's funeral.

When she was done, she waited in her room until Theo was sent upstairs to get her. They were already seated in the dining room when she came down. She stopped in the doorway.

Eva looked up first. 'Sweetie, you look fantastic!' she said.

Daisy was about to say thanks — lightly, regally — when Duncan said, 'I liked her better in Gracie's bathing suit, carrying a *big stick*.'

She looked at him. The smile she knew from their times together played openly on his face. She thought of his mouth, his teeth, loving her.

Gracie and Eva were on him instantly. 'Oh for

Christ's sake, give it a rest,' Gracie said, and almost simultaneously Eva was saying, 'Can't you ever play it straight, Duncan?'

Daisy looked levelly at him. She stood very tall, aware of her height, of her long legs, of her breasts in the sweater. She said, 'And I'd rather you didn't speak of me in the third person, since I'm right in front of you.'

'All right, Daze!' Gracie cried out. Duncan just grinned.

At the table, as they passed things back and forth, they started talking about salt — how much was good for you, whether it was an acquired taste or a primitive one. Eva was getting Theo set with the food he liked. Duncan explained the importance of salt in various cultures. Its religious uses. The pagan Roman custom of putting salt on a baby's mouth a week after birth to chase away the demons.

'It's a purifier, it stands for everything holy and clean, probably because it was used to preserve food, to keep it incorruptible, as it were.' He smiled, his faint, twisty smile. 'This is why Buffalo, where I grew up, is such a clean-living burg. It ran on salt. They kept mounds of it around, to spread in winter. Between the cold and the salt, there was no sin in Buffalo.' He raised a forefinger. 'Thus 'the salt of the earth.' Buffaloans. Me.'

'I didn't know you grew up in Buffalo,' Eva said.

'Someone had to.'

'But you — you seem unlikely.'

'Well, it gave me a keen nose for the hypocrisy

of life. Of salt. Of religion generally.'

They started in about religion. Eva was talking about its primitive pull, saying how just hearing a hymn could make her yearn for belief, for meaning in life.

Duncan said she was being sentimental. That there was no meaning to life. That it was a sign of immaturity to look for it.

Eva said that if she was immature (he smiled and began to shake his head), he was too. That his interest in fiction, in stories, was completely parallel, a parallel search for a *shape* to things.

He thought for a moment, chewing, swallowing. 'I might concede the point,' he said, 'except that Handke is one of my favorite writers.'

Eva said she couldn't stand Handke.

'There you have it,' he said. 'I think we can all guess why.'

'Well, yes. It's just, 'This happens, now this happens, now this happens.' And none of it . . . *goes* anywhere. None of it adds up to anything.'

He smiled. 'As opposed to life,' he said.

'But life *isn't* like that. Life does add up.'

His smile deepened.

'It *isn't*,' she said, passionately, and Daisy knew she was talking about John, somehow, about his death. 'You notice it everywhere,' she said. 'The shape of life, the coincidences, the way it makes meaning.'

'I have to say it blew *right* by me,' he said.

Eva turned to Gracie. 'How do you stand it?' she asked.

Gracie said, 'Oh, it was ever thus with

213

Duncan.' She lifted her wineglass and tilted it back and forth for a few seconds. Then she drank from it. 'It's what comes from his perpetual need to be dismissive. He's always reducing everything. Right, sweetie?'

Daisy watched as Gracie made a lascivious face, puckered her lips, and kissed the air at Duncan.

'I'm arguing here, goddamit!' Eva said. 'Pay attention, Gracie.'

'Oh, Eva, you're always arguing.'

There was a moment of silence while Eva thought about this. 'Well, maybe so,' she said. 'But he is too.'

Gracie laughed and set her glass down. 'Boys and girls,' she said. She clapped her hands. 'Time out.'

Theo grinned. 'Time out,' he echoed.

Daisy didn't like Duncan in this conversation. She didn't like his flirting with Eva, being coy with her, smiling at Gracie. What had happened between him and her wasn't included in any of this, hadn't changed any of it. And it ought to have.

Daisy felt put in her place, that was it. She felt dismissed. A child. Like Theo. She wanted to tell them, at this table, with their flirty, fake conversation, that she and Duncan were lovers. That he belonged to her as much as he belonged to Gracie.

But that wasn't true. And she knew it wasn't true.

But surely there was a way — wasn't there? — a way in which he *did* belong to her, maybe even more than he belonged to Gracie? Shouldn't there be some acknowledgment of that on his part anyway? Some signal to her?

Shouldn't he at least have told her he was coming to dinner?

As soon as they'd finished dessert, she excused herself. Homework, she said. Eva smiled at her, approving, and asked her to take Theo up too and get him changed and into bed.

Daisy carried her bowl to the kitchen sink. She didn't look at Duncan as she left. She and Theo went up the back stairs and she helped him into his pajamas and watched him brush his teeth. When he lay down, she lay down next to him and read him a book, a story about a bad little cat who wouldn't kiss his mother. He was leaned against her, his body seemed to radiate heat and energy. He laughed and pointed at the pictures, and Daisy lingered over the story with him. When she closed the book, she turned off his light. She slid down and lay next to him in the dim light coming up from downstairs.

When Theo's breathing changed, she got up and went into her own room. She changed her clothes. She did her homework with the door open, the sound of their voices drifting up.

Daisy heard their departure, Gracie's voice loud in the front hall, the thick thud of the front door. She knew that she was supposed to go down and help clean up, but she didn't. She waited for Eva to call her. And even then, she yelled back, 'What?' as though she didn't know the routine. She wanted to make her mother have to ask. She felt the meanness in this, but it

215

also felt like something she needed to do.

Her feet were bare and the tiles of the kitchen floor felt cool under them. Eva was moving around in her quick, darting way. She had put on an apron, a big old-fashioned apron, cotton with a flower pattern and rickrack trim, given to her by her mother. She had three or four of these, and Daisy opened a drawer to the right of the sink and took one out for herself. She pulled it on, she tied it in back, and then, while Eva started to put leftovers away, she padded back and forth to the dining room, bringing dishes with her, dishes she set on the counter by the sink. Dishes and glasses and the candlesticks and dinner napkins and silverware.

They worked silently, but there wasn't any tension in this. They'd done it hundreds of times by now. Eva looked tired; she was working fast.

Daisy was slower, thinking of Duncan. Duncan as he'd been with her today, and as he was at dinner. Duncan and Gracie and her confusion about that. Reaching over the big island in the center of the kitchen to wipe it down, she asked, 'Why do you think Gracie and Duncan got married?' She hoped her voice sounded casual.

Eva looked over at Daisy from the sink. 'Oh, the usual reasons, I suppose,' she said, and smiled.

That smile, and what seemed the assumption in her mother's remark of some common, perhaps commonly female ground, irritated Daisy. 'What does that mean, 'the usual reasons'? There's nothing usual about how *they* are.'

216

'Okay. I know what you mean. I was being flip. They are an odd couple.'

'So? why did they? You knew her before.'

'I knew them both before.' Eva had stopped what she was doing and turned to face Daisy. 'I introduced them. And I admit, I wouldn't have imagined what happened — that they'd ever, ever get together. Much less marry.'

'But they did! So?'

'I really don't know, Daze.' She frowned. 'I think any marriage is really a mystery in some ways. Why it works when it does, why it doesn't when it doesn't.' She turned back to the sink. It was full of soapy water. 'It's occurred to me that Duncan likes to be . . . the bad boy. I like him enormously, sometimes, but he can be so . . . just childishly nasty.'

'I'll say.'

Eva looked sharply over at her. 'Was he unkind to you, honey?'

Daisy shrugged.

'You know, if he's unkind, just ignore him. He's like everyone's mean older brother. He just needs a spanking, fundamentally.'

There was a silence while they worked. Daisy was drying the dishes Eva handed her, and putting them away. After a while, Eva said, 'I don't know. I guess one theory might be that by the time Gracie met Duncan, she knew she wasn't ever going to have kids.' She looked over at Daisy. 'That that was over for her, you know?'

Daisy nodded.

'So in some ways, *he's* like her child. She indulges him. She enjoys that bad-boy-ness, that rudeness.' She turned to the sink and pulled the plug. As the water drained out, she ran the disposal for a long, thunderously noisy minute. When it stopped, she said, 'But I think even Gracie has her limits. Or her moments, anyway.'

'What do you mean?'

'Just . . . well, you know, that *nastiness*. It can get very pointed, very personal. He has a kind of list of things about Gracie. That he uses. That he can use. You know, her weight, her size, her loudness, the way she makes her money, which he doesn't approve of, of course. Her . . . flabby arms, for God's sake. Things she wears. Anything will do, in a pinch. And then apparently, if she reacts or gets upset — if she should cry, for instance — he's incredibly disdainful of that.'

'Ugh.' Daisy is imagining this, Gracie crying, Duncan smiling, saying something sarcastic.

'Ugh is right.'

'So why would she stay with a person like that?'

Eva shrugged. 'At first, I suppose, because she was besotted.'

'Besotted?'

'Drunk. Drunk with love. Crazy with desire.' She looked at Daisy again, almost speculatively. 'She loved sleeping with him. Apparently he's quite the lover.' There was a half smile on her face. She was *enjoying* telling Daisy this. 'Are you surprised?'

Daisy shrugged and said nothing, though she was furious with Eva for saying this. For knowing it. For asking her to respond to it.

'But after a while, when that didn't weigh

quite so heavily in the balance anymore, she did leave him once. This was about two years ago. She left and she stayed with us for a few days. Don't you remember?'

Daisy shook her head.

'She'd really had it. She actually started looking around for a rental. She was going to let him have the house. And the funny thing was, she was relieved. She really wasn't sad about it at all. Oh, I'm sure she would have had some teary times if they'd split permanently, but she said she felt such relief. I remember she used the expression *out from under*.'

'But they got back together.'

'Yes indeed.'

'How come, if it was so great to get away from him?'

'Well, Duncan just fell apart, I guess. He came after her, he pursued her. He wept. He said he couldn't live without her.' She rinsed the pan she'd been washing and reached for a dish towel. 'Actually, I don't know what he said. I don't think he told her he'd never do it again. How could he have? He knew he would. But he gave her to understand that she meant everything to him. That he wouldn't be able to bear his life without her. And of course, that's very powerful. That carries you through a lot of bad times, knowing that. So that, now, I think, even when things are hard between them, she understands that it's just his darkness, his perversity. That he'd be lost without her.'

They worked silently for a few minutes, putting away the last cooking things. As Daisy hooked her towel through the ring hanging on the wall, she said, 'So Gracie *told* you all this?'

'Yes. I think . . . well, she was so thrilled by it. And I *am* her oldest friend.' There was an apologetic tone in Eva's voice. She was defending Gracie, her talking about the most intimate details of her marriage. 'And also, I think she might have felt I deserved to hear why she was going back, after I'd also heard how awful he was, how she never would, how this was it, and so on.'

She leaned back against the sink and crossed her arms. She was frowning. 'It's an odd dynamic, and one I've never been interested in, where you have such a difficult lover. And you feel, I guess, so grateful, so stunned by the moments of not-difficulty. I think people who love like that, the way Gracie does, feel this intensified sense of intimacy, because the intimacy is so hard won, so infrequent. It's like intermittent reinforcement.'

'And what does *that* mean, intermittent reinforcement?' Daisy hated it when Eva did this, set things up so she'd have the pleasure of making some elaborate explanation.

'Oh, it's behaviorism, the study of how behavior gets developed. And the theory is — or maybe it's proven: anyway, the idea is, if you reward someone for a certain behavior every *single* time, they become less reliable in that behavior, they figure they don't need to do it all the time because they know the reward will be there whenever they *do* decide to do it, so they don't learn it as well — the behavior. Whereas if

220

the reward is unpredictable — sometimes they get it, sometimes they don't — then they're more interested, more focused in their behavior, more anxious, more consistent.'

'So Gracie loves Duncan because he's only wonderful to her every little once in while.'

'Yes, I think that's right, actually.'

'That doesn't explain why *he* loves her, if he even does. Which I doubt.'

'Oh, I don't doubt it,' Eva said, smiling in a way that seemed smug to Daisy. 'Not for a minute.'

★ ★ ★

The next weekend, Daisy worked both days in the bookstore. Sunday, she took twenty dollars, a five, five ones, and a ten. That evening, after supper, she was sitting in her closet doorway, counting it again, when Theo burst into her room, calling her name.

For a moment they just looked at each other, Theo still hanging on to the doorknob, swinging a little with it; Daisy cross-legged in the open doorway to her closet, bills fanned out around her. Then Daisy whispered fiercely, 'Shut the door!'

'What are you doing, Daisy?' he asked.

'Shut the fucking door!' she said.

'Why are you having all that money?' he said.

'Jesus,' she answered. 'Shut the *door*, Theo!'

He shut it, and then came over and stood by the closet. 'You have *too* much money.'

221

Daisy was shoving the money back in the box now. She put the cover on. 'Yeah, well, it's a secret. I'm saving it up.'

'But how did you *get* all that money?'

'I'm big, Theo. There are lots of ways for big kids to get money.' Daisy got up on her knees, and set the shoe box in its place at the back of the closet.

After a long moment, Theo said, 'I can get money too. I'm big.'

'Yeah?' she said. 'And how is that? How can you get money?'

'I can get money whenever I want.' He thought for a moment, and then his face cleared. 'I can get money from my dad.'

'Is that right?' Daisy shut the closet door. She went to her bed and flopped on it. Theo came and stood next to it, right next to her head.

'Yes, that is right.'

Daisy didn't answer. She looked at him, at his pretty face, his perfect mouth, the down-sweeping eyelashes.

''Cause John's going to give me lots of money when I see him.'

'Is that right?' Suddenly Daisy felt an interested, rising meanness that had something to do with Theo's having seen her, his having seen the money. She lifted her head and propped it on one hand, turning sideways on the bed to face Theo. 'When will you see him, do you think?'

'I *think*, when I'm getting a little bit bigger, then I will.'

'And how much bigger will you be?'

222

'Oh, this much.' He raised his hand as high as it would stretch over his head.

'So when you're . . . ten, say. When you're ten, you'll see John and he'll give you money. *Pots of dough.*'

But there was no doubt in Theo's face. 'Yes. About around ten.'

'And will I see John then too? Or just you?'

Theo looked confused, but only for a few seconds. 'Yes. That's when we both will see John.'

'Do you know how old I'll be then?' she asked.

'How old?'

'I'll be a grown-up. I'll be twenty-two.'

'Oh,' he said.

'So maybe if I get married when I'm twenty-two, John will come to my wedding.'

This made Theo frown. 'But who will you marry, Daisy?'

'Oh, let's say I marry . . . Duncan. John would like to be at that wedding, don't you think?'

Theo looked uncomfortable. 'But. You're not . . . marrying Duncan.'

'Why not?'

'I know you can't marry Duncan, because he is too big, he's too grown up for you.'

'But I'll be grown up then too.'

'But he is *more* grown up.'

'Well, we're pretending a little bit here. We're pretending I'll marry Duncan, and we're pretending John will come to my wedding, right?' Daisy's voice was friendly, beckoning.

Theo's mouth opened for a minute. You could

see his small, even teeth. Finally he said, 'But John *will* come.'

'So, I will marry Duncan, right?'

Theo watched her. Then he got it. He smiled. His face relaxed in relief. 'It's a joke, right, Daisy? It's a joke about Duncan.'

'Right,' Daisy said. She flopped onto her back again and stared at the ceiling.

Theo turned and started toward her door.

'Theo!' she said.

'What?' He stopped and looked back at her.

'Don't tell about the money.' Her voice was low. 'It's a secret. If you tell, I'll kill you.'

'Okay,' he said cheerfully, and left.

11

Daisy was late, and Duncan didn't seem to care. He was moving slowly, poking through some drawings to find one he wanted to take home with him to work on there, then hunting for his keys. It occurred to her he was limping more than usual too — something she'd come to suspect he did willfully from time to time.

Daisy was standing by the open door. It was almost dark out, and she was supposed to have been at the bookstore about ten minutes earlier. There was a reading tonight, a reading she had promised to help with. Eva would be nervous, and then pretty quickly pissed off, when she got there to find nothing had been done — the chairs not set up, the books not unpacked and put out for signing. What Daisy hoped was that Callie might have started to do all this when her tardiness became clear — if Callie wasn't otherwise too busy.

'Come *on*,' she said to Duncan, even though she knew this was unwise. That in his perversity, the more she pushed him, the more he would resist.

He looked up and smiled, the smile you would have thought was open and sweet if you didn't know better. 'Ah, the impatience of youth.'

'The impatience of the *late*.' She smacked the door frame on the word.

'What won't wait for you, dear girl? The whole world waits.'

She made a face. The night air was chilly. In her mind's eye, she saw the bookstore, the front window with its light spilling out onto the darkened street, the first few customers already arriving for the reading, milling around self-consciously, choosing seats — if there were seats set up to choose.

'I'm going to wait in the car,' she said. 'I can't stand watching you dick around endlessly.'

She sat in the car with the door shut. From here she could see the yard full of old machines — crabbed, monstrous shapes in the fading light. Twice recently, someone from the family that rented the garage to Duncan had been in the yard when they arrived. Once the man, once the woman. They were both gray, lumpy, elderly. He had seemed busy with one of the machines as they drove past him, Daisy slouched low in her seat, Duncan cordially waving. But the woman had stopped in her progress across the littered yard — going from where to where? for what? — and had taken the opportunity to scrutinize them, her eyes squinted and mean, as they drove slowly in, as they got out of the car and went to the door. Duncan had slid his hand down Daisy's back and cupped her bottom before he opened the door. 'Might as well make it worth her while,' he said, and then he swung the door in and Daisy walked quickly past him. This had irritated her.

But lots of stuff irritated her now. Things had begun to change between her and Duncan, and

226

Daisy knew only some of the reasons why. Certainly Eva's talking to her about Duncan and Gracie had triggered part of it — talking about his needing Gracie, his begging her to take him back. But probably more important than that had been the sense Eva conveyed during that talk of how Duncan seemed to *her*, his being not quite adult in her eyes, his need to provoke being somehow childish rather than a sign of superiority, as Daisy now recognized she had seen it. So, there was that: the way her lover apparently existed in her mother's imagination; the echo of her mother's voice and the image of her face, slightly amused, slightly contemptuous, speaking of Duncan.

And there was the sex, which was still a matter of his looking and his touching and his kissing and poking her. *Poking her.* That's how she thought of it sometimes. Daisy was getting tired of it. Sometimes her body felt so ready for contact, for flesh, for something reciprocal, some muscular other body meeting hers, that she had the impulse to hit him hard, to bite him, to pin him down and make him fight her.

She didn't know how to understand their affair, if that's what you would call it. She didn't know what it was that he got out of their version of sex. Or why this *was* their version of sex.

Was it that he was ashamed of his body? She had considered this. There must be wounds, after all. Scars. She knew there had been many surgeries, plus the accident itself, a car crash, spectacular and flaming and meaningless, a dramatic event in one of those dumb car movies.

He was supposed to have walked away from it, that was the deal that went wrong. Perhaps his body was so wrecked, so ugly that he was ashamed to be with her — she pictured purple, gouged-out welts everywhere, missing musculature with the flesh stitched shut over the absence, crooked bony growths.

Or was he impotent? She knew this happened to old guys — though she always thought this meant really old guys — guys in their seventies, their eighties. And Duncan was fifty-three. Old, but not really old. But maybe that was it. He couldn't do it. Or maybe he couldn't do it because of the accident. Maybe something down there had been injured.

Though her mother had said Gracie liked having sex with him.

But maybe what Gracie liked was exactly the same thing he did with Daisy — the licking, the sucking, the fluttering fingers, the way they entered you everywhere. She had imagined them, imagined big flabby Gracie spread out like some beached sea creature, while Duncan, trim and neat and fully clothed, lay between her legs and worked on her. She had felt some jealousy, and then none — and that too must have been because of the changes that had come between them.

She hadn't seen him for almost a week after her talk with Eva. She made no real decision about this. It wasn't as though she wanted never to see him or be with him again. It was nothing absolute. It was simply that when she had a piano lesson, she went. When she was

228

supposed to be at the bookstore, she went — no lies, no excuses. Basketball practice started that week, so she really was busier than usual. She didn't look for Duncan; she didn't run into him on the street. When she left school, she avoided her usual route home, the streets he would cruise at the end of the school day, looking for her. Instead, she stayed on Main Street, and cut back up to Kearney a block from home. And being in the center of town lifted her spirits — the storefronts beginning to be decorated for the holidays, the twinkling lights in the dark afternoons.

He had called, finally, last night. He wanted to see her. He *missed* her, he said, his voice heavy with sarcasm.

She felt instantly the resurgence of her pleasure in his having chosen her, in her power over him. 'Sure,' she said. 'How about tomorrow?'

In the car as he drove her back to the reading, she sat silently, nearly twitching, as she felt it, with impatience.

'Are you so eager to get away from me?' he asked.

She looked over at him. He was smiling, but it was such a pathetic thing to say. 'Ugh!' she said loudly, and turned away from him in her seat. Turned to her window.

'Quite right,' he said. 'No whinging allowed.'

She didn't answer. The hills rode alongside them, the lights of a lone house fluttering here and there behind the leaves of the trees.

After some minutes, he said in a conversational tone, 'I didn't know this reading meant so much to you.'

'It's not the reading,' she said. 'It's that I said I'd *be* there.'

He was quiet for a while. Then he said, 'This is something I hadn't taken in about you, Daisy. Your punctiliousness.'

She turned back to look out the windshield. 'Yeah, well. There's lots you haven't taken in about me.'

'Hardly anything, I'd argue.'

'Nearly everything, I'd argue.' She pushed in the cigarette lighter.

'But you like to argue, Daisy. I *have* taken that in.'

'I like to argue with you, because you're always affirming the ridiculous.' The lighter popped out, and she pushed it in again.

'Daisy, is this kind?'

'Who cares? Have you been kind to me? Is seducing someone half your age — God, less than a third your age! — is that kind?'

'You would rather I'd left you to the tender mercies of some teenage clod who can barely speak, let alone read. Or think. Or bring you off.'

Daisy said, 'Yeah,' but she thought about it. The lighter popped out again. She actually thought about it. She knew he was right, she wouldn't have wanted that, wouldn't have wanted any of the boys she knew or could imagine. Noah? God, no. She thought of how Emily had described sex with Noah, how once he got inside her, he forgot all about her and

230

whumped against her and came within a few seconds. But she wasn't so sure she wanted the kind of sex she had with Duncan anymore either. Though she couldn't imagine not having him, not having his touch, his attention to her, to her body. He was all she had, she thought.

They were approaching the stoplight. 'Drop me off here,' she said.

He signaled, and pulled over. He turned to her. 'Shall we plan another meeting? A tête-à-tête?'

'I've got a lot of stuff happening between now and Thanksgiving. I think I'd better wait till after then.' She was already gathering her books, getting out. She shut the door and started walking quickly up the block, not looking to see when he passed her.

Eva's face was pinched and grim when she looked up and saw Daisy, but she was talking to people she knew, people arriving for the reading, so Daisy was spared for a bit. The sparkling water and wine and cookies were laid out. The chairs were set up, and people were already filling them, though others were still standing, looking at books or talking in little groups. Callie was at the register, and Daisy lifted her hands: What should I do?

Callie pointed to the signing table where the books were still stacked on a dolly and in boxes on the floor. Daisy worked her way through the crowd and began to unload them, folding the cover flap into the title page as she stacked them on the table, so they could be opened quickly to that page for the author's signature.

The author had already arrived, apparently — Daisy heard someone speaking of how much older she looked than her photo. She must have been back in Eva's office then. Eva straightened it up a little when there were readings, setting flowers and water out on her desk so the writers could sit there in comfort if they wanted to be alone before they had to perform. Some liked to hang around and talk to their fans. Daisy had more sympathy for those who fled, who waited until the moment they were introduced to appear.

The book Daisy kept opening was called *Creating the Life You Want to Live*. Drek. She hated self-help, and she'd forgotten that this was what was being read tonight. This was her punishment for being late, she supposed.

Now Eva was standing at the podium set up in front of the rows of chairs. She waited, smiling, while everyone sat down and slowly fell silent. She made some announcements — future readings, books that had come in. Daisy could see the writer, who had come down the hall and was standing at the entrance to the room, waiting for Eva to finish. She was fiftyish, carefully groomed. Her hair was stiff, her makeup perfect. She wore a beige suit, and a lot of jewelry.

Eva started her flattering introduction. Daisy looked at the book she had in her hands as she listened. The author photo was on the front cover. The woman faced the reader with her arms folded across her chest. The photo was slightly overexposed, so that everything distinctive about the face was erased. The author — her name was Joyce Garabedian — was neither young nor old in this picture, Daisy would have said. Just, perhaps, absent. Or abstract, anyway. An abstract woman.

Now Eva said her name and she came forward to the podium. She nodded, acknowledging the applause. When the room had quieted, she began to speak.

She wasn't going to read, Joyce Garabedian said. Instead she wanted to tell her story, the story of how she'd come to write her book. She held it up, as though the audience might not know what book she spoke of. Daisy, whose hands were moving more slowly now since she didn't want to make any noise, listened and watched her as she worked.

Joyce Garabedian described her life as it had been. A high-powered job that she hated, as an attorney; a high-powered husband who was rarely home, and when he was, was critical of her, of how she looked, of what she cooked, of how she'd furnished and kept their house. She described the house, a pretentious apartment on the Upper East Side of Manhattan. She said, 'But the point here is I didn't know I hated my job. Or my house. Or my husband. I would have said that everything was marvelous. Wonderful.' She smiled. 'This was your *classic* unexamined life.' She pivoted behind the podium and spoke to the other side of the room. 'And then one night I was having dinner with a friend, a friend who was seriously depressed — which I didn't feel I was, not at all. I mean look at all I was accomplishing, look at how busy my life was. Depressed people couldn't *do* all that stuff.' She lifted her shoulders, gestured with her hands while she spoke. Rings flashed on her fingers.

'And I was trying to focus her on the upside of things, so I asked her, 'Well, what makes you happy?' And she couldn't answer. I was shocked. She *couldn't answer*. She said to me, 'I don't know. I honestly don't know.' And finally she shrugged and turned the question around. She said to me, 'What makes *you* happy?''

She paused for a long moment, surveying the room, almost smiling. When she spoke again, she spoke slowly. 'And that was what did it. That's what changed everything. Those four words. What. Makes. You. Happy. Because, my dear friends, here was the hard truth.' She leaned forward and said in a lowered voice, an intimate voice, 'I didn't know either.'

Then she stood straight and looked around again at the audience. Daisy's hands, which had been moving steadily, lifting a book, opening it, tucking the flap in, setting it on the table, had stopped. Joyce Garabedian said, 'The honest answer? Nothing. Nothing made me happy. And I suddenly knew that. I knew. But of course, for the moment I faked it. 'Oh, certain things at my job.' 'Coming home to my lovely apartment.' I can't even remember what I said. I invented a couple of things. But all the way home in the cab that night, all the next day, the next week, I kept asking myself that question.

'And my answer scared me. Scared me enough

to start me on the long process of self-examination, self-questioning, and finally self-actualization that I record for you in this book.' She lifted it again and set it down, looked up once more.

'And that's where I want you to start. *What makes you happy?* What does make you happy?'

Daisy was thinking about her own life, about happiness. She remembered the paper she'd gotten a D on in the spring, the paper with the two sentences about happiness. She thought of John. She thought of Mark in the hillside house.

Joyce was saying, 'If you have even a fragmentary answer for yourself, you're ahead of where I was. You're in better shape. Maybe you've got kids, or you love to cook, or you play the guitar, or you go jogging among these gorgeous vineyards you live in.' Her sparkly hand lifted toward the front window. 'Maybe sex makes you happy.' She smiled and her eyebrows lifted, and there was general laughter.

Why? What was funny about that, Daisy wondered. Sex *did* make her happy — the moments as it began, opening herself, wanting it. And then when it happened, the feeling of it.

Then it faded; of course it faded. Was that what was funny? Daisy picked up another book.

'Whatever works,' Joyce Garabedian was saying. 'That's what tells you where to start. Do more of that. *Feed it*, I say in the book. And I tell you how to do that, how to make what gives you joy more central to your life. We even look at what you lie about for clues. If you say, 'Oh, my house,' while knowing full well that it doesn't, well, then you need to look at that. There are two possibilities as I see it that connect to that lie. The first is that you feel your house ought to make you happy. It ought to. And therein lies the problem. Because nothing, my dears, that you think ought to make you happy is ever going to. And the second possibility is that you would in fact like it to, but for various reasons it doesn't. And exploring *those* reasons will help you get there.

'But maybe some of you are like me, the way I was. When you ask yourselves that question, what you come up with, looking in the mirror, is a big fat blank stare. What makes me happy? *I don't know*. Nothing. And it's for you ladies especially,' she raised her finger, 'that this book will be most helpful.'

Daisy didn't know either. That was true. She didn't know what made her happy. But it was something that would come to her, that would arrive, she thought, and then she'd know it. She'd know it instantly. It would come into her life the way Duncan had come into her life. She'd look up one day, and it would be there. Only it would be real; it would be better than Duncan.

Duncan, having Duncan, had made her believe this, she realized with a start. That things could *arrive*, that things could change. Her hands began to move again, lifting Joyce Garabedian's book. Her life wasn't like Joyce Garabedian's, who was pushing the book hard now, laying out a series of steps she had taken and recommending them to her audience in

236

order to discover the life they truly wanted to lead.

But Daisy by now had tuned her out anyway. There was no connection. Daisy's life would be different. Special. There would be no steps, no strategies in this cheesy way. What good was it, after all, if you had to work at it?

The audience was asking questions now, and Daisy, listening half attentively, noted how skillfully Joyce Garabedian kept referring them back to the book, telling them just a little of what they wanted to know and then citing a whole chapter that would explain everything to them.

When she was finished, the applause was prolonged. She had trouble making her way back to the signing table, so many people stopped her and wanted to say something. Daisy pulled the chair out for her, and offered her a choice of pens, but she had her own, a fancy silver one with a real nib. Daisy began handing her the books, and the women stepped forward.

The line for signing was long, and Joyce Garabedian talked expansively to many of the audience members who stepped up opposite her and spoke to her of their problems, their hopes. It was late when Eva shut the door on the last customer and turned off the window lights. Callie had left to walk Joyce Garabedian and her escort to their car, so Daisy and Eva were alone.

Daisy had already begun picking up — she'd started as soon as the last book was signed, when there were still plenty of people in the store — and Eva came back from the front of the store and joined her. For a while they worked silently, staying as far apart as they could. But when they got to the chairs and began to pass each other going up and down the hall, Eva stopped in front of her and said, 'I'm so furious with you I can hardly speak.'

'I'm sorry I was late,' Daisy said. Her voice was cold, and Eva's face tightened. She moved away.

They each carried several more loads and then Eva, coming back, stopped in the hallway again as Daisy was approaching her. 'Why? Why *were* you so late?'

Daisy set down the chairs. 'Practice ran late.'

Eva looked hard at her. 'Daisy. I called over. Someone told me practice was done much earlier. At four or so.'

'Yeah, but a couple of us stayed on and shot around for a while after.' She shifted her tone. 'I'm not all that good, Mom. If I'm going to make the varsity team, I've really got to work on it.'

Eva sighed, and Daisy knew it was okay. She'd won. 'Couldn't you have called?' Eva asked.

'I didn't notice, Mom. There's no clock in there. And I was all sweaty so I had to shower and clean up and I didn't even *want* to take the time to call then, I was rushing so much.' She lifted her chairs again. 'I'm sorry. I said so, didn't I? I am sorry.' Daisy realized that she was actually feeling impatience with Eva — Eva, to whom she was elaborately lying, after all. Impatience for Eva's slowness in yielding to her lie, in forgiving her. But it didn't change anything to recognize the

238

unfairness of this — it was what she felt.

They walked home in silence. It was chilly out, and Daisy held her whole body rigid against the cold. The movie was still going — the marquee was lighted — but the rest of the town was as quiet as it usually was at this hour on a weeknight. Tourists and vineyard owners would still be dining in restaurants, but the shops were closed and there was almost no street traffic.

As they turned onto Kearney Street and approached their house, Eva said abruptly, 'Sometimes I can't stand it.'

Daisy, who had been thinking about happiness, about Duncan, about sex, was startled. 'Can't stand what?'

Eva was quiet for a moment. 'Can't stand how hard it seems, how complicated it is — life — without John.' Then, passionately, 'I hate coming home, sometimes. I hate it.'

'God, Mom.' Daisy felt that she was being blamed somehow, accused. That Eva wouldn't be saying this to her unless she was still angry. That her mother's sorrow was connected to her, to all that she didn't do, couldn't be, for her. And what this produced in Daisy was the impulse to turn away. She simply couldn't add her mother's sorrow or confusion or anger to her own. She didn't have the strength to carry any more than she felt she was carrying.

'Get a grip,' she said, and went ahead of her mother up the walk to the lighted house.

★　★　★

When Emily came home from college for Thanksgiving, Eva and Theo and Daisy all drove down to the airport to meet her. Daisy hadn't known what she would feel, how she would respond, but when she saw her older sister, small and pretty and frowning among the other passengers streaming toward them, she called out Emily's name and watched as she turned, trying to locate her, and then did, her face opening in pleasure. Daisy ran forward, ahead of the others, and she and her sister held each other a moment, and then backed away, laughing and awkward and embarrassed, so Eva and Theo could have their turns.

She had missed Emily, she'd been aware of that, but in thinking about it through the fall, she'd concluded that she'd missed her even more when she was still around, because of all that had changed between them. When she thought of being close to her sister, what she remembered was the early time in the house on Kearney Street when they still shared a room; or the years when they were little, in the house on the hill. And maybe most of all she missed the person she had been in those days too, before she had a sense of herself as awkward and clumsy, a sense that intensified as Emily became prettier, more elegant, more popular.

She remembered with a deep, inexplicable pleasure certain games they had played in their hillside home, prolonged fantasies in which they took parts — princess and wicked stepmother, orphan and kindly rich lady. There was a game in which they pushed the furniture into new

240

arrangements and had to cross the living room without allowing their feet to touch the floor — the floor, where crocodiles or skunks or dragons lived. Sometimes Eva let them make a house under the dining room table, draping it with sheets. They brought all their dolls and moved in, and often Eva let them take their meals under there. They would eat in the dim light in what felt like utter secrecy, worlds away from their ordinary life.

Emily, of course, directed all this. She made all of it happen. Left to her own devices, Daisy would have read, or made pictures, or, later, written stories or poems. And as she *was* more and more left to her own devices after the move to town — as Emily stepped into her own life — that's what Daisy had done, until John interceded. But even then, even after she herself had moved away from Emily, after she had come around to thinking of Emily as shallow, as bossy — even then when Emily beckoned her, as she occasionally did, Daisy had responded with a kind of eagerness she sometimes felt as pathetic in herself.

She had tried to prepare herself through the fall for Emily's return from college. She didn't want to feel so eager if Emily should pay attention to her or invite her into her life in some way. And there was a sense in which her relationship with Duncan connected to this resolve on her part. It was like armor against her sister. It was an adventure, an element in her life that Emily couldn't have guessed at. Something about it, about having this experience that Emily didn't know about, couldn't imagine, excited Daisy and made her feel in some way superior to her sister.

Lying in bed on Emily's first night home, she thought again of Emily's descriptions of sex with Noah, and it made her experience of sex with Duncan seem compelling. She thought of the strange, beautiful images that filled her mind when he played with her and she came — rain glittering like silver coins in the air, falling and falling on wide green meadows; or houses she was moving through which opened up, room after unexpected room, each one more full of light. She thought of how open and familiar her own body felt to her, all the parts of it that had frightened and disgusted her before, now so charged with power.

But when Emily asked her casually on Thursday night if she wanted to go shopping for Christmas presents with her on Saturday, Daisy said yes without even stopping to think about it. Yes. She did.

'There are, like, *huge* sales,' Emily said.

'Yeah,' Daisy said.

'Maybe we could get something for Mom and for Mark together.'

'Sure,' Daisy said. 'Cool.' She realized that she didn't care what they did. Just the idea of having been chosen by Emily again was enough. She felt, she realized, just as she had when Duncan had arrived in her life: rescued. Rescued from herself. It was like wearing the heavy makeup Maria had put on her at Eva's birthday party, and the black bathing suit with its too ample cups and the rhinestone belt. The sense of another self, another way of being in the world. It was news. News about herself. She remembered how everyone had looked at her that night, and how she'd wanted to stay in the costume because she felt suddenly that she could be anyone she chose to be. She remembered writing out the poem that Mark had asked her for, and then, on impulse, writing out that other one, the one that announced her feelings, the feelings of newness and possibility and happiness.

And she felt that way again, she couldn't help it, when Emily asked to be with her.

★　★　★

She was up early on Saturday. It was chilly out, and drizzly, but Daisy didn't care. She came down into the kitchen and turned on the overhead lights. Eva had left half of a baguette out on the island, and Daisy decided abruptly to make French toast. The butter smoked in the pan, the sopping bread sizzled. The kitchen filled with vanilla-scented smoke.

She took her plate to the island. She got the maple syrup from the refrigerator. It was cold and thick as she poured it on. She took a bite and chewed slowly, the sweetness and cold making her teeth ache. She was about to take another bite when Theo came in. He had dressed himself, clearly — nothing was tucked in and his fly was still open. He was carrying his wallet in both hands against his chest. This was a gift from Eva, bought for him last summer after he'd returned the money he'd stolen. A reward for having gone straight after having been a thief, Daisy supposed. She had smirked when she saw it then. She smirked now.

'Going *shopping*?' she asked sarcastically, weighting the word. It occurred to her that she sounded like Duncan.

His head bobbed enthusiastically. 'I'm going with you.'

Daisy shook her head. 'No, I'm going with Emily. Emily and I are going by ourselves.'

'Nuh-unh, Daisy,' he said with a teasing emphasis. 'Emily told *me*, and I'm going too. Mom said I could.'

Daisy set her fork down. Of course. Suddenly she understood it all. Emily *had* invited them both. It was a *project* of Emily's. *She* was a project of Emily's. Emily would manage them; she'd be in charge of their togetherness. She'd speak to friends of the day and of the time with them as a virtuous act. *What did you do on your break? Oh, I took my brother and sister Christmas shopping, you know, to get stuff for the parents.*

Daisy got up from the island, unhungry. She took her plate to the sink and watched the half-eaten toast slide from it. She turned the water on and punched all the food into the disposal. The machine roared and gurgled as she ran it.

Theo had climbed onto a chair. 'I am hungry,' he announced when Daisy turned the disposal off.

'Then *fix* something for yourself!' she said,

244

and left the kitchen.

She lay in her room and listened to the rest of the house wake up. She heard Emily in their bathroom, taking a shower, then the long silence while she fixed her hair and fussed with makeup. She heard Eva's radio in her room, tuned to the news. She heard them talking when they went down to the kitchen. Someone else made French toast too, she could smell it.

She was thinking of her options. She could just not go, but she'd have to explain why, and if she told the truth, she'd seem like a baby. 'I thought it was just going to be the two of us.' How pathetic! She didn't want to seem so foolish, so hungry for Emily's attention.

Which, of course, she was, wasn't she?

She was not going to admit to it, though.

She could lie, but a lie would lock her into all kinds of complications. If she said she didn't feel well, Eva would get involved — thermometers, no going out. If she had something else she was doing, she'd need to disappear and do it. Or disappear and do *something*. It didn't seem worth it. And she had to get the Christmas shopping done anyway.

When Emily called up that they were leaving in ten minutes, Daisy hollered back that she'd be there.

Eva left just before they did, headed to the store. She beamed at them as she said goodbye. 'Have a great time,' she said — and Daisy could tell that Eva was delighted by the very thing that was upsetting to her: that all three of her children were doing something together.

In the car on the way to the outlet stores, Theo needed to go over the math again and again. Since he had five dollars in his wallet and wanted to keep one for himself, he had four dollars to spend on a present for Eva. Emily was patient; Daisy was silent in the backseat, watching the silver rain streak across the windows.

They went first to the department store to look at clothes. Emily thought they could get her a blouse. Or maybe, as they passed a display of them in the aisle, a sweater. She held out the one she'd noticed, cashmere, widely striped horizontally in blue and white. It cost $120. 'We could all buy this together,' she said.

'I don't like it,' Daisy said.

'But Mom would, I think, and that's the point, isn't it?'

'Well. I can't afford it.'

'What's *afford it?*' Theo asked.

'I don't have enough money, dummy,' she said. She looked at him. He was holding Emily's hand.

'I'm not a dummy. *You* are the dummy.'

'Who cares?' She turned to Emily. 'Anyway, let's not.'

'You are the dummy, 'cause you do *too* have enough money, Daisy.' His voice was louder.

Daisy felt tense, suddenly. 'I just said I didn't, Theo. Shut up, why don't you?'

'But you do *so.*'

'No, I don't.' She turned to Emily. 'Let's go look at house stuff,' she said.

'House stuff! That's a horrible idea.'

'Well, it'll be cheaper.'

'God. I didn't ask you to go shopping so we could be stingy,' Emily said. 'God! What were you planning to spend on Eva anyway?'

'I don't know. I didn't think of it like that.'

'Well, what you said was, 'I can't afford it.' So you must have some idea of what you *can* afford.'

'What can *I* afford, Emily?' Theo asked. Emily had put his wallet in her purse for safekeeping. When he had it, he took the money out all the time, because he liked to touch it, to hold it.

'We told you, Theo. You have five dollars, and if you spend four on Eva, you'll have one dollar left, so four is what you can afford.' Daisy started ahead of them through the aisles, away from the sweaters.

'Daisy has much more than that,' she heard him say.

'Shut *up*, Theo!' Daisy said, without turning back to him. A woman passing her stared — a gigantic crazy girl talking to herself.

'She has hundreds and hundreds. I saw.'

'Hundreds and *hundreds*?' Emily said, in a teasing voice.

Daisy stopped and turned. She waited for them to catch up to her. 'You're a liar, Theo,' she said. Her voice was low and threatening.

Emily made a face at Daisy: let him talk. What's the big deal?

But Daisy wanted him to shut up. 'He's imagining stuff again.'

'I'm not 'magining.'

'Yeah? You're always imagining stuff. Just like you imagine John is alive, when he's dead.'

247

Emily said, 'Cut it out, Daisy,' just as Theo was saying, 'He's *not* dead anymore.'

'Yeah, and I have a lot of money. 'Hundreds of money.''

'Yes, you do so have it.'

'See?' Daisy said to Emily, her hand lifted. See how crazy he is?

They were standing in front of the perfume counter now, and Emily suddenly switched gears. Perfume, she suggested. Daisy, eager to end the conversation, quickly agreed. They knew Eva's favorite, Cristalle. Why not? And at the last minute, because the perfume cost them less than they'd planned on, they bought her a scarf too, the kind Eva liked and used as a shawl.

When they got home, Daisy went straight to the kitchen. She was starving, having thrown most of her breakfast away. She was standing in the open door of the refrigerator when she heard them above her, and knew instantly — knew because she saw it so clearly in her mind's eye — that they were in her room, that Theo was showing Emily the shoebox that contained her money.

She took the back stairs two at a time, and when she got to the doorway to her room, they were just as she'd imagined them. The double doors of her closet were flung open, and they were standing in it, as if on a stage. Emily was holding the shoe box in the crook of one arm, and in her other hand, she had some of the bills. They were looking across at her, agape. The word actually flashed in Daisy's mind, as words sometimes did. *Agape*. Stupid-looking. Theo

248

looked scared. They stood across the room from each other, and finally Emily said, 'There must be a couple of hundred dollars here, Daisy. Where'd you get it?'

In three steps Daisy was on her. 'It's mine. Give it to me.' Emily didn't resist. She held the box out, she held the money up to Daisy.

'I told you, Daisy,' Theo said. 'I *told* you you had a lot of money.' He wasn't scared now. He was excited. Daisy hadn't hit him, or yelled, and Emily wasn't backing down. He was safe. 'Didn't I tell you, Emily?' he said.

Daisy turned to him. 'Yeah, so what?' she said. Her voice was flat and mean. 'This doesn't mean anything. It doesn't mean you're right about anything. It doesn't change anything. John is still dead, you little jerk. Your dad is dead, Theo. Dead.'

'Don't tell me that.'

'He's dead.' Daisy's voice shrilled. 'And he's never, ever coming back. Not this year, not when you're ten, not ever. Ever. Ever.' Daisy was so angry she threw the money at him, and it scattered all over the floor.

'Don't tell me that,' Theo wailed.

Now he's going to cry, Daisy thought. And Emily will comfort him.

And she watched as that happened, as his face crumbled and the wailing started in earnest, as Emily scooped him up — he was like some animal, a monkey, clinging to her front — and carried him out of Daisy's room.

She could hear them down the hall in Theo's room, their voices — Theo's slowly calming

249

down, Emily's steady and reassuring. She stood listening for a while, and then Daisy got down on all fours and began to pick up the money, crawling around. She put it in the shoe box, and this time, put the shoe box in the deepest drawer at the bottom of her desk.

It was quiet in the house now. Emily's and Theo's voices were just an occasional murmur. Daisy lay down on her bed and almost instantly a desire for sleep came over her, a desire so profound it made her feel dizzy, even though she was already lying down. She was about to succumb, to fall heavily into it, when Emily was back, standing by her bed.

Daisy moaned. 'Go away,' she said.

'Where did you get it?' Emily asked. 'Where did it come from?'

Daisy groaned. It was like being tortured, this request to come up from where she wanted to be — to attend, to speak. To think.

'Where'd you get it, Daze?' Emily's voice was kind.

Daisy roused herself, she made herself answer. 'The store,' she said.

'The bookstore?'

'Yes.'

'Eva's bookstore?'

'What other bookstore is there? Yes!'

'It's what you earned? At Eva's store?'

A way out for Daisy opened here, but it felt too late, she was too tired to take it. 'No, I didn't earn it,' she said heavily. 'I took it.'

It seemed to her she might have slept for a while, but then she heard Emily's voice, whispering: 'So you just, *stole* it?'

Daisy opened her eyes and looked at her pretty sister. Emily was sitting down now, at the edge of the bed.

'Yes,' Daisy said. She closed her eyes again.

'And Eva doesn't know? She doesn't suspect?'

Daisy opened her eyes. Emily was frowning, earnest, concerned. Concerned for her. 'No,' Daisy said. Her eyes closed.

'We could put it back,' Emily whispered.

Daisy didn't answer. She wasn't sure Emily had really said this.

'Did you hear me, Daisy? We could easily put it back.'

Daisy moaned.

'Don't you think? Come on, Daisy, wake up.'

Daisy pulled herself up to a half-sitting position. She licked her lips. 'What's the point of that?' she asked. 'It isn't like she even noticed it was gone.'

Emily was chewing on her finger, frowning. Daisy could feel the nod of her own head, her eyelids yearning to close.

'You didn't even use it,' Emily said.

'Yes,' Daisy admitted. She sat up straighter.

'What did you take it for in the first place if you didn't want to spend it on anything?'

'I wanted it.' She cleared her throat. 'I wanted it.'

'But why, Daisy?' Emily looked anguished. 'You have enough money.'

For a moment Daisy smiled, thinking how Emily sounded just like Theo, thinking how everyone thought she had enough, how, of course, she did have enough, how that wasn't the point. 'Why indeed?' she said in a mocking tone.

And then suddenly she started to cry. It hurt, at first — her throat felt swollen and sore — and then it eased. 'I don't know,' she blubbered. 'I don't know.' And though she was speaking of the money, somehow everything else in her life — her aloneness with John's death, the solitary life she led at school, the secret of sex with Duncan, all the things she couldn't speak of to anyone else — all of these seemed part of why she wept.

Emily reached out and awkwardly rubbed her sister's shoulder for a moment. Then abruptly she swung herself up onto the bed and lay down next to Daisy. She put her arms around her in what they had called, a long time ago, a bear grip. They lay together as they had when they were little girls and their world was sliding out from under them and they had turned to each other for safety. And Daisy, because she knew there wasn't any safety anymore, even here, folded that memory into her grief and deepened it.

12

Mark was back home, in Nebraska, for Thanksgiving. He stood staring out the window over the sink as he did the dishes from the holiday meal. Three of his brothers were here too, at his mother's house, with their wives and some of their grown children. There had been fourteen of them at the table today, and his mother had gone all out: the old, worn white tablecloth, heavy linen napkins and her real silver, and the full array of traditional dishes, including sweet potatoes with marshmallows, and three kinds of pie. She had been up at five this morning; he had heard the noise in his half sleep from upstairs, in what was now the guest bedroom, and experienced it as he would have a dream, a dream of his boyhood, when he'd wake to the noise of his mother fixing breakfast for all of them — the distant clatter of pans and dishes, the steady low vibration of the radio tuned to the morning news.

His sisters-in-law and brothers were moving in and out of the dining room now, carrying dishes and what was left of the food. Mark had volunteered to wash, not wanting to have to keep up with the running conversation of the others as they passed each other going back and forth. Here, among his married brothers and their wives, he was thinking of Eva again, of Eva as he had spoken to her last more than a month ago, in the parking lot of the Auberge de Soleil — of her saying to him then that *this was all she wanted:* touching him, being with him. But then she'd left, quickly, and in some pain, it seemed to him. Pain brought on, he supposed, by what was hard, what was full of conflict for her in acknowledging that to him and mourning John at the same time. He'd watched her go, watched the car pull away, turn out of the parking lot, out of his sight, not knowing what to do, how to help her.

And he hadn't seen her again after that. They had talked a few times on the phone, arranging a visit with Daisy, and one with Daisy and Theo together. And there had been a problem Eva called him about — it turned out that Daisy had been cutting piano lessons without telling her. In fact, lying about it. 'That's what upsets me the most,' Eva had said. 'These completely invented *stories* about where she was, or what she was doing. Now I don't feel I can trust her at all anymore.' She'd asked him to pick Daisy up from the teacher's house on the night he was to have her over, just to be sure that she'd actually been there, she'd had the lesson. But through all these conversations, they kept their tone businesslike — or parental, anyway. They never mentioned their last time alone together or what Eva had said to him.

And then, of course, life seemed to intrude; or he let it. First there had been all the frantic work of the crush, the harvest; and then he went on a long-planned vacation; and now he was here on this visit home, which it would have been unthinkable to cancel.

254

He *had* considered, actually, canceling the vacation, but decided against it. And that had everything to do with Eva. He wanted to give her time. She needed time, he understood that. But he could wait. He would show her he could wait. The last thing he wanted was for her to feel he was putting pressure on her.

He looked up from the sink again, out the window at his nephews and one of his nieces playing touch football on the frozen ground. They wore puffy bright parkas. Their breath made quick clouds. As they shouted back and forth to each other, laughing, their voices carried in through the window, over the gossipy conversation moving from the kitchen to the dining room among the adults.

Beyond the young people and their game, the fields came up almost to the fence at the end of his mother's yard. He had been startled on his first day home — as he always was when he arrived — by the flatness, the monochromal quality of these fields, of the land generally. Shades of brown, gray, black, stretched for miles in every direction from the edges of town. Snow had fallen that day, just a light crust that melted by midafternoon of the next day, but enough to make him remember the cold, the desolation during the winter months of his childhood, when all you saw were the long hopeless planes of white, broken here and there by tree lines along the creek beds or at the margins of someone's land. How did they endure it? How had he endured it?

He had known early on that he didn't want to

stay. He'd gotten out as soon as he could, going to California to work for a year after high school, and then enrolling at Santa Cruz. Before he had left, he had sometimes dreamed of California as he thought it would be — the warmth, the light, the sea — but the reality of it had surpassed anything he could have imagined. He was stunned by the touch of the air, by the lushness of the vegetation.

And in the early days of his life there — before the malls sprang up at the edges of every town, before the vast sweeps of cheap housing blanketed the lower reaches of the hills — there was a sweetly old-fashioned quality to the dazzling pastel cities, to the sleepy little villages he drove through with his friends. Plus of course, he had no past, no history in California. He felt a sense of possibility for himself there that the landscape itself seemed somehow to confirm everywhere he looked.

And even though he no longer thought of California in quite that way — or at least not often — he was still stunned in reverse sometimes when he came home. Before his brothers had arrived, he spent a couple of long days in the car with his mother, doing errands. Driving around in the emptied, sere landscape, you'd catch the whiff of a hog farm every now and then, or stronger yet, the stench of the feedlot some miles down the highway. When this happened, he'd look over at his mother's face and see nothing in it change. She was, simply, used to it — how it looked, how it felt, how it smelled.

Only three of his five brothers were around for the holiday — the other two lived too far away, on the East Coast. Of the three who were here, one — Bill — had stayed in town and taken over their father's small lumberyard. The other two had come from Lincoln and Chicago, respectively. Eric was a lawyer, Robbie an editor for the *Herald Tribune. Distinguished men*, Bill and Mark joked, casting themselves as yokels, guys who worked with their hands. Though even Bill, Mark knew, did more of his work in the office at the back of the big lumber shed, and most of that work was numbers, figures; and over the years they'd all come to understand that Mark's work wasn't anything like the farming they'd grown up with. Eric and Robbie actually knew something about wine and sometimes sought out labels that bought grapes from Mark's clients. And Mark's mother, having read in her AARP magazine that a glass of wine a day was good for her, had asked his advice on what to buy.

But on these visits they all fell into the old patterns, they pretended that nothing had changed. That Bill and Mark were hopeless students who would do physical labor for the rest of their lives, that Robbie and Eric were intellectual escapees, but escapees tied to the treadmill of overwork, overachievement. Mark participated easily, he knew his role, but it weighed on him; it reminded him of all the old feelings of inadequacy and failure that had been part of growing up here. Impossible, though, to reinvent any of this. It would be seen as shocking, offensive, if he were to say, 'You know,

I'm tired of this, I'm tired of pretending I'm slow, I'm nothing but a good old boy.' It was why you had to leave; it was why you sought a new place, a new set of terms under which to live your life.

He was remembering how much Eva had disliked coming home with him, partly because of the way he was treated in the family, and partly because of her sense of the closed circle he and his brothers and mother made. Once when they were still married, she hadn't come for the holiday, she'd sent him with just the girls. His brothers had teased him about his 'liberated' wife, about his doing all the work while she took a vacation, about being pussy-whipped. (When they divorced, nothing had been said. It wasn't even as though she had died; it was as though she'd simply never existed.)

'The boys,' 'you boys,' as his mother called them, had been there for two days now with their families — all but Mark would leave tomorrow. Their mother's joy in their presence was palpable, though it mostly took the form of the presentation of food, as it always had. Mark had been the first to arrive, and he'd been able to take in the scope of her effort in its pristine, untouched state: the jars of cookies, the pies and a cake ready for snacking, Rice Krispies treats, and something his mother called TV mix — pretzels, Corn Chex, nuts, and a few other dried cereals tossed with oil and Worcestershire sauce and toasted. The dinner she prepared the first night they'd all eaten together — last night, Thanksgiving Eve — was one they'd always loved: meat loaf and mashed potatoes with gravy, green beans with slivered almonds, and creamed corn. They were all skinny men, except Bill, who'd stayed in this world and whose stout wife cooked the way Mark's mother did. At the end of the meal, the four brothers had sat with their chairs pushed back from the table, their hands resting lovingly on their swollen stomachs, and let their mother bring them cups of the strong coffee she drank through the evening, right up until bedtime. The three wives, restless and perhaps bored, had cleaned up, leaving the family to their old habits.

Now his mother stood next to him, drying dishes, putting them back on shelves, in cupboards and drawers. She was a slender woman, and she'd been pretty, he would have said, until only a few years earlier. But she'd had a cancer scare then — one breast had been removed — and the illness, and perhaps the treatment too, had altered her. He hadn't seen her when her hair was gone, when she had lost almost thirty pounds. But even partly recovered, she was diminished, aged. Her face seem collapsed, her skin hung in new pouches, over new emptinesses. Mostly, though, a kind of determined energy that had always marked her had vanished. Even her eyes, which had signaled that energy — a hard, snappish blue — seemed faded. Sometimes over these three days, he'd looked at her when she hadn't known she was being watched, and her body, her face, seemed abandoned to him, like something she'd left behind.

Now, though, animated by her sons' presence, she was teasing the 'boys' as they tried to help — flirtatious with all of them, as always. It struck him that she had loved having sons. What would she have done with a daughter? with a Daisy, an Emily? Her wiles, her way of being maternal, all these were aimed at men. Today, at the end of the meal when they could eat no more, she had scolded them, and compared them to their father. 'Now there was a man who knew how to put it away,' she had said, bright, teasing.

No one had mentioned the series of heart attacks, the untimely death, her long widowhood.

He looked at her. She was holding a large platter now, drying it, smiling as she listened to the two younger wives in the kitchen, who had adopted something like her tone as they mocked their husbands for their gestures at helping — gestures that the husbands themselves had consciously made minimal, inept, as part of the joke.

'Oh, ya mean these dishes are *dirty?*' Linda asked in a voice like Goofy's. 'Gee, a-*huh*! A-*huh*!'

Suddenly there was an explosive crash.

Mark looked up, around, in confusion. His mother stood, her hands empty, her face sagged in open-mouthed shock.

And then she wailed, a sound of such deep pain, such loss, that his hands lifted from the water in response.

But Linda was already there, holding her, and then Kate was kneeling on the floor, starting to pick up the pieces of the platter that had slipped from his mother's hands, that had broken into hopelessly small shards which were scattered all over the kitchen.

'Oh *no!*' his mother cried with a grief so powerful you would have thought she'd lost a child, a lover. '*No, no.*'

Her sons had come to the kitchen door and stood, like Mark, stupid, helpless, before this sorrow that sounded so bottomless, that must connect to their father's death, to her fears for herself, to all she'd lost or never had; but that came from a part of her she would afford them no knowledge of, give them no access to.

And so, once it was over, once his mother had reappeared from her bedroom, recovered, her lipstick newly applied, cheerful once more, no one spoke of the scene again; and the next day the goodbyes were cheerful, teasing, and full of references to next year.

That night, Mark's last night home, he and his mother were quiet together. She seemed deflated to him, but maybe she was just tired. She served Thanksgiving leftovers for dinner, with scalloped potatoes she'd made that afternoon. The crusts of what was left of the pies were a little soggy by now, but Mark had a thin slice of each.

'I keep meaning to ask about the girls,' his mother said after dinner. They were sitting in the living room, their coffee cups resting on TV tables she'd set up by each of their chairs. 'I wish kids wrote letters anymore.'

'You need to get on the phone,' he said. 'The phone is what kids understand. Why don't you call whenever you feel like it and let me know what it costs? I'll reimburse you. Or just charge it

261

to my number. It can be my Christmas present to you.'

'Oh, I'm not going to start calling long distance at the drop of a hat now.' Though she was smiling, her voice was slightly testy, certainly dismissive. 'I'm too old for that. In my book, long distance is still a luxury.'

'You're only as old as you feel, Ma.'

She smiled. 'Like I said, I'm too old.' The television sat across the room from them, turned on low. A report on the fall of the Berlin wall, with the images they'd seen many times before — the young people dancing on top of it, the crowds, the joy. Both of them watched it for a moment. Then she said, 'But they're good, the girls?'

'They seem great to me. One's a winner socially, one's a loser, but that could change any time. Daisy's coming on strong. She's almost six feet tall, you know. Well, five-ten or so.'

'Oh my. Five-ten! That could be hard on a girl that age.'

'Yeah, for now it is. But the thing is, she's going to be gorgeous. She's going to turn heads. Emily, of course, already does, but Daisy's going to turn all the heads, 'cause she's going to stand way, way over anyone else.'

'And they're both doing good in school?' Meaning, at least in part, that she wanted her usual reassurance that the girls hadn't inherited his problems.

'Fantastic. Daisy's making straight A's, just about, and Emily seems to be doing fine at Wesleyan. We don't see her grades till the semester's over.'

'I bet they grade real hard there, given how hard it is just to get in. I hear it's just as bad as Harvard, or Yale or any of those big ones.' And she began to talk about local kids, the grandchildren of friends, her grandchildren by Bill, the children of Mark's cousins who lived nearby, all of whom were far more vivid to her, he knew, than his own children — details of where they were going to school, where they were applying, where they might get in.

When she stopped, he waited a moment, and then he said, 'Eva seems better.' She didn't look at him. He said, 'It's been hard for her, this last year, but she seems to be doing okay, finally.'

Why had he brought Eva up? To prepare his mother? To accustom her to hearing Eva's name, to having her be in his life again? He wasn't sure actually; but it didn't matter, since it was as if he hadn't mentioned her. His mother said only, 'Hnnh,' and then, a moment later, asked him if he wanted more coffee.

He said no, he was fine.

The house was silent around them except for the murmur of the TV. The windows were black. He imagined her here alone night after night. He thought of the sound she'd made crying out the day before, of her nameless grief. He said, 'You're happy, Mom? It seems . . . kind of quiet now. Your life.'

'Well, I don't know that I'd say happy, exactly. But I'm *content*,' she said.

He could feel something rehearsed, something self-satisfied in the way she summoned and used the word, and he understood that she'd said this before, perhaps more than once. That she'd used it to sweep aside any need to look at herself and her life, to try to change things.

She went on. 'I think this happiness business is ridiculous, really. I'm *content* with my lot, and I hope to stay right here, among my friends and dear ones, until they carry me out.'

'Feet first.'

'Is that the way?' She smiled. 'All right, feet first.' After a long moment, she suddenly began to sing, an old song he remembered from his youth. Her voice was thin, but she had perfect pitch — she still sang in the church choir — and she clearly loved the words, the story the song suggested.

> *Oh when I die*
> *Don't bury me at all.*
> *Place my bones*
> *In alcohol.*
> *And at my feet*
> *Place a white snow dove,*
> *To tell the world*
> *That I died for love.*

They sat for a moment, and then she got up and started to clear their cups away.

★ ★ ★

He had been to Santa Fe before he went to Nebraska. This had become his practice since he and Eva had been divorced — to reward himself for the work of the harvest and for the trials of the coming Thanksgiving visit home with a trip to a place he'd never been before.

At first he had liked Santa Fe — for its exoticism, its beauty. You could have been in another country, he thought. But after the second day, he felt himself too much a part of the economy: a cog in its wheel, a tourist, meant to move from one commercial destination to another. And there was no destination, it seemed to him, that wasn't commercial. It was hard to tell where people lived, or even whether people actually did live in the town anymore.

He wondered if this was Napa's destiny — to be there for the viewing, the purchasing. To be preserved in this way. Of course, the towns in the valley were less historic, less exotic than this one, and people *did* live in them. But more and more they needed money to do that. Big money. And though it was true that the agricultural preserve kept it in vineyards — so it would go on being farmed indefinitely — it was also maybe the only kind of farming in the universe, he thought, that could be a tourist attraction. He'd felt it as an irritation several times during crush, driving a truck laden with grapes, pulling a gondola full, waiting in the long lines of tourist traffic to make a turn, fretting about the rising heat, the time wasting. And yet, without the tourists, his work would have been worth less. Far less.

He had a rental car in Santa Fe, and when he got tired of strolling into the shops and galleries and churches and restaurants near the plaza, he drove out into the surrounding country on several days, watching the dry land roll and change. He stopped three times at Indian pueblos and walked around, taking in the small stone-and-adobe buildings that had been there for centuries, looking at what remained of that ancient way of life. Several places charged admission, but one seemed utterly derelict; and even though several families, anyway, were still living there, he was apparently free to wander anywhere he wanted, unchecked. But this was the pueblo where he felt most the intruder, in the end, where he was most aware of his false relation to the life he looked at — it seemed so sunk in poverty, so helpless.

He had talked about all this to a bartender in Santa Fe one night. He was in an expensive restaurant where the waitstaff was all white, and the runners, the bus boys, were Mexican and Indian. 'Yeah, they work it different,' the bartender said, speaking of the pueblos. He wore a heavy brocade vest over his white shirt. 'Some of them, okay, you can look all you want for five or ten bucks, but they don't even live there anymore, it's like a museum. They've moved onto their lands now, they're out there in ranch houses with big dishes. But some others are right there, living there, even selling stuff, charging you an arm and a leg.' He shrugged. 'Some of them, you can come in for free and take all the pictures you want; but go near their kiva, man, you're in trouble. And then there's a couple so disorganized that they don't even think of making money. Just, whatever. Got a drink? Got a buck?' He crossed his arms and leaned back against the wall counter. Behind him, in front of

266

the antique mirror that lined the bar, was a display of expensive malt liquors, most of which Mark had never heard of. 'It's all over the map,' he said.

Mark had liked Albuquerque better, what he saw of it on the day he spent there before he caught his plane to Lincoln. People were living there anyway, a mix of people, and the sense of high tourism was absent. It made him think of the valley again, the valley as it had been when he got there and as it was now. It made him think of all that was for sale in Napa, of all the big arguments about the wineries: should they be selling caps and T-shirts and jars of mustard? What corrupted? What was sufficiently connected to the making of wine to belong?

He was grateful, he thought, to be just a grower, a manager. Life was easier when you stayed free of those questions. He sold grapes. He sold his knowledge of the soil, of farm machinery and trellising techniques and pruning and irrigation and the timing of things. He didn't have to think about the tourists, about the *presentation* of wine, about the art on the labels, about whether aprons were a wine-related product or not. He was removed from all that. It was true that he didn't very often anymore have dirt under his nails or embedded in his skin, dirt that you couldn't wash off, dirt that said, I'm a farmer first of all. But he was a farmer. It was all he'd ever been really good at. And he was glad of his work.

★   ★   ★

Mark thought of this again as he drove back up the length of the valley in the light late-November rain, coming home from his trip. He passed the expensive restaurants, the new, huge wineries, and he thought about it, what he'd made of his life, what he'd done. When he'd come to the valley, there had been perhaps twenty-five vineyards. Now there were at least three hundred, and scores of other small, private ranches that made their own wines or sold grapes to wineries or a little of both. He had contributed to that. That was his job, and he had done it well. But land, which had cost three or four thousand dollars an acre when he and Eva arrived, cost forty or fifty thousand now, and the price would only go higher. His clients, even the ones with the smallest ranches, were rich, and there were things about most rich people that bothered him, that he didn't like to deal with.

Still, the work was the same, and the pleasure of moving around with the workers, of laboring beside them, was always there. He didn't much like the paperwork or the sense of being on call when a machine broke down, when someone didn't like the way an irrigation pond looked from the back deck; but he liked his ability to fix things, to make things right. The soil, the machines, the tools, the seasonal patterns of work — these were all the same, were familiar and comfortable to him.

Was he happy? He thought of what his mother had said, that she was *content*: her self-satisfaction in announcing that. He hadn't liked her in that moment, he realized now. She had said what she did because she didn't want to try, because she'd always been afraid to try. She never wanted to risk changing anything. And that probably connected to her unresponsiveness when he mentioned Eva's name. His saying Eva's name, his reintroducing Eva, was asking his mother to acknowledge or comment on the risk he was taking. To react to it somehow. And she wouldn't, or she couldn't — because that kind of effort, that kind of risk and hope, was something she'd turned away from in her own life.

But he wanted more from his life than she did from hers. He wanted happiness. If Eva would come back to him, he thought, he could be happy with his life. That's what he wanted to try for, wanted to risk himself for.

But he knew — he had seen it when they were last together — how hard it would be for Eva to want to try that. Even without John and his death, it would have been hard for her. How could she trust him again, or want him? When he'd been such an unreliable jerk? He had to give her all the time she needed; he had to let her be in charge.

He fisted his hand and punched the steering wheel. This was it. He'd been thinking of Eva the whole time he'd been gone, he'd been planning various ways they might have their next encounter, but now, no: he decided now that he wouldn't call her. He'd wait in this way too. He'd let her call him when she was ready.

The valley was wider now, and beautiful in spite of being at its darkest, at its most drained of color. Some of the lower hills were green with pine, some were rolling bare fields studded with the sculpted trees that looked like the ones you saw in the background of Renaissance paintings. The rhythm of the vineyard rows planted across the valley floor was deeply, humanly satisfying. This was home. This was where he wanted to be. With Eva.

With Eva and Emily and Daisy and Theo.

★ ★ ★

A few nights later, a Tuesday, he saw Eva with a date at the movies in town. He was there with a date himself — or at any rate, with an amiable, sexy woman he had slept with occasionally. Lorie Douglas. She slept with a lot of people occasionally. She was known for it. But they were just friends now. Each of them called the other when he wanted company, wanted a partner to do something with. Lorie had called him last night and asked him to meet her at the theater. They planned to have a drink afterward and compare Thanksgivings. She had spent twelve hours stuck in the airport in Columbus, Ohio, when her connecting flight couldn't land at O'Hare. 'So you'll be buying, my friend,' she said. 'I'm *owed*, by someone, and it might as well be you.'

He and Lorie had already bought tickets and popcorn and had taken their seats when Eva and the man she was with walked past them and moved into a row about halfway down the theater. They hadn't seen him, Mark was pretty sure. While he and Lorie talked, he watched Eva. She was attentive to this guy, a large, solid man, almost totally bald. You might even have said she was flirty — Mark recognized the behavior: the too-bright laughter, the toss of her hair. He watched them during the film too; he had a clear sight line down to the back of their heads. Twice she leaned over to whisper to this guy, something she used to hate when others did it, something she had chastised him for in the deep past.

When the movie ended, Mark stood up immediately. He wanted to get out of there, to get Lorie out of there, before Eva saw them.

But it wasn't going to work. Lorie was in no rush. She was fussing around, she'd lost something — her scarf. She bent down, flipping seats up around her. He was still standing there when Eva and the man she was with walked past, up the aisle. Mark was facing away, so he wasn't sure Eva had spotted him, but he looked over at them just before they reached the open door to the lobby, and Eva turned to him and waved. She was smiling, mischievous.

He wasn't certain what to do about this. Over the next week, over the next several weeks, he pondered it. Should he call her? Should he explain himself when he saw her?

But he didn't see her, that was the problem. Daisy was busy with work and basketball and the last tests and papers before the Christmas holidays, so she canceled several visits with him. He did call Eva once, but when Theo summoned her to the phone, he was suddenly confused about what it was he wanted to explain, what he needed to tell her; and he made up a question about the girls' schedule over Christmas to cover himself.

He felt that everything he'd worked for over the past year was slipping away from him. He felt powerless to help himself.

Ten days before Christmas, there was a sudden return of warm weather. The sun was low and buttery, the air was soft. That afternoon, Mark stopped into the cantina for a beer after work — Amy had long since left her job there. The door was open to the sunny street, the bar was noisy and friendly, a warm breeze rode through every now and then. There were guys playing pool, Mexicans, and they kept feeding the jukebox and dancing around the table to the Latin music. Mark settled into the odd valley conversation at the bar, the combination of standard rough stuff about women ('You can't get pussy in the valley anymore, the whole place is too upscale for fucking around the way we used to') which veered suddenly to what would be sophisticated anywhere else, but here was just talk about farming: the nose on a certain wine, its bouquet, its rating in the last *Wine Spectator*. It always amused him, this incongruity.

He was listening, smiling, when he saw Eva walking slowly by — Eva and Theo. She was holding on to Theo's hand, her head bent down to hear what he was telling her.

Mark pushed his glass forward along with a five-dollar bill, and walked quickly to the door. He called her name. She stopped and turned. She smiled at him, the slow smile that caught his heart. Theo smiled at him.

He caught up to her and lightly kissed her cheek, touched Theo's head.

'How are you, Mark?' Eva asked. 'We haven't seen you forever.' They were going to the store, she said — her bookstore. She had just picked Theo up at day care, and now she was going to close up for the night. Theo was going to help her. 'Won't you, my sweet?'

Theo was carrying a small motorcycle in his hand. He wore a brightly colored backpack. 'Yah,' he said.

They talked about the amazing weather, the sense of blessing, as Eva put it, in the touch of the sun.

'Listen,' Mark said after a moment. He'd adjusted his pace to their amble. 'Remember that woman I was with?'

She frowned. 'What woman?'

'That woman, the one I was with at the movies when I saw you.'

'Oh! Well. Sort of.' She grinned at him. 'Not really.'

'Well. That was . . . ' He gestured uselessly. 'She was, just a friend.'

'Mark!' Eva stopped walking. Her hand rose to her chest. She saw his intention, what he was thinking. Something in it surprised her, clearly.

'Oh, Mark!' she said. 'But you see, I thought you understood. That's really, it's not, any of my business.' She smiled and lifted her hand dramatically. 'She could be your *paramour* . . . '

She saw something in his face and stopped. Her hand fell. When she spoke again, her voice had changed. 'Mark,' she said gently. She touched his arm, a light touch. 'It's truly *not* anymore — it isn't — my business.' She shook her head, her lips pressed together.

They were at the corner now, at the light. The walk signal came on, and Eva suddenly turned to Theo. 'Hold my hand, sweetie,' she said. Her voice had changed again. It was no-nonsense, strict.

What was it? what convergence? — the shift in Eva's tone, the presence of a man who might have been Theo's father, the car that swung suddenly around the corner — which of these made Theo remember, at last? Which made him look up at his mother and gravely announce, 'My dad *flew*.'

Standing next to her, lost, confused, Mark heard her breath rush in.

'That time he died, remember?' Theo said. Mark looked at him now. Theo was frowning, laboring. He was working to call it up. 'When my dad flew?'

And Eva sank to him suddenly, grasped his head, kissed him twice. 'Oh, darling,' she said. 'Yes! Yes he flew.' Her voice was thick with sorrow, alive with love for his memory.

'Like an angel, didn't he?' she said. 'He flew.'

13

Cleanly, sharply, his ankle broke. He heard it and felt it.

Up until the second it happened, he had thought he wouldn't fall, that he'd be able to catch himself, to hold on to the limb he was slipping from. He had been pruning, late in the afternoon, cutting off the low-hanging tree branches that were encroaching at the edge of a small vineyard he managed on a hillside above St. Helena. He had been sitting too precariously, as it turned out, on the branch he was sawing off. Now he was half lying on the ground below the tree.

Though his ankle hurt, he was surprised it didn't hurt more, that it was a pain he could bear. No, what was flooding his mind, even as he lay there waiting for the first wave of pain to ease, were images of how amazingly inconvenient this was going to be. Driving. Working. A big *how?* loomed. It can't be, he thought.

Maybe it was just a sprain. When the first pain had ebbed, he struggled to get up, keeping his weight on his good foot. His hands were muddy, his pants damp. He tried shifting his weight onto the other foot, his injured one, and knew instantly he was in trouble. It hurt like a sonofabitch. It was already swelling, he could feel it. There was no question of even hobbling to the truck.

He was standing at the edge of the vineyard, near a small stream that was running freely with thick brown water. It was dusk, perhaps a little after dusk, and he probably shouldn't have been in the tree by himself out here in the first place.

He tried hopping. The jounce sent the pain shooting into his ankle. And the ground was treacherous — too uneven to try getting around this way in any case. The truck was maybe sixty feet away, he had walked over here in a matter of seconds, a few strides; but it was going to take him a long time to get back to it. Gingerly, grimacing, he got down again to his hands and knees.

The earth was wet and rocky. His pants soaked through instantly. His hands and knees were chilled and wet. His ankle, dragging, shot pain when he slid that leg. Placing his knees was difficult, there were so many rocks. It was cold out, but he was very quickly in a sweat: fear of the pain, the pain itself, the effort it took to move forward slowly. He had to stop every three or four feet to let his body get ready to be hurt again, and it was dark — night — by the time he straightened his back and pulled himself to a standing position by his truck, holding on to the door handle. It had taken him almost an hour to get here.

He opened the cab and pulled himself up, using the steering wheel. In the seat, he slowly turned, moving his legs in. He sat there for some moments. He was so grateful to be in this familiar space — a kind of home — that he almost wept. He rested his head on his arms while he considered his next move.

He couldn't drive, that was clear. The foot and ankle were huge now and throbbing with pain. They were going to have to cut his boot off to treat him. Or he hoped they would. The idea they might slide it off came briefly to him in an image too excruciating to think about. In any case, he couldn't use his foot on the accelerator. He reached for the car phone and called Gracie.

Half an hour later, he was lying across the cab with his hurt leg elevated through the open window on the passenger side, his jacket resting under his calf where it touched the door. The emergency lights were blinking steadily, the engine was on, the heat high, and the radio, turned on softly, was bringing him news of Noriega's surrender, in Panama. He had unlaced his boot, and that had eased the pressure on his foot slightly.

Suddenly Gracie was there, in the passenger's-side window by his foot. She smiled in at him. She was wearing no makeup, and her big face looked girlish and sweet and infinitely welcome to him.

'Hey,' he said.

'Hey, yourself. You look entirely too comfortable for a man who just interrupted my dinner preparations.'

'Well, I'm not, if that makes it any better.'

'What's the plan?' she said.

'I don't know. You're the one who used to be a nurse. You tell me. The hospital, I guess.'

She was looking at the foot. 'This mother's big, huh?'

'It is. It's a big foot. Big-foot syndrome.'

She touched his ankle, delicately. Her face was concentrated, thoughtful. She looked up. 'You're sure it's broken.'

'*Oh yeah.*'

' 'Cause even a sprain could swell up like this.'

'No, it's broken. I heard it. I felt it.'

She was shaking her head, smiling ruefully. 'Markie, Markie, Markie,' she said.

'Help me out here, Gracie.'

'Okay. I'll come around that side, and you try to get yourself up. We'll go in my car, I think, so you can lie in back and keep it elevated.'

'Okay,' he said. He smiled. 'Boss.'

She disappeared, and he began, as slowly as he could, to pull his foot in, to sit up, to bring the leg over to the driver's side and turn his body to the front. Gracie was behind him now, he heard her through the closed window. 'Tell me when I can open the door.'

'*Okay,*' he said, and she did. He leaned forward. The night air was cold. His jacket had fallen out the window on the passenger side, and he told her this. She went around the truck again and retrieved it while he pushed the button to roll that window up, while he cut the engine.

It was silent suddenly, the sounds gone — the hum of the heater, the ticking rhythm of the warning lights, the muted radio.

Gracie was there again. 'Let me get my backseat set while you maneuver out of there,' she said. 'I'll use the coat for a cushion again. Mine too.' She moved away, struggling out of her jacket.

He was already feeling the increased pressure of the blood in his foot now that he'd lowered it. He turned completely, dangling his legs out the side of the truck, and then dropped down onto his good foot. 'Christ!' he said, bending over in shock.

Gracie heard him. 'Hold on, stay right there,' she called. When she came back, she lifted his arm around her shoulders and put her own arm around his waist. He could smell her hair, a Gracie smell. 'Now use me like a crutch,' she said. 'Stand on your good foot. Then all your weight on me and swing yourself forward. I'm a big dame, remember. Lean on me. We'll go slow.'

She *was* big, and she didn't buckle under his weight, but she grunted loudly with every step. It took six to get him to the open back door of her car. Then she stepped away from him and he laboriously crawled in. When he was on his back, wedged half sitting against the far door, she put his coat and her own, rolled up, on the seat. He stretched his leg out and rested it on them.

'You're an angel,' he said, as they pulled away.

'Not by a long shot, sweetie,' she said. 'But it's fine for you to pretend to think so.'

At the hospital, he waited.

He waited in a wheelchair in the emergency room with Gracie for his ankle to be X-rayed, and then, when the break had been revealed and discussed, he waited for the cast. He'd been drugged by then, though, and he was lying down in relative comfort in a space made private by curtains hanging from a curved track that encircled his bed. Outside this space, beyond it, he could hear the noises of other accidents, other catastrophes. Gracie sat in a chair next to him. When he came up from his doze, she set aside the copy of *People* magazine she'd brought from the waiting room, and smiled at him.

'What did I interrupt?' he asked.

'I told you. Dinner. Well, dinner preparations.'

'But what were you having? Let me imagine it.' Gracie was a famously good cook.

'Pork. A little roast. A nice pasta dish with white beans and wilted escarole. That was the plan anyway. Duncan'll have to have a sandwich, I guess.'

'He'll survive.' As soon as he'd said it, he worried that she would have heard his dislike of Duncan in his tone, in the remark itself.

'Oh, that's not the issue,' she said.

'What *is* the issue?' He sat up a little more. 'What issue?'

'Oh, I don't know,' she said. She made a face, an odd shape with her mouth: I don't want to talk about it. 'I was going to fix a nice dinner, that's all. Something's up, with Duncan. One of those . . . bumps, in matrimony.'

'Ah, those,' he said. He sank back on his pillow.

She grinned at him. 'So well known to you, my darling.'

He smiled weakly. It seemed to him that he drifted off for a while. When he came back, his mouth was dry. He licked his lips. 'What kind of bump?' he said.

She looked up from the magazine. 'Damned if

I know,' she said. 'Just, something's up. He's gone far, far away from little me.' She rolled her eyes, but he could hear the worry in her voice. 'I mean, the guy is unreadable anyway. But now it's like — he's unreadable in another fucking *language*.'

He laughed. And then sobered. After a minute, he asked, 'An affair, you think?'

She sighed. 'Maybe. Maybe something exactly that trite.'

'It never feels trite when you're in the midst.'

There was a silence. Mark shut his eyes.

'Didn't it, Mark? Didn't you know how dumb it was, how little it mattered, really?' He looked at her. She was earnestly asking.

'I didn't,' he said. He was thinking of Amy, of how much he had wanted her, while never not loving Eva. He closed his eyes again. After a while, he said, 'If it is an affair, Gracie, what will you do?'

She pulled her chin in and stared at him. '*Do?*' she asked. 'What do you mean?'

'I mean, will you leave him?'

'Why would I leave him? I love him.'

'You left him before.'

She smiled. 'I love him better now.' She turned back to her magazine.

Mark drifted off, woke again. 'So what *will* you do?' he asked.

'I will *not know*, darling. I will assiduously not know, something you didn't allow Eva.' She started to read again.

'You would rather not know?' he asked.

'Are you serious?' Now she folded the

281

magazine and set it down. 'Why should I want to know?'

'Because. To love someone, you need to know them.'

'I know him. I know Duncan.' She smiled ruefully. 'That's hard enough. I don't need to know everything he does, too.'

'But how can you love him — really love him — how can you say you do, if you don't know everything he does?'

'I know *him*,' she protested. 'I know his . . . capacity. His capacities. I know what he's capable of.'

Mark thought for a while. He thought of Gracie and Duncan, and himself and Eva. He said, 'But what if he *wanted* you to know?'

'Why would he want that?'

He felt almost dizzy from the drug, but he struggled to say what he meant. 'So you would *know* him.'

'But I do know him, I just said that.'

'But he might feel you didn't, unless you knew certain things about him.'

'He would be wrong then. He would be, I would say, indulging himself.'

Mark lay still, resting. His eyes closed and opened, closed and opened. Some time passed. Someone dropped something metallic outside the curtain and loudly defamed all the members of the holy family.

He could feel Gracie lean forward. He turned to focus on her. She was resting her arms on the bed. She said, 'Look, Mark, we know we were talking about you and Eva. I'm not saying you meant to hurt her or you were deliberately cruel. But don't you think that what you did, finally, was selfish? Oh, I don't mean the sleeping around. We all know *that* was selfish.' Her head bobbed in agreement with herself. 'But you wanted some fucking drama, of estrangement and reconciliation. You wanted some recognition of *your* drama. Of what you had renounced or something.' She sat back. 'But sometimes happiness is . . . less dramatic than that. Is just keeping your mouth shut and making the pork and pasta for dinner. Is putting one foot in front of the other and going forward, day after day.' She caught at a strand of hair that had pulled loose from her clip. 'Is a kind of preemptive forgiveness, I suppose, that doesn't need the drama of the instance.'

He was shaking his head. 'But it's the particular, the instance that . . . '

'That what?'

'Needs forgiveness.'

'No, no, no, no, no. It's the particular *person* that needs forgiveness. You.' She tapped his chest. '*You*, you sorry son of a bitch. Not so much what you did, but that you did it.'

'I'm too tired for this, Gracie. I don't get it.'

She sighed. 'Oh, forget it anyway,' she said. 'You're a good person, Mark. You just keep barking up the wrong trees. And mostly I'm talking about Duncan anyway. And Duncan and I are going to be fine.'

The next time he rose from his druggy sleep, they didn't talk. She insisted on reading him a short article on Mia Farrow and Woody Allen, on

283

their ideal relationship, distant and close at the same time.

★ ★ ★

It was Gracie who thought of having the girls come and live with him for the rest of the time Emily was home on her Christmas break. He didn't know what she said to them, he didn't know whether she had to pressure them or whether they came willingly, but they showed up the next day, in his truck, which they'd retrieved — Emily was driving. They carried in suitcases and their backpacks and the bags of groceries Gracie had helped them buy. He would never have asked them — he probably wouldn't even have thought of it — but he was grateful for their arrival, for their noise and attention.

Still, it made him feel his life was not his own. And that feeling only intensified when, on Sunday night, he called Angel, who'd been his work boss for six years, and asked for his help. The next day, Angel pulled into Mark's driveway in his old Chevrolet and parked. Mark hobbled out and they both got into the truck, Angel in the driver's seat.

And that was how they worked it. Angel drove him to client meetings, to get supplies, from vineyard to vineyard, to the wineries. At first, Mark tried to get out of the truck at the vineyards, he tried to move around at each site to see what the issues and problems were; but it was clear that this wasted everyone's time. So after the first day, it was Angel who got out, who checked the work and reported to him as he sat in the truck. Mark asked questions, he made suggestions and requests, and then Angel walked back out into the vineyards and passed the orders along. This meant Mark lost the use of his best worker, which was an enormous loss, but Angel had called down to his hometown in Mexico and found him two extra workers, second or third cousins of his, who would be up in a week or so. In the meantime, work was a little slow anyway. If he'd had to pick a season to break his ankle, Mark thought, the only better one would have been late fall — November and December.

It seemed to him as though he ought to come home at the end of the day with almost as much energy as he'd had when he started it since he'd done nothing but sit on his ass the whole time, but he was exhausted when Angel dropped him off each night and he hobbled in. And so he was glad for the girls, for their noisy presence in the kitchen, for the food they made, even for their arguments and routines at dinner.

After they'd cleaned the kitchen, they went their separate ways. Emily almost always went out. Sometimes with female friends, sometimes with a young man, but either way, she left. For Daisy, school had started again after the Christmas break. Every weekday night, she spread her books on the dining room table and worked, talking only occasionally to Mark. For the first couple of nights, Mark watched TV with the volume turned low, but he could tell this bothered her, so finally he turned it off and read, slowly but with some pleasure, a novel Eva had sent over with the girls, *The Mambo Kings Play Songs of Love*, one of a box she'd put together for him. She'd tucked a note into it, on top. 'Now that you have so much time on your hands, maybe there's enough to work your way through these. I think you'll like them.'

Eva. He was almost grateful for the accident because it made a sensible context for her kindness to him. Her pity, as he felt it. He couldn't forget her hand on his arm in consolation in the moment before Theo spoke of John and she knelt, so grateful and excited to have John remembered as he'd been, even as he'd been, dying; to have Theo begin finally to grasp what it was he'd lost.

'Like an angel.' She'd said this, of John, and Mark had understood by her voice, by her eagerness and joy, that she still loved John. That anything he could offer her would simply not be of enough importance, of enough use to her.

* * *

For the next week and a half, until Emily went back to Wesleyan, the girls had a kind of routine. Eva or Gracie helped them, writing out shopping lists, making suggestions for meals when they ran out of ideas. Only once were things thrown off, when Daisy arrived late one afternoon after a basketball practice, and Emily had to do everything herself. He heard from Emily about this, partly because she was going out that evening. He tried to excuse Daisy.

'Dad,' she said. 'This is not a *little* late.'

'Well, maybe she had trouble getting a ride home.' They were already eating — grilled mozzarella cheese sandwiches with tapenade and basil leaves, and a soup Gracie had brought over.

'She said she had a ride. She was supposed to have arranged everything ahead of time. She could have called, at least.'

'Well, it's not as though it killed you, Em. Gracie made the soup.'

'That's not the point, Dad.'

'What is the point, then?'

'Just, she said she'd be here.'

He looked at her, her pretty small face, so full of indignation now. Maybe they shouldn't have gotten her the braces, he thought. They made everything about her too regular: the pretty dark eyes, the perfect small nose, the even, straight teeth. 'You're not her mother, Emily,' he said. 'Don't get all bent out of shape.'

'But you *are* her father, aren't you? Why aren't you at least a *little* bent out of shape?'

'I don't know. I guess it just doesn't matter that much to me.'

'Well, it should.'

Should it? he wondered. Was this something Eva would have worried about, would have felt required discussion? Or even, perhaps, punishment?

It was going on seven when Daisy showed up. He was reading and Emily was already gone, picked up by the guy she seemed to have settled on to amuse her on this visit home. George somebody. He seemed years younger than Emily

287

to Mark: a goofy kid with running shoes as big as milk cartons on his feet, and a strange dent in his hair that Mark assumed was from a baseball cap.

He hadn't heard Daisy's approach; she was just suddenly there, letting herself in at the front door. The dogs, startled out of sleep, barked halfheartedly.

'Hey,' he said, when she stepped into the hall.

She was flushed. Her long hair was wild, tangled. She looked sexual to him, her lips reddened from the cold. 'Hey, Dad,' she said. 'Sorry I'm late.' She turned away, taking her jacket off. The dogs had padded over to her and were milling around, hoping for attention.

'Yeah, we missed you at dinner. Em left a sandwich for you.'

'Oh. I could have made it.'

'Well, she was already doing ours.'

She went into the dining room and set her books on the table.

'I didn't hear the car,' he called.

'Oh. Well. Natalie dropped me at the road, and I walked in from there. She was in a big hurry.'

'I see.'

Daisy went into the kitchen, the dogs following. He heard the clunk of dishes. The refrigerator door opened. In a few minutes, she appeared in the living room, carrying a plate and a glass of milk.

'Emily was pretty pissed,' he said. 'She left the dishes for you.'

'I saw.' She sat down opposite him, set her plate on the coffee table, and picked up her sandwich. The dogs were sitting at her feet. They

288

watched her hand, holding her food, with rapt attention.

'How was practice?' he asked.

She shrugged. The long strands of cheese stretched from her mouth to the sandwich, and she didn't answer until she had broken them off and brought the ends to her mouth. 'Okay,' she said, chewing.

'He's working you pretty hard, for a girls' high school team.'

She chewed a moment more, and swallowed. 'We don't mind.'

In the night, he waked. Something had broken into his sleep. For a minute he thought it was Emily, arriving home — some noise outside — but that wasn't it. It was inside, somewhere in the house. His door was shut, but he sat up in bed and listened, hard.

It was weeping. One of his daughters was weeping. It must have been Daisy — he was pretty sure Emily wasn't back yet. He sat and listened. He thought perhaps he should go to her, and then decided he shouldn't. The weeping, or his ability to hear it, was intermittent. After a while, it stopped, and he lay down again and went back to sleep.

At some point later, a car waked him. He looked at the clock. It was two-thirty. He lay there awhile, and then he had to take a piss. He sat up and grabbed the crutches, made his way to the bathroom in the dark. There was a small, high window next to the toilet, opening out onto the driveway and the backyard — the cement pad, the shed, the fig tree. After he flushed, he turned his head and looked out through it. He could see the car, George Somebody's car. The windows were silvery with fog. Shapes moved inside, they pushed rhythmically against the driver's-side window. Mark knew he should turn away, but he didn't. He stood leaning on his crutches and watched for a while, feeling a response that combined arousal and shame.

These were his daughters' lives, their real lives. The deep, submerged nighttime world of love and pain and sex. And he knew nothing at all about it. Nothing. Where had he been living? Why hadn't he understood any of this before? Or cared to understand?

He'd left it to John, he thought. All of this. Because he didn't *want* to understand this. Because he wouldn't have known — because he *didn't* know — how to be a father to them through all this. That was it, wasn't it? It was why he had stayed in bed when Daisy was weeping, why he couldn't begin to imagine what she was weeping about. It was why he was standing here in a kind of prurient shock, watching Emily fuck this unattractive idiot.

When they were little, when it was easy to love them, he had loved his daughters. He'd entered their games, he'd roughhoused with them, he'd been tender to them. He'd loved being their father then. But now, now that they were young women, he felt confused about how to do it, not ready yet to be a parent to them.

'Not *ready*,' he muttered as he turned away from the window, full of contempt for himself.

The next Saturday night, he and Daisy went to
Eva's house — Emily was out on her last date
with George. Eva was having a small party, what
she called a post-holiday party. Gracie and
Duncan, and Maria and Fletcher were there, and
several of Eva's neighbors had been invited too
— the Bauers, the Fields.

When they arrived, Eva asked Daisy to help
serve wine and drinks, and she began to move in
and out of the butler's pantry, carrying glasses to
the adults. She was wearing a white blouse and a
black skirt and heels — high heels. She had
lipstick on, which he'd noted in the car on the
way over. She looked years older than she usually
did. And lovely, he would have said. Somehow
the stillness, the heaviness that had seemed part
of who she was when she was younger had lifted,
who knew how or why. Now a kind of nervous
animation livened her face, made it striking.

Everyone was milling around, greeting one
another, talking about their holidays. There was
much discussion too of the Fields' dog, a
chocolate lab, who had had puppies three days
before. Naomi Field invited Theo to come over
and see them, and somehow, within the first
fifteen minutes or so of the party, it was decided
that the whole group would make a pilgrimage.
Mark, who had just laboriously made his way up
the front steps, who had gratefully sunk into one
of Eva's overstuffed chairs, leaning his crutches
against its arm, who had just been served a
drink, shook his head *no* when Eva ducked back

in to the living room to ask if he wasn't coming along.

She raised her eyebrows at him.

'It's just too much work, Eva.' He held his hands up: This. Me. Life.

'Okay,' she said. She left.

He heard them all troop out the kitchen door; he heard their voices and laughter crossing the backyard. He sat back in his chair and drank his wine. The living room was picked up for the party, the usual books and objects put away somewhere. Eva's tree was still up, by the front windows. It was strung with small white lights, and decorated, as always, with old small toys of the children's — tiny stuffed animals and dolls, little cars. He remembered the ritual of decoration, and Eva's insistence on certain ways of doing things. It had irritated him occasionally. Now he felt sorry for himself for having lost this, too.

When they returned, they stayed in the kitchen with Eva, talking, as people often did at her house while she cooked and assembled the meal. They had forgotten him. He'd have to get up and go in there in a minute. He heard someone in the butler's pantry behind him again, opening the small refrigerator there. Daisy, no doubt. It wasn't Eva. She was still in the kitchen — he could hear her talking.

And then he heard Duncan's voice behind him too, in the butler's pantry, pitched low, for Daisy alone to hear. 'Perhaps you could pour me a glass of gin while you're pouring. Gin lightly touched with vermouth.'

There was what sounded like a too-long silence. Then Daisy said, 'Well, perhaps I could. But would I? Will I?' Her voice was light, teasing.

Mark was electrified, suddenly.

'Let me rephrase, then,' Duncan said. 'Under what conditions would you consent to pour me a glass of gin, Daisy, my dove?'

After a moment, Daisy said slowly, 'Well, first of all, you'd have to say please.'

Mark's heart was pounding. But why? None of this was so remarkable. Daisy had spoken in something like this slightly snotty way even to him.

'Ah, how could I have forgotten?' There was a silence, and Mark had the conviction — he would have sworn it — that Duncan was touching Daisy. 'Please.' This was spoken softly, like a caress. 'Please, Daisy.'

Daisy was almost whispering when she answered him: 'And then you'd have to say, 'Pretty please.'' There was something so sexual, so breathless, and to Mark, so horrifying in this that his hands lifted involuntarily.

Duncan's voice was low too when it came, intimate. 'Pretty please, Daisy.' Mark waited for a long moment. '*Pretty* please,' Duncan said. 'Will you?'

Mark was up before he thought about it, and in his sudden motion, he knocked his crutches off the edge of the chair where he'd leaned them. They clattered to the floor. He picked them up laboriously, and set them under his arms. By the time he'd hobbled around the corner, there was no one in the butler's pantry; and when he entered the kitchen, Daisy was standing with her back to him, filling Naomi Field's wineglass from the bottle she carried, and Duncan was leaning against the counter, seemingly listening to Gracie talking to Harry Field.

'Oh, Mark! What you missed!' Eva cried, spotting him. 'They were adorable! Enough to make you believe in the possibility of perfection in this life.'

His heart was still pounding in his ears, his breath still felt short, but he smiled at his ex-wife and said, 'Well, that's something I'd like to believe in. I'm sorry to have missed it, then.'

14

Daisy and Mark were the first to leave — he was tired, he said, and Daisy didn't mind, she was ready to go. They drove in silence, Daisy at the wheel of the truck, laboriously shifting when she had to. She was glad to get out of St. Helena so she could just drive.

Her thoughts were jumbled, moving around fast, partly because of the two glasses of wine she'd had. She was thinking of the events of the evening. Of Duncan and the terrible fight they'd had a few days before. Then of his touch tonight, his hand moving up her leg under her skirt in the pantry — thank God they'd heard Mark in the living room and gotten out of there before he saw anything!

She was thinking of something Andrea Bauer had said to her — that she looked ravishing tonight. *Ravishing*, Daisy thought, and smiled. Then she was thinking of the puppies, helpless and dependent, curled blindly together against their mother, and of how they smelled, sweet and slightly urinous, when she picked them up and held them. She was thinking of how glad she was that she no longer had to invent things to talk about with Mark. Of how she'd gotten used to being with him, these last few weeks. How she liked being with him, her handsome father. She looked over at him, and met his gaze, looking back. His face seemed sad, somehow. His hair was a little too long, curling over his collar.

He said, 'Know what I think, Daisy?'

She smiled. 'You know, Dad, I can't say I do.'

'I think we should make this arrangement permanent.'

'What arrangement?'

'This one. Where you live with me.'

She was startled. It was inconceivable. Where was this coming from? She had a room, a life, at home. She stared at him for a few seconds. He was watching her steadily. 'Have you talked to Eva about this?' she asked. 'Is this something you guys worked out together?'

'Not a word. I swear.' He seemed to be thinking for a moment. He said, 'But would that be so bad, if Eva and I were concerned about you? Talked about you?'

'But why *would* you be concerned about me?'

'Why.' His voice was toneless.

She looked over at him. 'Yes. *Duh*. Why?'

Again that steady gaze back. He didn't say anything. Then he looked away from her, out the window. His hand came up, his chin rested on it. His crutches, riding between them, had slid over and were resting on her arm, she was suddenly aware of their touch.

'I mean, I'm doing fine in school. I help out at the store.'

He said, without looking at her, 'There were the piano lessons.'

'Well, yeah.'

'*Yeah*,' he said.

So Eva had told him. They *had* talked.

'Why did you skip them?' he asked.

'I already discussed this with Mom.' She had lied. She had said she hated the lessons, that they bored her, that she'd cut them to have more time for basketball. Eva's eyes had darkened, she knew this was bullshit; but she hadn't argued, she hadn't contradicted Daisy.

'So I *should* be talking about you with Eva, if I want to know what's going on.'

'That's not what I meant.'

They drove in silence for a while, through the green light at the end of Lincoln Avenue, past the lighted gas station and the drive-in. Then it was night again. 'Coming back to my idea,' he said.

She didn't answer.

'The arrangement.'

She was suddenly aware that he seemed nervous, maybe because he was, after all, asking her for something. 'I don't know, Dad,' she said. She was trying to make her voice kind. 'It seems . . . wacky.'

'Lots of kids whose parents are divorced live with their fathers.' He was looking out the window again. Maybe he could see the moon out there. Everything seemed touched with its silvery light.

'But I haven't,' she said. 'I've lived with Mom. I mean, it would be bizarre to change at this point.' Though Daisy was thinking about it, just trying to imagine how it might be.

'But maybe it would be good for you to change.'

She pulled up at the light at Petrified Forest Road and put the truck in neutral. She looked

297

over at him. 'Good, why? Why good?'

'I don't know. I think maybe you and Eva have more or less . . . run out of gas, in terms of your relationship.'

'God! What does *that* mean?'

'I suppose, that there's not much communication between you.'

'Oh yeah. And there's, like, *so* much between you and me.' The light turned green, and she put the truck in first, grinding the gears slightly.

After a moment he said, 'There's more, I think, than there is between you and Eva. And there might be even more than that. Sometimes we really talk.'

She snorted.

'This is a stupid idea? Is that what you're telling me?'

'Well, it's just like we've *really talked* about three times in my life.'

'But maybe that's 'cause we don't live together.'

She didn't answer. She couldn't even believe, in some ways, that Mark was serious.

'Who *do* you talk to, Daisy?' he asked, after a minute or two had passed. 'Who do you let into your very private Daisy-ness?'

There was something almost sarcastic in his voice, and she looked over at him, hurt and startled. He was sitting back, his arm along the back of the seat, looking at her appraisingly.

'*Dad,*' she said, a complaint, a request.

Then they were passing Tubbs Lane. She remembered to signal, and she pulled into the long dirt drive Mark shared with his neighbors.

Under the beam of the truck's lights, the jackrabbits, with their absurdly long ears, froze, then scuttled off to either side. Daisy had to steer carefully to avoid the ruts and potholes left by the rains. The truck jolted and rattled. She turned into her father's driveway and pulled up on the cement pad. She stopped the engine. They sat a moment.

'Why is this coming up now?' she asked. She had turned in her seat to look at her father, pushing the crutches back toward him.

He lifted his hands. 'You've been living with me. I like it. I'd like more of it. I like you.'

She made a gesture, dismissing this.

'What? You don't believe me?'

'Oh, sure, Dad. And what about when you can drive again and I'm living with you and Emily is gone and you want to resume your *dating* life again. Where is that going to leave me?'

His mouth opened; she heard his breath draw in. Then he said, 'I think we should both try skipping the dating life for a while. That would be my plan, anyway.' His voice was neutral, careful.

'That's like a ... someone who drinks, promising to go on the wagon.'

'Speak for yourself.'

'Who, me? I don't *have* a dating life, Dad.'

'Then what would you call it?' He leaned forward a little now.

'Call what?' She was aware of the dogs barking in the house, a distant hysteria.

'Your social life,' he said. 'Your social interests.'

299

She made a face. 'I think you have me confused with some other daughter of yours.'

'I'm not confusing you with anyone, Daisy. I'm concerned about you.'

She hated this. She hated that word. She hated the way his face looked, so intent on her, so *serious*. She said, 'The dogs are barking.'

'Fuck the dogs!' His fist hit the dash on the first word. 'Talk to me!' He was almost yelling. He was ugly.

She had jumped when his fist made its noise. After a few seconds, she was able to yell back, 'I don't *want* to talk to you! I don't want to talk to anyone! I have nothing to talk to you about.'

'*I* want to talk to you, though!'

Daisy got out of the truck and slammed the door behind her. She crossed the cement pad and walked the few steps to the back door in the moonlight. She opened it, and the dogs streamed out past her. Before she started into the dark house, she looked back and saw Mark struggling with his crutches, the dogs jumping around him.

She crossed the rooms around the familiar black shapes of the furniture without stumbling, went into her room — her room and Emily's — and slammed that door too.

In a minute or two he was there, outside it. 'Daisy?' he said.

She didn't answer.

'Open up, Daisy.'

'I'm tired!' she said loudly. 'I'm trying to sleep. Go away.'

The door opened. He stood there a moment, shifting his crutches around; she could see his shape in the faint light of the door's rectangle. He came in slowly. He lowered himself laboriously onto Emily's bed, facing Daisy. In the dark she was more aware of him physically than she'd been before — his size, the sound of his breathing as he sat there. She lay still. The moonlight came filtered into the room from the window behind him. She couldn't see his face at all.

'I wanted this to be positive, Daisy,' he said. He sounded almost hoarse. 'I wanted it to be — that I want you with me. That I think you need a father, and I want to be your father.'

She made a noise, dismissive and rude.

'That's fair,' he said. 'I know I haven't been there for you.'

Been there for me, Daisy thought. How corny.

'But that's what I'd like to change. I want a chance, I want you to give me a chance, to make a difference in your life.'

'Don't you think it's a little late for that?'

'It seems it might be. But maybe not. I'm hoping not. I'd like to help you.'

This all seemed familiar to Daisy, maddening. 'What does that mean, *help me*?'

'Well, it seems you've gone about . . . making your own life, without me or your mother, in ways that I think — ' He stopped, as if waiting for the right words to come to him. He looked away, and for a moment she saw his profile against the window. Then he turned back to her. He was almost whispering. 'In ways that seem . . . really dangerous to me, Daze. Really . . . not good.'

What did he know? Had Emily mentioned the money to him? That would be just like her, to let it drop somehow. Her big *concern* about her troubled younger sister. 'Whatever's not good in my life is something I can fix myself.'

'I'm not so sure of that.'

'Well, tough. I am.'

One of the dogs — it was Henry — came into the room, his paws clicking on the tile floor, his tail swinging. Mark reached out to touch him for a moment. Then he drew his hand back. The dog sat.

'Daisy,' Mark said. 'Let me say that I think Duncan. Duncan is . . . a bad choice for you.'

Daisy felt her heart stop. It seemed she might have made a noise.

'I know you might . . . ' Mark cleared his throat. 'I think what you might feel is that you need someone.' He was speaking haltingly. 'What I see, what I think I understand, is how much you needed someone. And you know, Eva is so sad right now, and I've been. The way I've been . . . you know *me*. But Duncan. To get involved with Duncan. I don't know how far it's gone, but — '

'I don't know what you're talking about.' Daisy was trying to make her voice steady, sure, categorical, but it didn't sound that way to her.

'Don't you, Daisy.'

'No.'

There was a long silence between them, in which they could hear a coyote howling, far in the distance; and then, a moment or two later, in

302

nervous response, Mark's neighbor's cattle lowing.

'Maybe *he* would,' Mark said. His voice had gone cold. 'Maybe Duncan would know what I'm talking about.'

'I don't know why.'

'Why what?'

'Why he'd *know*,' she said sarcastically.

'Don't jerk me around, Daisy,' he snapped.

'Who's jerking who around?' she said. 'You start off asking me to live with you because you *want to get to know me*,' her voice mocked the idea, 'and you end up accusing me . . . of some sort of . . . relationship with Gracie's husband.'

'They're not unconnected,' he said flatly. 'And that's some of the point, surely. That he *is* Gracie's husband.'

Daisy didn't answer.

'Shall I call him?' Mark said.

'Do what you want.'

'I'll call him then,' he said.

'Fine.'

'Maybe he's still at the party.'

'Maybe.'

When she didn't say anything more, he got up. Her eyes had become accustomed to the dim light in the room. She could see him clearly, hunched on the crutches, making his way to the door. She heard him, the dull plunk of the crutches, sometimes not quite in unison. A lamp went on in the living room, and then she heard the faint tonal clicking sound of the push buttons being worked on the phone. The dog yawned and put his head on the bed near her.

303

And suddenly her father's voice, loud: 'Eva? Eva, it's Mark! No, we're home. We're fine. Yeah. No. No. I just wanted . . . is Duncan still there? Yeah. Well, I just wanted to talk to him for a minute. Yeah. I'll wait.'

Daisy was up now, she crossed to her desk and picked up the phone. She could hear the noise of the party, people talking — someone close to the phone said, 'But you never gave one to *me*' — and then Duncan's voice suddenly on the line. 'This is Duncan. Is it Mark?'

'Hang up, Dad,' she said in a low voice.

Duncan said, 'Daisy?' He sounded startled. When the extension clicked off, Daisy hung up too, just as Duncan was speaking her name again.

She heard her father coming back to her room. He stood in the doorway, a dark silhouette against the living room light.

She turned at the desk to face him. 'What were you going to do?' she asked defiantly. 'Beat him up?'

'I might have,' he said. 'Depending.'

'Depending on what?'

'Depending on what he said. On what I understood about where things stood between the two of you.'

'He's very strong,' Daisy said; and this was the closest she would ever come to acknowledging the affair to her father, this knowledge of Duncan's body, and its power.

'Well, that would only have made it more pleasurable then,' Mark said. He sat down on Emily's bed again, again facing her. She was still

304

standing at the desk, her arms folded. He watched her for a long time without speaking.

'So,' she said finally. 'I'll live with you.'

'If Eva says it's all right.' He was nodding.

After a moment, she thought to say, 'Will you tell Eva? About . . . Duncan?'

'No. No, I won't tell her,' he said. Then his body straightened, he was taller. 'Did you think I would? Unless you agreed? There's no *deal* here, Daisy. You don't need to come live with me to buy my silence.'

'No, Dad. That's not what I meant. I didn't mean that.'

He sounded exhausted when he spoke again. 'I want you to come because I think we need each other. I think you need me.'

After a long moment, Daisy said in a quiet voice, 'I don't need anyone.'

He looked at her sharply. 'You needed Duncan. That's about the worst thing that anyone could say about me as a father.'

'I *didn't*, 'need' him.'

'Ah, no.' There was an odd smile on his face. 'You chose him, freely. Of all the people in the world, you decided, quite logically, that the warmhearted, the generous, the . . . expansive Duncan Lloyd was the very guy to be your . . . your best friend. Your pal.'

'Okay, Dad.'

He groaned, suddenly, and shook his head quickly from side to side. His face, in the light falling in from the living room, looked old to her, seamed.

'What *will* you say to Eva then?' she asked

after a few moments had passed.

'*I* don't know.' His hand lifted, ran through his hair. 'Maybe the truth.'

'What do you mean, the truth?' She heard the fear in her own voice.

'The truth about *me*, Daisy.' He smiled, sadly. 'The truth only about me. That I want to be your father, somehow, in a way I haven't been. And I'll just ask her to give me that chance.' He pulled his crutches up to his chin. After a moment he said, 'Maybe it would help if you told her you wanted to.'

'Okay,' she said.

'You don't have to.'

'No,' she said. 'I will.'

'It's just . . . It will raise fewer flags, fewer questions, I think, if it's something you want too. Or *say* you want.'

Daisy looked down at her folded arms in her white blouse, at her hands, resting on her own elbows. She was wearing the bracelet her father had given her for her fifteenth birthday, the one he'd forgotten about.

She knew what this would mean, agreeing to this. She knew that part of what her father was asking for was that she give up Duncan. She had felt it would be impossible for her to give up Duncan, to give up sex, to give up the sense of power he gave her. But she couldn't have guessed that this was the way the choice would come to her. That it would be her father. That he would be *asking* her for something. That she would be turning from Duncan to something else that would have arrived in her life, that would change it, in ways she couldn't begin to guess at. 'I want it,' she said softly.

This was so costly to Daisy, acknowledging this to herself, and to him — she had the sense of it as a gift she was making him, an expensive, precious gift — that it was a moment before she even thought about his response, about what she might be expecting him to say back to her.

But he didn't answer, and he didn't answer, and when she looked up at him and saw his face in the half-light falling in from the living room, it was transformed by what she could only have described — did describe, years later to Dr. Gerard — as anguish. She felt she was looking into his soul. It was as if everything superficial was stripped away, and she was seeing her father, her real father, for the first time.

15

E-mail, the telephone, this is how they stay in touch now, they live so far apart from each other. Daisy thinks of their communication as a kind of network, a spider's web, a sociogram, laid over the entire *U.S. of A.*, zinging with news that engenders more news.

Emily writes to Daisy from Phoenix about her two-year-old son, Gideon. She makes fun of her own nearly rabid devotion to him, she calls him 'The Little Prince.' She says that her brain has turned to hominy, 'whatever that is. I can't remember anything.' Except that, inadvertently, she's memorized entire children's books, and can summon them whole if need be — 'and unbelievably to me, Daze, need *does* be, from time to time.'

She worries that when she has the new baby, due in six months, she will not be able to love Gideon as well as she does now. Or love the new baby as well as she has loved Gideon.

Sometimes I think of Eva and Mark and how careless they seemed about us, how they were just happy (were they ever?) or miserable (yes!) and didn't seem to worry very much about what impact any of that might have on us. In a funny way, that seems like a kind of gift to me, from the vantage I have now. But I suppose there's a part of me, too, that simply doesn't believe they loved us as much as I love Gideon.

I know I'm wrong, that every parent feels this way. That this amazing love, which I feel has happened to me, me, and only me in this miraculous way, is just utterly ordinary and predictable and the *way things go*, unless things are terribly wrong somehow.

Eva summarizes the news of the valley for them all. The weather, the traffic, the new shops and restaurants, the doings of people they know, the health of the bookstore — which has new co-owners, a young couple who've bought into it and will slowly buy Eva out. She threatens, in every fourth or fifth e-mail, to sell the house, but no one takes her seriously. She's the one who loves it most.

Every now and then she becomes *pensive*, as Daisy thinks of it. She writes of John, or of her failed marriage with Mark. She's thinking, it seems, of the course of her life; she's wondering, perhaps, if her story makes sense, if it means anything, or amounts to anything.

Once she writes to Daisy about Daisy's hard adolescence, her going to live with Mark and the difference that made:

I still wonder from time to time if it was the right thing to do. It seems that it was, that your life was better and easier after that. But I worry that I gave you up too easily, that there might have been something hurtful in that to you.

309

Daisy doesn't know how to answer this, how to tell her mother that she did the right thing, that she was only grateful. She finally writes Eva that she thinks living with Mark was something she needed to do at that stage of her life, that it seems generous to her that Eva allowed it.

Theo writes from college, from Duke. He writes of courses he's taking, of concerts he's planning to go to, of basketball games he's seen, of peace rallies he's participated in. Does he have an inner life? It's hard to know. He doesn't write anything that might reveal it, but this is how Theo is, having grown up alone with Eva, who worried too much about him, who made his life the center of hers. It seems to Daisy that he realized at some point that to have thoughts and feelings that could survive Eva's probing concern — her wish to shape and control the lives around her — you needed to keep things buttoned up. She feels that her own moving in with Mark, battling openly with him about who controlled what, has somehow released her from that need.

But Theo, more loving, less angry perhaps than Daisy, seems to have flourished in his own way with Eva, even if he is a private soul.

Once though, in an e-mail he sends around to all of them, he writes that a folklore course he's taking has made him remember the stories they used to tell him around the dining room table.

I don't really remember the stories *per se.*

(Theo is fond of Latin words, which endears him to Daisy: *quid est, lacunae, ipso facto, passim*

310

— these stud his e-mails.)

Maybe occasionally an image. A threatening old woman, an animal that helps a lost child. Mostly what I remember is that they all had happy endings. Were they from folklore? Were they old tales? Or did you make them up just for me?

Daisy writes back.

They were created for you of course, you schnauzer. John started it when you were maybe a little over two. You were usually the main character — didn't you notice that? Never Hansel *and* Gretel, just fucking *Hansel*. Sometimes you were the superhero, rescuing yourself — the subtext here being *brave, competent Theo*. Sometimes you were rescued by kindly forces: 'Yes, Theo, the world IS a good place.' Anyway, always, always, always, the happy ending — though because we passed them around, because we each got to tell a part of the story, sometimes Emily or I would try to subvert things — set it up so you *wouldn't* make it back from the cave, or escape the wicked witch or the dark forest. But the grown-ups, natch, always made sure you did. I envied you, occasionally, being the center of all that loving invention.

Daisy's own letters mock her life — this is her way of presenting both the bad and the good things that happen to her.

311

I finally realized that Rob was more in love with his dog than he was with me. Though to call this creature a dog is misleading. A small demented horse who happened to have canine teeth he really enjoyed showing off is more like it. I had to arm myself with steak bones when we had a date. Twice the dog bit me.

Nipped me, Rob said.

At any rate, his teeth broke a barrier I like to keep between myself and the world. I drew the line: the dog or me.

Well, there are some people who when they draw the line are left standing there with only the line to keep them company. That's the story here. Goodbye, Rob. For a while I felt a certain *tristesse* whenever I opened my purse and the faint odor of raw meat floated up to greet me, but it passed.

And more recently:

A *part*, guys! in the new play at the Court Theatre. Small, yes, but noticeable. I'm a memory, really, a dream woman who gets to step forward off and on through the action and remind the main character of another aspect of himself and his life. She's maybe a little too good, a little too idealized (well, she's a pill, really), but I'm going to try to make her as salty as I can. I hope maybe one or two of you can come and exclaim about my excellence in this role at some point during the run.

I didn't, by the way, get Phebe at the Shakespeare Theater. The guy cast as her suitor was shorter than me by a mile or two. For a while I think they were pondering the joke of that, the joke I've so often and so painfully lived through offstage — huge me, shrimpy him — but in the end they said, 'Nope, but try us again.' Which you may be sure I will.

Mark doesn't write. He calls. Mostly he calls from his cell phone while he's driving around. They are all used to the fuzzy static that comes and goes, to the sudden absolute silence on the line. They can imagine the terrain that blocks the signal. They hang up and they don't wait for another call right away — that's not his style. It will come in three days, or a week, with no sense of urgency. When they ask how he is, he says, 'Same old, same old.' It's *their* lives he's calling about. He wants *them* to talk to him.

Listening to himself, Mark sometimes thinks of his mother saying to him once that she was content. Not happy, but content. He wonders if that's what he means when he says 'Same old.' Content.

But then one of his kids makes him laugh on the phone, or tells him something that surprises or pleases him; or he catches the smell of smoke from the burning vines drifting across the fields in January; or he takes a turn in the road and sees, spread out below him, the vineyards in spring, vibrant with the soft green leaves opening in the rows, with the pure, cold yellow of the mustard flowers; and he is flooded with happiness. Same old, same old: happiness.

They also *don't* write, of course. Certain things stay private.

When Emily's husband, Ted, moves out for three weeks, she falls silent. She feels that to mention it will make it more real, more permanent than it is, and she is holding herself in a state of almost unbearable tension, insisting to herself that it isn't real, it isn't true, it won't last.

And it doesn't — he comes back — and she writes again, about the shifts in her body during this second pregnancy, about maybe moving to a larger house after the baby is born.

When Eva has a small lump removed from her breast, she writes to none of them about it. Gracie is the only one she tells. After a year has passed and things still look clean, she finally tells Elliott, and they go out for a celebratory dinner.

She's continued to see Elliott all these years. Twice they have broken up, when he decided to date someone else — for a long time he wanted to get married again, which Eva had told him was out of the question for her. But they have come back together each time, and now that Theo has left home, he often spends the night, though rarely two nights in a row.

She doesn't write either of starting to attend church again. This is in part because it's an experiment for her — will it seem in any way relevant? will she feel anything? And then, as she goes on attending, as her attendance becomes regular, it's because she doesn't know exactly what this means or how to explain it, and she doesn't want them to think of it in certain ways: as a born-again experience, as a revelation, as a consolation for herself now that she's alone.

Gradually though, references to her involvement in the church's activities, to events in the Christian calendar, creep into her e-mails, so that her children, almost without remarking it to themselves or each other, come to understand her as a believer. Perhaps even to misremember her as someone who was always a believer.

Daisy never mentions her abortion, or the depression, the sense of the uselessness of life, which followed it. She never mentions, either, the several years of therapy with Dr. Gerard — except to Mark, who pays for it; and even then, all she says by way of explanation to him is, 'Apparently I've got some chickens coming home to roost.'

'These wouldn't be chickens I know, would they?' he asks.

'It wouldn't make any difference whether you did or didn't,' she says.

'Ah! Touché,' he says. The cell phone connection fizzes a little.

'I'll pay you *back* eventually!' she says, more loudly.

'You better not,' he says.

'Why *better not*?' she asks.

'Because. Because I'm paying *you* back, sweetheart.'

★ ★ ★

Mark doesn't call and doesn't call about getting married, and by the time he does, it's so close to his wedding date that Daisy isn't sure she can make it. She has to ask the director at the Shakespeare Theatre to rearrange the rehearsal schedule — she's playing Miranda in *The Tempest*. But it's early in the process; they're still sitting around working over their lines, so the director tells her okay, she can be away for a long weekend, they'll arrange things around her.

It's January, seventeen degrees out in Chicago when Daisy leaves, and the sight of the green hills as the plane comes in to land in San Francisco is more beautiful than she remembered.

Mark meets her in the baggage area, and they walk through the airport to the garage together. Daisy is happy to walk next to him. She knows they are a striking pair. It was only after she'd come to live with him that she realized that he was the one in the family whom she resembled — that she had his long, narrow face, so different from Emily and Eva. That she had the same wide-set light eyes, the strong nose and brows, the high forehead. She had come to think that she too was handsome. Not pretty, but handsome.

They stop in at Eva's to say hello to her and Theo, and to Emily and her family, all of whom are staying in the big house. They make their plans for the weekend. Tonight, they decide, Emily and Daisy will have dinner together, by themselves.

316

At Mark's house, Daisy unpacks and changes into jeans. Kathy, Mark's wife-to-be, comes over — Daisy has met her only once before, a tall funny woman who does publicity for a winery — and they talk, easily. At six, Emily comes for her and they drive into Calistoga, to the All Seasons Café.

Emily and Daisy haven't drawn any closer as they've gotten older. They're still too different, still headed in more or less opposite directions in life. But tonight they speak directly about that, about the different ways they grew up, about their parents. Emily talks about how being a parent herself has given her a whole new perspective on Mark and Eva. As she talks, her hands are in constant motion, down to stroke her immense belly, up to touch her own face or to move gesturally around her shoulders, as if calling attention to her prettiness, her animation. Daisy, who has learned to love her own capacity for *stillness* as an actress, can't help thinking of the cheerleading motions Emily practiced over and over in high school. Boom chicka boom.

But now Emily's asking what it was like to have Mark as a father, something she never really experienced.

Daisy tells her about the way they struggled with each other. 'I think we were more or less growing up together,' she says. 'There was this one night, I remember, where he got so mad at me for something I'd done and he said something like, 'And until you can learn to fuckin' respect me, you are fuckin' grounded!' Which struck me as so funny, so incongruous,

317

that I couldn't help it, I started laughing. And he did too, and he said, 'That's not what the dad says, is it?' and I said to him, 'Oh, *that's* what you were after? Dad-ness?''

Emily was grinning.

'I was still grounded, I want you to know.' Daisy looks past Emily to a couple walking past outside. It's raining, and they're huddled against it. 'He really tried,' she says, thinking of Mark in those days. 'He tried, and I tried. It was as though we both knew it was a kind of last chance for us.'

'What do you mean?' Emily asks.

'Oh, who knows?' Daisy smiles. 'I'm just being theatrical. As is my wont.'

The next night, the night before the wedding, the whole family, Eva and Theo, Emily and Ted and Gideon, and Mark and Kathy along with her two sons, both in their twenties, all go out for a festive meal together at Tra Vigne. Afterward, after their prolonged goodbyes outside in the parking lot, Daisy goes home alone with her father one last time. As they are saying goodnight, standing in the living room, she grins at him and says, 'Some bachelor party, Dad.'

He smiles back, shaking his head. His hair is gray now, and he keeps it cut very short — 'the bullet look,' Daisy calls it — which makes him look different from the handsome cowboy he used to resemble. 'My *life* has been the bachelor party,' he says.

★ ★ ★

318

The wedding will be at Kathy's house, and the only people invited are the group that gathered for dinner — family. Not friends, and certainly not Gracie and Duncan. Mark has explained this to Daisy on the telephone ahead of time, to reassure her. And Daisy has been relieved to hear this, though it makes her wonder, as visits home often have, how it would feel to see Duncan again, to be in a room with him, to speak with him. Coming home only rarely through college and even less afterward, and always staying with Mark when she did, she has managed to avoid seeing Duncan for almost a decade now — and it seems she will this time too.

But Eva has wanted Daisy 'sitting at my table at least once,' she says, and has planned a brunch for everyone but the bride and groom for Sunday morning, before the wedding. And when Daisy walks in, she sees Gracie down the long hall framed in the kitchen doorway. Gracie sees her too. She gives a loud whoop and charges Daisy. It's a little like being tackled, Daisy thinks; though Gracie seems smaller than she used to be. Smaller but plumper.

Now she steps back and openly appraises Daisy, even as Daisy is taking her in; and of course is thinking simultaneously of Duncan, who must be waiting in the kitchen with the others.

Daisy has dressed up for this occasion, as they will all go directly from Eva's to the wedding. She's wearing a red dress with long sleeves, high-necked and simple, but beautifully fitted. When she tried out for Miranda, she made an

319

effort to tone down all that was strong and powerful in her appearance, so she looks softened today, *prettier* than she usually does. Her eyebrows are plucked into a thin line and lightened. She's wearing blush in the middle of her cheeks to fatten them. She's had her hair highlighted. She likes this way of looking, for the moment. This disguise.

And Gracie does too. Her wide fleshy face opens in appreciation of Daisy. 'You are fabulous!' Gracie pronounces in her booming voice.

'Same to you,' Daisy says, and laughs.

Gracie takes her hand and leads her back to the kitchen. It's jammed with people, and for a few minutes Daisy is able to ignore the small, trim man with white hair who stands on the other side of the island and watches her, his face still, his dark eyes expressionless.

Finally, though, she has to acknowledge him. She steps toward him, her hand out, and he raises his hand, shakes hers formally. 'Good to see you,' she says, and he nods.

'Yes,' he says. He is the only man in the room wearing a suit, a suit of a beautiful, subtly striped fabric. *Bespoke*, Daisy thinks.

'Oh come on, Duncan,' Gracie says. 'Work up a little more enthusiasm for this absolute *babe*.'

He turns to his wife. 'Enthusiasm has never been my forte.' He pronounces it correctly of course: *fort*.

Daisy smiles and takes the opportunity to move away, over to hug Eva, to pour herself a mimosa.

There are ten of them around the table, and Daisy is glad for the sheer numbers, for the buffer they provide between her and Duncan. She has maneuvered herself between Gracie and Kathy's older son, Kevin. Duncan is across the table from her, on Eva's right hand. Looking at him from time to time, Daisy sometimes catches him looking back, his face unreadable. He seems frail, she thinks; she noticed how much more pronounced his limp was when he walked to the dining room. But the frailty is something separate from that, and it seems characteristic of someone much older than he is now — and, of course, she knows his age: sixty-seven.

He still feels compelled to weigh in with his opinion from time to time — on the Democratic primaries, on Michael Jackson's face — but no one here is under his spell any longer. Or maybe it's simply that his age has changed the way these pronouncements are received. In any case, no one pays much attention to him — they're too busy talking about their own lives, about what comes next for all of them.

Emily has center stage for a while, describing a house they're thinking of buying, discussing mortgage rates and real estate. Gracie asks Daisy about work, and she talks about her role, about Miranda, about how even though she's an important character to the play, it's not a large part. 'But she's so incredibly difficult to act,' Daisy says. 'Because she's grown up on this enchanted island with no one else but her father and this . . . monster, really. And so she's astounded, she's amazed, when other humans

321

arrive. And you have to *get* that — her innocence, her amazement — without making her seem stupid.' She runs a finger around the edge of her mother's familiar plate, its bumpy rim. 'And I have to say, she has — *I* have — one of the greatest lines in Shakespeare. And one of the hardest, because it's so familiar. It's 'O brave new world, to have such people in it.'' She opens her hands. 'I mean, how do you say it, and make it *new*? Make people really hear it, instead of the book title, or whatever.'

'You know, I'd forgotten that's where that title came from,' Eva says. 'Shame on me.' This last is so typical of Eva that Daisy smiles at her, and is rewarded by that warm smile back.

And now Kevin is asking her how she gets by, how she makes a living. He has asked this of Ted too, and Emily. He will graduate this June and he needs ideas.

Daisy laughs. 'You know those cheesy circulars that fall out of the Sunday paper? where bright young things are standing around casually in their underwear, looking as sexless as they can while also being half naked?' He nods. She gestures at herself with her thumb. 'That's me. Underwear queen of Marshall Field's. Underwear, and voice-overs, and a little bit of hand modeling. Stuff like that.'

After this the conversation fractures, multiplies. Gracie wants a recipe from Eva. Gideon is fussing, he doesn't *want* to stay in the high chair, and Emily and Ted are deciding whether he has to. Through the noise, Daisy hears the voice directed at her.

'Where would one get one of those circulars?' Duncan asks.

She looks at him. He is smiling, a smile that's like a parody of the way he used to smile at her in his studio, a kind of stagy lasciviousness.

'Oh for Christ's sweet sake, Duncan,' Gracie says, offended and indulgent at once.

'What?' he says, a vast feigned innocence on his face. He turns to Daisy. 'Can't an old man let a young woman know how lovely he finds her?'

Daisy stares levelly back. Her voice is flat and cold when she speaks. 'No, I don't think so,' she says.

'Daisy!' Eva says to her child. And then she hears herself and says more gently, in a self-mocking tone, 'I didn't *raise* you to be so rude.'

'No, you didn't, Mom. I know that. This is something I've achieved all by myself.'

There's a silence that stretches perhaps a few seconds too long.

'Well,' Theo says. 'This must be the time for a story.'

Emily says, 'Oh yes! Let's. For Gideon.'

'You start then, Theo,' Daisy says. 'Return the favor done so often to you.'

'Gladly,' Theo says. He's pierced his ear at college, and the diamond twinkles as he turns to her. 'The start is the easy part. They all start the same, right?'

Gracie leans toward Daisy. 'At some point I'm going to get what's going on, right?'

'Right,' Daisy says.

Emily is asking Gideon if he wants a story. Yes,

he says almost inaudibly, he does. He is shy. Even stuck in his high chair, he is trying to lean against his mother, to bury his face in her shoulder.

'Okay. Once upon a time,' Theo begins, 'there was a little boy, a brave little boy named . . . *Gideon*!' He raises his eyebrows at his nephew.

'Me,' Gideon says. He almost smiles.

'Yes. And this boy was walking in the woods one day when he met an old, old woman.'

'Me,' Eva says.

'No!' several others chorus, Daisy among them.

Theo describes it, the woman, the house she takes the little boy to. He is overacting, Daisy thinks, he should pull it in.

He passes the story to Daisy. She adds candy to the house, and a magic bird who can talk to the boy. Then she passes it to Emily.

But Gideon won't let Emily talk. He puts his small hand over her mouth and says, 'No, no! Mumma.' She is his, not theirs.

So Eva takes it up. The bird flies out the window and through the forest to town, where he finds the boy's parents, and they come and get him and they all live happily ever after. Gideon tilts his head against his mother and a vague, pleased smile lights his face.

Brunch breaks up. Emily and Ted and Gideon go upstairs to get ready for the wedding. The others clear the table and load the dishwasher. It isn't until everyone is milling around in the hall getting coats, preparing to leave, that Daisy finds herself almost alone next to Duncan, that he turns to her and lowers his voice to be heard by only her.

'I'm surprised you came,' he says. 'Surprised. Delighted. I'd gotten used to the family parties where you were conspicuously absent.'

'*Conspicuously* to you alone, I suspect. But this one could hardly be avoided. I needed to be here.' She has straightened her back; she's at her full height, taller than him.

'Still, it had come to the point where I expected never to see you again.'

She nods. Then she says, 'I'm surprised you would give it — that you would give *me* — a moment's thought.'

His smile, his ironic smile. 'You underestimate yourself, Daisy.'

'*That* I do not do,' she says, firmly.

'Well, you misunderstand *me*, then.'

'I think, actually, that I *don't* understand you.' She turns her light green eyes fully upon him. 'I didn't, and I never will. But I don't need to, really. Because whatever use you were making of me, I made *use* of you, too. Good use.' Her voice is hard as she says this. She smiles her own ironic smile. 'I should probably thank you.'

'But you won't.'

'No, I don't think I will.'

★ ★ ★

After the wedding, after the dinner at Kathy's house, Kevin drives Daisy down to the airport.

She's catching the red eye to get back to Chicago in time for rehearsal, and he's headed back to college. She has planned to sleep on the plane, but she doesn't. She's wide awake, thinking about the wedding, about her father and Kathy, about her family. And then, inevitably, about Duncan.

She felt nothing for him, and this surprises her. Seeing him was easy. He was an old man she used to know. She is a grown woman — a *grown-up*, she thinks, and smiles — who used to be under his spell, somehow, when she was a child. A child like those in Theo's fairy tales, held in some cottage in the dark forest, unable to imagine escape.

'But you did escape,' Dr. Gerard had said to her when she used this analogy once in therapy.

'Not exactly.' She looked through the thin aureole of Dr. Gerard's white hair to the bare tree outside the window behind her. 'I was rescued. The noble woodsman. The prince. My father.'

'But how did this figure, this rescuer, know you were there if you didn't somehow signal him, if you didn't somehow find a way to call for help?'

They had sat in silence for a while. Then Daisy said, 'I know what you're saying. You're saying I somehow deliberately let Mark know about my affair with Duncan.'

'I would call it *his* affair with you.' Dr. Gerard had her ironic smile too.

'Okay, point taken. But the other thing, that I somehow knew what I was doing — '

'I *didn't* say you knew what you were doing. I said you managed to signal him, to make your life speak to him.'

Daisy thought for a minute. 'Unconsciously,' she said.

Dr. Gerard grinned. 'Why not? Why not the unconscious: the thing I believe in and you pretend not to.'

'It's *not* that I don't believe in it,' she argued.

'No? Then what is it?'

'It's that that's not how it *felt* to me. I was *angry* he found out. I was upset.'

'And *then* relieved.'

'Yes.' Daisy was reluctant, and it made her sound sullen.

'But all I'm suggesting is that you take some credit for having relieved yourself, for getting what you needed from your father.'

'Oh, that's all.'

'That is all,' Dr. Gerard said, and smiled across the room, across her strange magic carpet, at Daisy.

It was Dr. Gerard who suggested she read *Lolita*, who felt it might help her to think about what had happened to her, how she had been abused. And Daisy had read it, she had considered what Humbert imagines Dolly Schiller, his transformed Lolita, wants to say to him at the end of the book: that he broke her life.

But that's not what she felt, or feels, Daisy is thinking on the plane. Her life was already broken. There was a mystery in it when Duncan took up with her, a mystery she didn't understand. It had to do with Mark and Eva, with Eva and John, with those things that hold people together in a sexual union, or push them apart. It had to do with how that is so deeply part of who they are, an expression of something central in them. And it had to do with the way the grown-ups are reckless with that, the way that others, even their own children, can simply *not matter* to them in the face of that. When she first heard the words *collateral damage* to refer to innocent people killed in war, Daisy had laughed at the inept horror of the phrase — and then realized those seemed the perfect words too, for herself as a child, as a teenager.

Duncan exposed the underpinnings of adult life, sexual life, to Daisy, though there wasn't a way for her to have articulated that at the time. He completed a kind of dark education that had begun in her with the divorce, and continued with John's death. She'd been mired in confusion for all those years, unable to take in any of the events that shaped her life except as pain to herself. Duncan had made her see what else they meant, what they might have meant to Eva, to Mark. Even to John.

She remembers saying once to Dr. Gerard of John that she hadn't really accepted that he and Eva had a sexual relationship until after Duncan. She hadn't understood that essential part of Eva's grief. She hadn't known how much she stood outside the lives of her parents, her stepfather.

Duncan had made her understand her insignificance. He had toughened her and hardened her, and that was wrong; but she was lost, and he had, almost certainly inadvertently, shown her a way out. Or he and Mark had, working unwittingly together.

Looking out the plane's window at the blackness below, Daisy remembers a terrible fight she and Duncan had in the week or so before Mark had found out about them, a fight that had shaken her deeply. She had been pushing him again to tell her what she meant to him, and if not that, then to beg her for sex. To *give* her something, as she felt it. In her confusion about what he was doing with her, what they were doing together, she wanted to understand his feelings, to be able to measure them somehow. Finally, in exasperation with her he'd turned away, walked to his work table — she could remember watching his hitching process across the room — and picked up his wallet. He'd taken out a handful of bills and come back to her, tossed them on her naked belly.

She stood up, not even brushing them away, and came at him, hitting him twice before he simply held her arm, and she felt how much power he could have exerted over her at any time he chose.

When he finally let go of her, she turned away and got dressed, wordlessly. She walked out to the car to wait for him to come and drive her to her father's house.

She had wept that night, alone in her room at Mark's, wept until her head ached.

But she would have gone on with it; she

wouldn't have given Duncan up, even then — except that somehow she must have been ready to. Somehow she *had* signaled Mark. On the plane, now, she thinks maybe even her weeping had been a signal intended for her father. She was thinking of it while she cried, actually, she remembers that now. She was thinking that her father might hear her and come to her, and she was wondering what she would say if he asked her why she was crying. Wondering if she would have to tell him the truth.

But he hadn't come, and after a while she had stopped.

★ ★ ★

Before they land in Chicago, the pilot comes on the intercom to tell them that it's four degrees out. When Daisy comes up out of the train station in the Loop, her eyes tear up instantly, her nose starts to run and pinch with freezing. Her hands hurt, even in her mittens. She has the sense that the bones of her face are in danger of cracking.

She catches a lone cab, drifting by on the empty street. In the backseat on the way home, she suddenly realizes she's making a little moaning noise with each inhalation, and she stops herself.

There is no new snow, she's grateful to see. But at her apartment she has to clamber with her suitcase over the blackened, frozen bank of old stuff shoveled up at the edge of the sidewalk.

Inside, she's grateful for the scorching heat in the hall, the burned smell in the dry air. It's the same in her apartment, except in the kitchen, where the window always slides open a crack, since the two sides of the latch, one on the upper sash, one on the lower, can't be forced to meet. Strong men have tried it and failed, as has Daisy.

She closes it again now — the creep to open is gradual — and bends to scratch her cat, Charley, who is rubbing back and forth against her legs, his spine arched, his tail whipping in pleasure. The digital clock over the sink says 6:37. The windows are still dark. Two days of mail are piled on the kitchen table, mail brought upstairs by the same neighbor who's fed Charley while Daisy was away. Daisy opens the cupboards. There's not much here — there never is, Daisy eats badly — but she finds part of a package of Chocomallows and carries it with her into her living room, along with the mail.

Daisy loves this apartment. She's lived in it since she came to Chicago eight years ago, drawn to the city by its reputation as a good town for young actors. It's a tiny space, two rooms and a kitchen on the fourth floor of an old town house on the near north side. It smells faintly of cat piss. This is her fault. She made the mistake of leaving the unscreened window open one night when the weather was nice so Charley could go in and out off the fire escape and catalpa tree that brushes against it. She waked to find four strange cats plus her own hunkered motionless as ornaments in the apartment — some sort of cat standoff, apparently — and the terrible odor everywhere. She laundered everything, she even washed the walls, but it lingers still, delicate and occasional.

In the living room, the streetlights' harsh glare is falling in, empurpling everything, making ugly what it touches. Daisy pulls the curtains and turns on a light.

One other thing Daisy has told no one in her family about is the set designer she met last summer who has recently moved in with her — David. The magnitude of this step has been tempered for both of them by the amount of traveling he does for his work, but even so, she feels astonished by this decision, on her part and on his. She has been in love before, but has never thought she could live with anyone. There's a line she learned as Miranda that she whispered to David the first night after he moved his few possessions in: 'This is the third man that e'er I saw, the first that e'er I sighed for.'

This had caused him to lift her nightgown up and press his lips to the white flesh of her body here and there for a while. When he was done, when he was lying next to her again, he frowned in exaggerated thoughtfulness and said, 'Only the third, Daisy?'

'I may be a *little* off on the math,' she said.

He's due home Tuesday, and Daisy has spent some of the two weeks of his absence sanding and polyurethaning the beat-up, dark floor in the living room. Now, in the lamplight, this space is transformed. It looks light and clean and fresh. The last thing she did before she left the house three days before was to move the furniture back

332

in, including David's one contribution, an Eames chair that makes everything else look shapeless and provisional. Now she sits down in it. Charley joins her, warming her thigh. She should try to sleep, she knows, but she's too keyed up. She goes slowly through the mail. She eats another Chocomallow. Charley licks up a little piece of the thin chocolate skin that falls on her leg.

Daisy is thinking of her father, of how his face looked saying his vows to Kathy — opened, hopeful. Daisy had looked at Eva then, she couldn't help herself. Tears had been streaming down her mother's face. Daisy had no way of knowing what they meant, but her own throat had knotted too.

Her script is lying on the cedar chest she uses as a coffee table. She's pulled out her own pages, highlighted her lines in yellow. She picks up the sheaf of paper now, and flips to the ending, to her own final speech. 'O wonder!' she cries out in the nearly empty room. 'How many goodly creatures are there here! How beauteous mankind is! O brave new world, that has such people in't!'

The fluorescence has faded behind the curtains — Daisy can see the wide stripe of pale daylight beginning where they don't quite meet. She thinks of being Miranda, enchanted by her father into a capacity for love, astonished at what life has brought her — an innocent, open to everything. She reads the lines over and over again to herself, whispering, looking at the rhythm, the repetition in the words and in the ideas, as she's been taught to do. It's the people, she realizes, that Miranda is wondering at, their sheer numbers, and their beauty. The *creatures,* the *mankind*: the *people*! *That's* where she should put the emphasis, that's what will make it new.

She looks up at the slant of sunlight entering the room, reflecting brightly off the floor she's made shiny for her new love, and takes a breath to start again, sure that this time she will get it right.